# TRETJAK

# TRETJAK

MAX LANDORFF

translated by
**Baida Dar**

Originally published as: *Der Regler* by Max Landorff
© S. Fischer Verlag GmbH, Frankfurt am Main, 2011

First published in English in the United Kingdom in 2013 by
HAUS PUBLISHING LTD
70 Cadogan Place, London SW1X 9AH
*www.hauspublishing.com*

English translation copyright © Baida Dar 2013

ISBN 978-1-908323-24-8
eISBN 978-1-908323-35-4

Typeset in Garamond by MacGuru Ltd
*info@macguru.org.uk*

Printed in the UK by TJ International, Padstow, Cornwall

A CIP catalogue for this book is available from the British Library

# Prologue

*He looked across the smooth, lead-grey surface of the lake and watched the ship come towards him, bow first. The invisible line along which she had been approaching for the past few minutes stood exactly perpendicular to the bench he was sitting on. It was a Wednesday in October, the first Wednesday in October to be precise, and it was a quarter past six in the evening. Apart from him and the employees of the ferry line, nobody was awaiting the arrival of the ship, which was called* Alpino *and which criss-crossed the Lago Maggiore on a regular schedule year-in year-out. In the summer, sometimes she was so packed with tourists and lay so low in the water that it looked like a refugee boat, pounding the water heavily. In this season, however, she appeared to be fast and elegant, and one could make out her white colour, white with dark blue lines at the side and around the doors and windows.*

*At the pier, two round signs indicated the arrival times of the next two ferries, one from Cannobio and the other from Luino: they looked like big white clocks with red arms on the dials, which were moved by the ferrymen – both showed these ferries were due at five past six. The sun had already set behind the mountains and the lake lay in shadow. The bow of the* Alpino *had appeared from the mist which had descended onto the water's surface. The ferry was late.*

*In the last few days, the weather had changed. The warm autumn had become a harbinger of winter. Up on the mountains the first snow had fallen, and down below freezing cold water flowed into the lake. Gabriel Tretjak wore a black cashmere coat and a dark grey scarf. He stood up, walked a few steps along the pier and stood next to the signs, his hands in his pockets. He was not wearing gloves, but the metallic surface of the gun in his right pocket felt warm.*

*In his line of business one could not avoid occasionally threatening people, and he had got himself into some quite dangerous situations. On principle, however, he did not use any weapons. Never. He did not even own one. However, this was something else. Never in his life had he been so afraid of anything as he was of the events which were about to unfold in the next few minutes on this pier.*

*The* Alpino *swung around and moored alongside the pier. An aluminium landing bridge was put across to let the passengers come ashore. There were only three of them. The first one was a tall man, who was holding a young boy with one hand and the child's yellow bicycle with the other. Then she came ashore. She was smaller than he remembered, somehow more fragile. The brown woollen coat, which she had wrapped around her, seemed a tad too big, the cap made her face look gaunt.*

*When she reached him she put down her bag on the wooden planks, looked up at him and asked in an almost embarrassed way: 'Did you wait long?'*

*He nodded. 'Twenty years.'*

*She threw him a strange glance. He picked up her bag*

*from the ground and headed into town. She walked beside him.*

*'There is only this one hotel in town,' she said and pointed at the cream-coloured building ahead. 'What is it like?'*

*'Not up to your usual standard,' he replied, 'but alright.'*

*By the time the Alpino set off again, to cross the lake in the direction of Cannobio, they had reached the entrance to the hotel. In golden letters it said Torre Imperial on the glass door. And below were painted three stars.*

*PART 1*

# THE DECEPTION

# First Day

## 11 May

### *Galle, Sri Lanka, 7.30pm*

Gabriel Tretjak was sitting in a deep English armchair watching the waiter fixing him a G&T. The steward was dressed properly: black trousers, black jacket and a neatly buttoned white shirt. He was quite old and something about him – maybe his nose, slightly squashed and pushed upwards – reminded Tretjak of the rhinoceros he had observed in the Hellabrunn Zoo. The director of the zoo had been blackmailed by one of the keepers and had hired Tretjak to put an end to the unfortunate business, which concerned the administration of illegal drugs to exotic animals. Tretjak had waited next to the rhinoceros enclosure where the keeper was on duty that day. He loved rituals, so they kept on meeting in the same place from then on, until everything was settled. That is how Tretjak had learnt such a lot about the rhinoceros. They were quite touchy about even the slightest alteration of their environment: they immediately became suspicious and their actions became unpredictable. They had this in common with practically all animals: change spells danger. Gabriel Tretjak knew that it was no different for human beings. With humans, change brought about alertness, something he had often been able to use to his advantage. But compared to the rhinoceros, for human beings the transformation had to be on a larger scale. If only details were altered, if there were only small digressions from business-as-usual, human beings remained docile, good-natured, almost naïve. They misinterpreted and dismissed these details, and only understood their true significance later. Sometimes there were only a few minutes between misinterpretation and the realisation that something was wrong; at other times, decades lay between these two points.

The waiter asked him whether he would like something to eat. Tretjak declined. He had already made a reservation in the restaurant adjacent to the lobby area for 9pm, where the tables had been laid with white linen.

Tretjak was pretty sure that the man he was waiting for in the lobby would misinterpret the small change in his daily routine. The small alteration was the fact that his wife had not yet called him. If Tretjak knew the man well enough, he probably had not even noticed that the call had not been made – despite the usual routine on his business trips. Never mind, he would soon find out the significance of this vicissitude.

Tretjak looked at his watch: it was a quarter to eight. Suddenly he had this 'feeling' again, a feeling which he had experienced quite often lately. It was a kind of tiredness, a sense of tedium and over-satiety. In the past, he had enjoyed precisely these moments, the moments of critical importance, the approach of a dramatic turning point in the life of the other, who as yet had no idea what was to happen to him. But for a few weeks now he had caught himself wishing that these moments would pass without any interference.

Tretjak was sitting with his G&T in the lobby of the New Oriental Hotel in Galle, a harbour town in the south west of Sri Lanka. An eleven-hour flight lay behind him – Lufthansa LH 2016 from Munich to Colombo – as well as a four-hour car ride. The short, silent driver of the Peugeot had smoothly negotiated huge potholes, donkey carts and swarms of *tuk-tuks*, as well as seriously dodgy lorries. In a few hours time the same driver would take him back the same way, to the airport in Colombo where he would board flight LH 2017, which would take off for Munich at sunrise. Tretjak was here only for this one evening – to tear a human being out of his lethargy.

It was hot in the lobby. The old wooden ceiling fans were going round and round rather drowsily. The one directly above the black piano in the left corner of the lobby, where the bar was located, was squeaking. A group of three Englishmen was sitting there, each with a cocktail in front of him, at times emitting short bursts of a strange hissing noise as one of them cracked a joke.

At this moment a brawny man in khaki trousers and a green Ralph Lauren polo shirt came through the wide open entrance door. He was sweating, his face was flushed, and he was wearing aviator sunglasses. He purposefully strutted towards the reception and said in a deep voice and with a slight German accent: 'Room Number Seven, please.'

Tretjak got up and stood behind him, slightly to his side, at a distance of about two metres. 'Congratulations, Mr Schwarz,' he said. 'Number Seven is the best room in the hotel.'

The man turned around, pushed his sunglasses up, and looked at Tretjak with inquisitive blue eyes.

'Are you enjoying your short holiday, Mr Schwarz?' Tretjak enquired.

The man was now obviously searching through his memory. Did he know this stranger from somewhere? 'Yes, as a matter of fact, I am,' he replied in the end, 'may I ask…'

'We've got to talk, Mr Schwartz,' Tretjak interrupted. 'I've booked a table in the restaurant for 9pm.'

'I wouldn't know…' The man shook his head. 'I don't know you and I have no idea what we should talk about.'

'I beg your pardon. My name is Tretjak. We've got to talk about your life, Mr Schwarz. I've come here to change it. With your help, of course.'

The man, whose name was Schwarz and whose life was an open book to Gabriel Tretjak, was losing his patience and becoming indignant. 'Look, you are mistaking me for someone else. I have no intention of changing my life. And even if I had I wouldn't talk to *you* about it.' An amused twinkle was noticeable in his eyes, a sign that he was regaining his composure. This was a madman he was confronted with, nothing else. 'You know, this country offers many attractions. I am not one of them. Good evening.'

With these words he turned to the receptionist, took the brass key for Room Number seven from the counter and was halfway to the staircase on the left when Tretjak spoke: 'If you can't work out the deal with Union Carry, you are going to lose your job as CEO. At least, that's what your Board of Directors says.'

Schwarz stopped in his tracks and turned around to look at Tretjak.

'Shall we say 9pm?' Tretjak resumed. 'And don't worry. We'll sort everything out.' He turned to the receptionist behind the counter: 'Room Number Five, please.' Tretjak took his key, smiled at Schwarz – who was still standing there, dumbfounded – and walked past him towards the staircase.

That went alright, he thought. Schwarz was irritated enough, and in his room he would notice that his wife had not called him and he would call her. Or rather, he would try to call her. This attempt would only increase his irritation, because dialling his wife's mobile number he would only get the answer, 'this number is not operational'. And nobody would answer the landline.

Tretjak went to his room, put down his briefcase, moved the chair to the window, sat down and closed his eyes. The windows of this hotel had no glass in them, only wooden shutters. One could hear the noises from outside, of the chirping insects, of screaming kids. The

New Oriental in Galle was an insider's tip, an old hotel in the English colonial style. The big, dark, wooden four-poster bed was at least two hundred years old. It was covered by a light mosquito net, which came down from the high ceiling all the way to the floor. Tretjak was not going to use the bed. He got up, went to the bathroom and took a long, cool shower.

Looking into the mirror, he decided he should become fitter. Now, with summer around the corner, he could go for a run again in the mornings, directly from his flat to the Isar, along the river and over Montgelas Bridge, then enter the English Garden and pass by the Haus der Kunst on his way back. Tretjak took pride in keeping his weight in check. He was 44 years old and for the past 25 years he had always worn size 50 suits. There was no trace of grey in his black hair and it would probably stay that way. He had inherited his hair from his mother, and in her whole family there was not a grey strand in sight. Tretjak's hair was thick and he wore it a bit long. Now it was wet and he combed it back, out of his face.

He took a new pair of underpants from his briefcase and proceeded to get dressed. A pair of synthetic navy trousers and a long-sleeved beige tee-shirt. He slipped his bare feet into his dark brown slippers. The room was perfumed by freshly-cut papaya, arranged on a flat dish on the table. Tretjak sat down again on the chair at the window and thought about how to start the meeting down in the restaurant. He must not lose the pace which he had set in the lobby, he must keep up the tension.

Tretjak decided to go down a tad too late and to use as an excuse: 'I just had your wife on the phone, Mr Schwarz, and… well, you know her.'

The success of the mission, he knew from experience, depended on the beginning of the conversation. In this case the matter seemed not to be terribly complicated. It was actually a fairly routine assignment. Tretjak had considered turning it down, since he was in no mood to be bored. But then his client, Melanie Schwarz, had uttered a sentence which had made him smile. And it was because of that sentence that in a few minutes he would taste the 'Great Curry', the speciality of the New Oriental's restaurant. He had pre-ordered the meal so as not to waste any time studying the menu. The Great Curry, it had been explained to him, consisted of numerous small dishes of the most delicate vegetables, meat and fish and an assortment of sauces, which were all already hot and would elicit beads of perspiration from your forehead.

Melanie Schwarz felt trapped in a life from which she longed to escape but could not. A web of guilty feelings, responsibilities and a lack of courage were holding her back, as was the fear of failure in her new, her own, life. In her youth she had been a starlet with two songs on Top of the Pops: 'You Are Alone Now' and 'Truth Hurts'. But her career had been a short one and soon there was nothing going anymore. She had once reappeared in headlines reporting an alleged suicide attempt and then finally she had disappeared completely from the limelight. Then she met Peter Schwarz, who erected a secure castle around her made out of family and a high standard of living. In the meantime, their grown-up daughter had left home for London where she was studying Dance. Melanie and her husband lived in a fantastic penthouse overlooking the Gendarmenmarkt in Berlin and owned a small, restored estate outside Potsdam with a stable attached. Melanie had loved riding even as a child. Peter Schwarz had fulfilled her dream. But now she had a new dream. At the end of their conversation she had stared at the piece of paper on which Tretjak had jotted down his notes and said: 'I don't have any money of my own. I can't pay you.' Tretjak, who had been tempted to turn down the assignment, had pricked up his ears. He looked at her and observed how she gathered up all her courage to conclude: 'you've got to make my husband pay you for your work.'

The lentils had been the hottest dish. Even Tretjak, used to hot food from childhood, felt his eyes fill with tears. Schwarz had tasted a morsel and then refused to touch the rest.

The waiter with the rhinoceros nose was busy cleaning the little dishes off the table. When he had finished, the only things left on the table were a glass carafe filled with mineral water, a scarcely touched bottle of *Haut-Médoc* and a few glasses.

'Would the gentlemen like to order dessert?'

Tretjak looked at Schwarz enquiringly.

Schwarz shook his head. 'Espresso. A double.'

Tretjak nodded to the waiter and motioned that he would have the same. Then he reached for his briefcase, which he had placed on the floor next to his chair, put it on his lap and took from it a single sheet of white paper and a dark blue ballpoint pen, placed both in front of him on the table, and returned the briefcase to the floor.

'So she wants to start a new life,' Schwarz said, more to himself than to Tretjak. 'But she can't tell me herself… she needs somebody like you to tell me. How did she find you?' He looked Tretjak in the eyes. 'Are you sleeping with her?'

Tretjak did not bother answering that question and remained silent. He gave Schwarz time. Some people fell apart when they received bad news. Others needed to utter the words, needed to repeat them in order to comprehend. Schwarz belonged to the latter group. He was hurt, one could recognise that much from his face. His hands were shaking as he poured himself some water. The bull was swaying.

'Spread her wings one more time, well, well… were those Melanie's words, or did you make them up? A peaceful divorce… a small flat… just a small sum for a fresh start… What kind of start? And is that what we are now going to talk about? What do you hope to gain from all this, if I may ask?'

The coffee arrived and both men, facing each other, let it grow cold in the cups. The whole restaurant was now empty except for one table in the back corner. The elderly lady sitting there was engrossed in a book. There was a faint clatter of dishes coming from the kitchen, a sound common to every restaurant all over the world at the end of a long day.

Tretjak was satisfied. Now he only had to clearly explain the rules to this man sitting opposite him in a restaurant in Sri Lanka, who was soon going to disappear from his life again.

He had to make it clear that there was not going to be any contact with his wife for the time being. That his wife was on holiday and only he, Tretjak, knew where she was. That she would only return when everything had been arranged the way she wanted. One more hour, that was Tretjak's estimate, and he would step out onto the terrace and beckon the driver.

At this moment the hotel's receptionist came to the table. And it was this moment which Tretjak would go over in his mind later, again and again. He had caught sight of the man from the corner of his eye as the man had briskly crossed the lobby, stopped briefly when he reached the restaurant, looked around and then determinedly headed towards them. Tretjak was even convinced that he had seen him hang up the phone at the reception desk before setting off. With hindsight Tretjak knew full well that he had been annoyed at what was bound to be an unnecessary interruption.

'Mr Tretjak, there was a call for you,' said the receptionist.

The human brain is a decision-making machine. It continuously processes a huge amount of data, literally every second, to make decisions in a flash and for one purpose only: to secure survival.

'A call? For me? Are you sure?'

'Yes, no doubt about it. The caller said he had an important message for Gabriel Tretjak. He didn't leave a name.' He looked at the piece of paper in his hand. '"Winner in the fourth race, horse number six, Nu Pagadi." That's the message.'

Even when crossing the street the human brain performs a massive achievement. It estimates the distance to the other side and calculates the time needed to cross, including stepping down and mounting the curb. It estimates the distance and the speed of the approaching car and calculates the time needed until it reaches the brain's position, also considering the condition of the ground in the calculation and the two cyclists approaching from the right and then decides: to walk or not to walk? If only one of these calculations is incorrect it would mean the end and this particular human being's brain would be splattered as grey matter all over the asphalt.

In the New Oriental in Sri Lanka, Gabriel Tretjak decided, in this very moment, that this call did not signify any danger, that it must have been a mistake. Nobody knew where Tretjak was at this point in time. And he had never in his life attended a race.

'Thank you,' Tretjak said, waiting until the receptionist had left before taking up his pen again and leaning forwards to break the silence between himself and Schwarz.

'Now listen carefully, Mr Schwarz,' he began, 'I know that you are planning to fly to Mumbai the day after tomorrow. There you want to close a cooperation deal between your company and a chip manufacturer.' He paused for a second. 'I also know that this deal involves a conspiracy in your own executive board. The cooperative deal will not happen and the supervisory board has already made up its mind that the failure will cost you your job as chief executive.'

Across the table from Tretjak Schwarz looked at a complete loss. Three hours ago his life had been orderly, easily comprehensible, well-lit to the smallest corner – a good life on the horizon without any major problems. On 11 May he had taken a little boat ride, with a guide of course, upstream in a canoe all the way into the interior of the country. He had walked on a small island full of mango trees and had seen alligators on the riverbank. He had sent a text message to his daughter in London from the canoe. She had given him the stay at the New Oriental as his birthday present. She had stayed there on her way to a trip to Sri Lanka, and when she had heard that her father was going to India on business, she had decreed that this was the perfect opportunity for a mini-break. 'Something else, Dad, not the usual fully-air-conditioned anonymous hotels. Something new, something just for you for a change.' That evening he had returned to the hotel in high spirits.

And now he was sitting across the table from a stranger who had just announced to him that his wife wanted to leave him – in fact, had already left him – and that he was about to lose his job. The company he worked for as the CEO manufactured cooling units. The deal with Union Carry concerned electronic conveyor chips, which would make the cooling units compatible worldwide. At least that was what his experts had told him and had backed up with a very impressive presentation. In the past there had been a board member who dealt with international cooperation deals like this one. In the course of some cost-saving and streamlining of operations, which had been extended to the executive level to make a point, that responsibility was now assigned to the CEO, who in turn had to rely on his experts. What did this Tretjak know about cooling units?

'In my bag I have some files which will prove to you what I say is true,' Tretjak explained. 'Emails, minutes of meetings and telephone conversations, proof of secret conferences. I will leave them here for you to study carefully at your leisure later. Not an easy read. I am now going to propose a clear deal to you, Mr Schwarz.'

Tretjak folded back the tablecloth, put the piece of paper on the hard surface of the wood and drew a line on it, from top to bottom, exactly in the middle. 'On the left side of the paper, we will write down what *you* have to do,' he said. 'On the right side we will write what *I* have to do. Let's start with your tasks.'

Tretjak now spoke quite urgently, taking short pauses between sentences and never letting his opponent out of his sight. When he had finished explaining a part, he jotted down a few notes on the paper.

'Your wife is from Heidelberg, and that is where she wants to return to. You are going to open a little book-shop for her there, with an esoteric focus. This shop is probably never going to be economically viable, but you are going to support your wife and make sure she has a modest income. That and a small flat in the centre of town, two rooms and a balcony, that is all she wants. You will also talk to your daughter and tell her that her parents are splitting up, but that everything is OK, and that there was no bad blood. Her lawyers are going to draft the divorce papers and you are going to write your wife a letter. In it you will assure her that you are not angry, not even because of the method she chose to make her decision known to you. You will write to her that she has a friend for life in you. You will sell the two horses in Potsdam, but find them a good home where your wife can visit them; you know how attached she is to the animals. You will talk to Melanie's parents and you will speak to your own parents. You will start now with the preparations for a family Christmas. Maybe in the beautiful country house at the Schaalsee your wife loves so much. Everybody will come and celebrate Christmas there together and everybody will get along. Call me if you think there are any problems with any of those tasks which I haven't anticipated.'

The left side of the paper was now full of notes, care-fully written on straight lines with little dashes at the beginning. Tretjak again leant down and took out of his briefcase a dark, brown file held together by a leather string and placed it on the table. 'Those are the papers I spoke about to you,' he said and again picked up his pen.

'My part of the agreement: I will save your job. I will make sure that your two opponents on the board will leave the company. That the advisory board reunites behind you. All this, of course, will work only if you do exactly as I tell you.'

He wrote on the right side of the paper: *eliminate enemies.* And below that, new dash: *turn Board of Directors.* And then he added a third dash below: *double annual bonus.*

'You should have a little more money in your account at the end. Not least because you will have to pay me.'

Tretjak was sitting in the back of the Peugeot, on his way back to Colombo. In the dark the trip was even more nerve-wracking, but the diminutive, silent driver gave the impression that he knew what he was doing. It was just before midnight, and he calculated the time difference with Europe: there it was only afternoon. He picked up his phone and dialled the number of a hotel on the Parhijuese Atlantic Coast near Sintra. It was called Palacia de Seteais and was a little castle which had been turned into a hotel, beautifully placed on a hill in the middle of ancient trees with a view of the sea. Melanie Schwarz was not in her room, so he left her a message: *Made good progress on the way towards your bookshop.* T.

Later on, in the plane, LH2017, first class, first row, he thought back to this Peter Schwarz fellow, who by now must have read the papers. He kind of liked the guy, even if one of his working principles was not to think in these categories. 'You once were an excellent squash player, Mr Schwarz,' he had said at the end of their conversation. 'You know, in other words, that you have to capture the centre of the court, and should not let go of it again.'

There was only one sensible way to manipulate a person in the future: go back to the past. Tretjak had learned this from a CIA psychologist. 'If you fly to Mumbai tomorrow you are definitely leaving the centre of the court, in fact you would be moving to the furthest-most corner,' he had told Schwarz. 'You shouldn't do that, if everything is supposed to go according to our plan. You have to return to your headquarters tomorrow…'

Tretjak turned down the meal, only drinking a glass of water, placed the back of his seat in a horizontal position and fell asleep with the reassuring feeling that things were developing just the way he had planned them.

When he unlocked his flat's door in Munich, the next morning (local time), he noticed a small change. The pile of read newspapers on the floor in the hallway was still there. That meant that his cleaning lady, the reliable and faithful Frau Lanner, had not shown up. But there could be a thousand different reasons for that. Tretjak did not pay any attention to this small change in his daily routine.

### *A8 Motorway, Berlin–Munich, 6pm*

Max Krug had been on the road for almost eight hours. He had driven exactly 611 kilometres in his black horse-box – Krug had bought himself the most modern one of all – a twin-cabin with electronically secured doors and inside walls which could be moved remotely at the touch of a button. To the left of the steering wheel there was a small monitor, on which he could observe what was going on inside the transporter. He had installed the highly sensitive webcam himself. It was a brand of high security transporter and that was precisely what Krug wanted; after all he was ferrying around a golden treasure. The best racing horse in the whole of Europe, just four-years-old. What a future lay ahead of this horse. Nu Pagadi was its name, a Russian saying roughly translated as 'Just you wait.' Krug had come up with the name himself.

Many moons ago, as a soldier of the East German Volksarmee he had studied at the Military Academy in Leningrad. Even back then, he had loved to hear these words, a phrase uttered in a slightly mocking way: 'Nu pagadi.'

The horse had already won almost half a million euros for Krug. He was too superstitious to think about what money was still to come. Anything could happen to a horse. And that's why he had insured it well, just in case, and invested over 100,000 euros in this transporter.

Nu Pagadi always travelled alone; the left-hand box remained empty on the trips. The camera was focused only on the right-hand box. This is why Krug did not see the thick grey blanket which had been lying on the floor of the left box since the last service station stop and which was covering up something big, which wasn't moving.

About 20 kilometres down the road, Krug noticed for the first time that Nu Pagadi was getting nervous, unsettled. He snorted, scraped the floor with his hoofs and danced around. Krug was getting nervous as well, as Nu Pagadi was normally calm on these trips. Was the drive just too long this time? Or what was the matter?

Krug was well aware of the stories about the little quirks of great racehorses while travelling. The French super stallion Ourasi would only into the horsebox if a little white goat entered the wagon before him. Others calmed down only when a certain other horse accompanied them; their best friend, so to speak. Was Nu Pagadi now also starting to display such airs and graces? Krug saw on the monitor that his horse was getting more fidgety by the minute. It become clear that he had to stop. There was a sign for the next rest area in 5 kilometres. Maybe Nu Pagadi was just hungry. Krug was well prepared for that eventuality. He had brought all his favourites: carrots, bananas and his sweet milk pudding.

The exact location of the small restaurant where Max Krug turned off the motorway was 22.6 kilometres north of Munich city centre. He was going to consult a psychologist there, a trauma specialist, who was going to chase away the images of those few moments at the rest area which had been haunting him ever since and robbed him of all his sleep.

After stopping, Krug got out, walked around to the back, entered the security code and the back door of the horsebox opened. He immediately saw the blanket, which did not belong there, which he had not put there. He was the only one who had access to the box. Krug lifted up the blanket and saw the man, brown suit, white shirt, no coat. The man was lying on his stomach; he did not move. A slim, bald man. 'I don't know the man,' Krug immediately thought, 'this is a stranger.' Maybe one always thinks that when faced with a dead man. Dead men always look like strangers.

Krug tried to feel a pulse. But there was no pulse, and then Krug made the mistake of turning over the body. There was only a tiny bit of blood, an insignificant amount. But something awful had happened to the face. Something horrible. Again and again Krug would repeat this scene to his therapist. Again and again he would have to relive this moment. That was the only way, according to the therapist, that these images would ever leave his brain.

Everything else, everything that had happened at this rest area that night, was pretty much a blank in Krug's mind. Obviously the police had arrived at one point. At another point a second horsebox had arrived, into which he had led Nu Pagadi. He must have left a sorry impression all around, he thought later, as he had explained to everybody how precious this horse was. And in the face of a dead body... Oh, yes, he could also remember the name of the police inspector who had taken his statement. He could not really recall what he looked like except for a noticeable scar on his cheek, but the name had stuck: Inspector Maler, August Maler; Maler had been the name of a famous racehorse, who had won the German Derby many moons ago. Krug told his therapist that he really hoped he had not blubbered that bit of trivia at the time as well.

Nu Pagadi did not show any signs of post-traumatic stress. Krug had him checked, because you just never know. But everything was in order, physically as well as psychologically. Only two days after the horrible experience Nu Pagadi won his next race at Munich-Daglfing, convincing as usual. It was the fourth race of the evening. Krug's therapist would later repeat the well-known saying that a seriously insensitive person was as unfeeling as a horse.

# Second Day

## 12 May

### St-Anna-Platz, Munich, 2pm

August Maler was wearing grey corduroy trousers, a beige shirt and his light, beige canvas jacket. Beige and grey, those were his colours, and no matter what clothes he bought they always ended up being grey or beige. His wife had bought him a red shirt for a change, but he did not wear it very often.

St-Anna-Platz No. 9, that was the address of Gabriel Tretjak. On this warm afternoon August Maler afforded himself the luxury of sitting down for a few minutes on a green park bench just outside one of the churches, the big one, and opposite the other, the little one. August Maler had no special relationship with churches, but St-Anna-Platz was his favourite square in Munich. The two churches, the mighty chestnut trees, on the right the button shop, next to it the bakery run by the fat Turkish lady and her even fatter son. The school, the café, the gallery and the butcher. Maler often passed by the butcher and bought himself two sausage rolls. Not today though. This morning a cursory glance at the scales left him a little disillusioned.

On the corner of St-Anna-Platz there was a restaurant, which once upon a time had been a rotisserie, then had been taken over by Italians and then became a café. Now it was an Italian restaurant again. But the real significance of the place lay in the fact that it had been the backdrop to a cult TV show called 'Münchner Geschichten', but that was a long time ago. August Maler had loved that show, and still did today: he owned all the episodes on DVD. A group of young people, specialists in the lightness of being, big dreams, no rules – that was roughly the plotline. Thinking about the dialogue from the TV show made August Maler smile: Charley, the main character, gets into a taxi. The driver asks: 'Where to?' 'Anywhere,' Charley answers. 'Anywhere,' the driver retorts, 'that's tricky.'

Sitting on his bench August Maler thought again: one should live here, on the St-Anna-Platz, that would be a dream; but the Lehel district was one of the most expensive ones in expensive Munich. How would a policeman ever be able to afford that? But he also thought something else, and he surprised himself by that thought: if that guy with his horse had decided to pull in and stop 40 kilometres away, his colleagues from Ingolstadt would have had to deal with the gruesome murder. With the body in a horsebox. And a mobile phone. And he could stay seated on the bench, now lit by a beam of sunlight, which had come up behind the little church's dome. Inspector August Maler, 51 years of age: had somebody grown a bit tired prematurely?

*

A few minutes later August Maler rang the doorbell. The response came quickly over the intercom: 'Who's there?'

'My name is Maler, I am from the police. May I have a word?'

Maler had become used to introducing himself as an ordinary policeman. The acronym CID always sounded so dramatic.

Tretjak was standing in the doorway when Maler came up the stairs to the second floor. A good-looking fellow, dark, an almost southern European type. He was wearing jeans and a white shirt. And he was grinning. 'What a day. Inland Revenue is already here. And now the police…'

The inspector was led into a big room, a kind of kitchen-living room. He saw a stove, a big fridge, a bar and in front of that a black table on which lay a few files, one of them open. A young woman was sitting at the table, whom Tretjak introduced as a tax inspector from the Inland Revenue, Division Munich II: 'Ms Neustadt is doing a complete investigation of my tax affairs. We are right in the middle of it, so to speak.'

'Maler,' he introduced himself, offering his hand to Ms Neustadt. Then he turned to Tretjak: 'you must be tired. You had an exhausting flight, only landing this morning. How long is the trip from Colombo exactly?'

'How do you know that?' Tretjak asked.

'That's why I am here,' Maler answered, 'but I must speak to you in private.'

'Understood,' Ms Neustadt got up and gathered her

things. 'Then let's draw a line here and continue where we left off the day after tomorrow as discussed. I'll give you my card.' She laughed and also gave her card to the inspector. 'Who knows, maybe one day you'll need the Inland Revenue.'

After she had left, Tretjak put a bottle of mineral water and one glass on the table. 'Well…?'

Inspector Maler opened an envelope, took out two photographs and placed them in front of Tretjak. Both showed the same man. 'Do you know this man?'

'No.'

'This is Professor Harry Kerkhoff from Rotterdam, a well-known brain specialist. I should add: this *was* Professor Kerkhoff. Yesterday he was murdered.'

'My God,' said Tretjak, 'but I don't understand. What has all that to do with me?'

'We found a mobile phone on the body. A very strange mobile, I would have thought. Nothing on it, no saved numbers. In fact it was only used once, to place a call yesterday. The call went to Colombo, to your hotel. With this mobile phone a message was passed to you, that much we have been able to piece together.'

'That's right. I was at dinner and the guy from reception came over to say that a man had left an urgent message for me.'

'And what was that message?'

'It was weird, total nonsense. I didn't understand a thing. It alluded to a racehorse, a tip off that it had won some race or other. I have never in my life been to the races. I thought the whole thing was a mistake, a mix-up.'

Maler took a sip of water. 'Do you remember the name of the horse?'

'As a matter of fact I do: Nu Pagadi. Once upon a time I knew what that meant, something Russian. A strange name for a horse, I thought. That's why I remember.'

'Nu Pagadi. That means: "Just you wait."' Maler paused. 'Mr Tretjak, we found the body of the professor in a horsebox at a motorway service station. The dead man was lying in the left box, and in the right stood the horse. Nu Pagadi. A very special horse, by the way. Worth a lot of money.'

The conversation between the two didn't last very much longer. Maler asked who knew that Tretjak was in that hotel in Colombo and enquired after the purpose of the trip. And then he added: 'you have to think about what this message could mean.'

The big church bell on the St-Anna-Platz tolled half past three when Inspector Maler left the house. Two chimes, as always, every half hour. Maler had had a great teacher in the police, his long-time boss, who had taught him a lot. One lesson was: try to avoid, as far as possible, judging people who you are investigating. Don't evaluate, hang everything in the balance, don't decide whether you like them or not, whether you find them credible or not. Because every judgement narrows the perspective, limits the observation. A good policeman hasn't got any drawers for thoughts like that, his boss used to say.

Maler climbed into his car, a beige BMW, and for once listened to that inner voice: don't jump the gun about Tretjak. Only one observation registered in his memory: normally people who are given such dramatic news ask questions. How did the man die? How was he discovered? Are there any leads the police are following? These kind of things interest people. With Tretjak it was different. He listened and responded. Nothing else.

When Maler turned into the Mittlerer Ring he could not help passing one tiny little judgement. It concerned the slim blonde tax inspector whose hand he had shaken in Tretjak's flat. He remembered his roommate in the cardiac clinic who had shared his two-bed room for weeks. They had thought up a little game. With every woman who entered the room or who they met in the clinic they connected profession or nationality with looks. Clichés like 'nurses are prettier than cleaners' were predictable, but nevertheless interesting, but more fun were remarks such as 'for an English girl she is pretty, but not for a physiotherapist.' Maler was certain that his roommate and he would have agreed about the lady from the Inland Revenue: for a tax inspector, she was damn good looking.

## St-Anna-Platz, Munich, 5pm

There is only one thing the human brain cannot do, and that is *not* to learn. That's what he had always said. That had been the standard opening line to Kerkhoff's famous lectures. Tretjak looked at the picture on the screen. Harry Kerkhoff smiled his arrogant, flashing smile; it was an old photograph, at least ten years old, taken at some festivity or another, at a late hour. Kerkhoff in dinner jacket, Tretjak as well. He was standing next to him in that picture. Kerkhoff still had a full head of hair back then. Later, when he started to lose it, he had immediately had his head shaved. Now he had more of a patch which he needed to shave each morning, he had joked, when Tretjak almost did not recognise him – one shouldn't delay good-byes too long. Tretjak moved the mouse and clicked through a few more old pictures of Harry Kerkhoff, which Google had found – until a newer one turned up. Tretjak picked up the phone and dialled the number of Kerkhoff's son in Rotterdam. But nobody answered.

The room Tretjak was in was originally meant to have been a living room. It measured almost 60 square metres. It had two bay windows and a door leading to a balcony. Tretjak did not need a living room and had therefore had it redesigned. He had had the parquet floor sanded and oiled but not sealed. In front of the windows and the pale balcony door blinds came down to the floor in aluminium strips. Most of the time they were closed, just like now. There was not one single picture on the white walls. Even the steel girders holding up the ceiling where walls had once stood were painted white. When entering the room one noticed two areas, like small islands in the middle of this sea of white. To the right stood a table by the Danish designer Hein van Eek, made up of tiny pastel-coloured wooden pieces, glued together and thickly coated with varnish, 3 metres 20 centimetres long and 1 metre 40 centimetres wide. There were no chairs, only a bench in front of it without a backrest. The whole surface of the table, and the seat of the bench as well, was covered with piles of paper, books, newspaper clippings, files, all neatly arranged, flush at one side, obviously following some kind of order.

On the left side of the room, the other island looked a little bit like the cockpit of an airplane. That is where Tretjak was sitting now, on a simple, grey office chair, with three flat screen monitors arranged on a sort of crescent-shaped base. The connected hardware, modems and printer were hidden underneath, behind light grey lacquered panels.

Tretjak had turned his chair to the left, moved the mouse with his right hand and looked at another over-sized monitor mounted on the wall. It was showing the official University of Rotterdam photograph: Professor Doctor Harry Kerkhoff, 50, Vice-President of the university, Dean of Faculty for Bio-chemistry. On the smaller desktop screens Tretjak had called up several files. Kerkhoff's bibliography, a podcast of his appearance in front of the ethics commission of the EU when he was asked about stem cell research, and media reports about the discovery of his body yesterday. One monitor showed the minutes of their last meeting. That had been eight years ago.

When the brain receives information it immediately processes it, and it will always learn from it. You cannot turn back the clock to the moment when the brain did not have that information. It had been Kerkhoff's great talent to condense his knowledge into short messages, which were easy to understand.

When do you give what information to whom – and what is the result? And the effect? That had been the theme of their meetings over the years: Tretjak had provoked the scientist with questions – and had noted down his answers, analysed them, used them to fine-tune his techniques. When does who get what information?

Maybe his 'No' in answer to the inspector's question about whether he knew Kerkhoff had been a reflex. The reflex of a man who liked to have the advantage over his opposite as far as information was concerned. Tretjak regretted his answer. Maybe it had been the fault of the tax inspector that he had made the spontaneous decision not to reveal that information.

He rolled his chair back and got up. The wall behind him concealed one single, big cupboard. All the files about his clients and their special cases were contained here. An archive full of connections and intrigue, full of personal secrets, full of information, which at some point somewhere had been useful – and could be again.

Behind one of the doors was a fridge. Tretjak opened it and took out a small bottle of still Hildon mineral water and a strip of tablets marked Tavor. He swallowed two and drank the water in one gulp. He closed the door, placed the bottle on the floor and sat down in front of the monitors again. He looked into the eyes of the scientist on the big screen and wondered: what were you doing in a horsebox, Harry? What has your death got to do with me? Who called me? You?

Our brain is constantly looking for order. It wants to recognise structure – in everything which life dishes up. Kerkhoff had written a remarkable book on that very subject: *On the Correlation of Emotion and Structural Thought.* We search for the structure of a story, of a movie, the structure of the character of a person we meet, we want to understand a sequence of events by recognising its pattern. 'Feed the brain of a human being with structure,' Kerkhoff had said, 'then you take away his fear.'

Tretjak decided he would call the inspector whose card was still lying on the kitchen counter later and tell him the truth: yes, he had known Kerkhoff. In fact, he had known him well.

The digital clock below the screen was showing 7.20pm; it was time, he had to go. The table in the Osteria was booked, as per usual the second booth from the entrance. A client was waiting there. Or to be precise: a man who wanted to become his client. A member of the Bavarian parliament, not a well-known one, more a back-bencher. Tretjak knew only a few titbits so far. The man's name appeared on the client list of some group of call girls or other, who supplied young women from the Ukraine to men for sex, and this group had now been busted. 'Help this man, Tretjak, fix it. Please.' This was the message he found in his mailbox on his return from Sri Lanka. It had been the voice of a minister, a member of the Federal Government in Berlin.

Tretjak keyed in a combination and all screens went black. For a few moments more he stayed seated and stared at the big black space on the wall. It had been Kerkhoff who had, back then, helped him come up with what he later called 'the seven commandments' of his job. It had been Kerkhoff who had said to him: 'what you are doing is interfering in people's lives, interfering with their value system... you are playing fate, you do realise that, don't you? If you want to continue doing this job, then you need firm principles which structure your action, a kind of inner constitution. A few immovable pillars, which you can hang on to. If you don't have those pillars, you'll find yourself at sea, and then things will turn dangerous. Not just for your bank account, but for your soul.'

Tretjak got up, went to his walk-in closet and changed. He chose a clean, white shirt and the dark navy suit he had bought in Milan in March. He put his phone in his pocket and slipped into a light black summer coat. He did not need anything more. Pen and paper would be waiting on the table as usual.

The bell gave off a melodic ring. And the voice on the intercom said: 'your taxi is waiting, Mr Tretjak.'

When Tretjak left the Italian restaurant Osteria, Schelling Street 95, almost four hours later, he decided to walk home. It was not really warm, but the air would do him good. He paused outside the restaurant, buttoned up his coat all the way, looked up to the sky and saw the stars, despite all the pollution. For a very short moment he had a flashback to his youth. That happened rarely, very rarely. And when it did, it happened without warning, as if it assaulted him. Back then, when he was eleven, twelve years of age, a starry night had been an opportunity to escape. Then he knew that that night he could escape the misery of his existence and go away, far, far away. When he went to his room to fetch the suitcase with the telescope he had the blessing of all those who ruled his life back then. They would say something in a language he did not understand. But they said it with a smile and he realised it was something nice.

Tretjak turned his face from the sky and walked in the direction of Ludwig Street at a brisk pace.

The member of parliament had disgusted him. A sweaty man with a fake and at the same time obsequious expression, who had tried the whole evening to win his sympathy. Maybe, Tretjak thought, he really believes he deserves sympathy. Again and again he had outlined, for Tretjak's benefit, what would happen if his name was associated with this group of call girls. His family, his reputation as a politician, his whole life would be damaged.

Tretjak had asked right after the starter, 'What do you want me to do?' and had repeated the question twice. 'You are supposed to help me,' the man had answered again and again.

During those kind of meetings in the Osteria, Tretjak always sat with his back towards the entrance. That is why he did not notice the very attractive lady in a black trouser suit entering the restaurant. Only when he got up to go to the gents – in fact, he just wanted a break from the exhausting conversation – did he notice her. She sat at the bar, long, straight brown hair, unobtrusive make-up, no jewellery except a big silver ring. For a split second, when he passed her, he had the feeling that she wanted to say something. But then Mario, the waiter, pushed himself between them.

'You don't want to change your life, do you, not at all,' Tretjak had told the member of parliament at the end of the meal. 'You just want to get away with it.' He had thought of Kerkhoff and the first of the seven commandments, the simplest one: a job you don't want to take on you turn down. 'I have no access to police files, I can't manipulate evidence, do you understand?' he realised that most people did not believe him when he said this. Was there anything Tretjak really had access to? 'All I could do for you is to get you a new telephone number. How old did you say the girls were?'

Tretjak saw in the parliamentarian's face that he had

not cottoned on to his irony. Back in the old days he wouldn't have made such a remark. He would have stayed polite and cool. The guy would complain to the minister but that would not matter. The minister knew Tretjak's principles – from his own experience.

'I am sorry, sir,' he finally said. 'I can't take this job. You can remain seated, finish your wine. The bill is paid. You are my guest.'

When Mario brought him his coat, he noticed that the woman from the bar was now gone. Mario noticed his glance and smiled. 'She urgently wanted to talk to you. She said it was very important.' The waiter had strict instructions not to interrupt any conversation at table two.

When Tretjak reached Ludwig Street, he walked towards the Feldherrnhalle and the illuminated Theatiner Church. Just as he turned into the Hofgarten his mobile phone rang, indicating that he had received a message. Tretjak took the phone out of his pocket and read: *I am the woman from the* Osteria. *I need to talk to you.*

Tretjak was not overly surprised that a stranger had found out his number. But he decided not to react, put his phone back in his pocket and walked on. The phone rang again. The message was exactly the same. Tretjak paused again – this time he wrote back: *you can speak to me only on recommendation.*

*I have a referral,* the answer shot back. *From your father.*

Tretjak froze. A passerby might have mistaken him

for a newly planted tree. Then he raised the phone to his ear, making a connection to that unknown number. A woman's voice answered.

'Hello?'

'That is the wrong recommendation. I haven't spoken to my father for 20 years and I intend to keep it that way. This is the end of our conversation.'

Tretjak was determined to push the red button but hesitated for a split second. That was how he still caught the beginning of the sentence: 'You are making a mistake, don't you understand...' before the call was cut.

He was still standing between the trees. The pale blue light of the phone's display illuminated his face, when he entered a service code, which instantly changed his mobile phone number – and automatically sent a message with the new one to all his registered contacts. It would take this woman some time to reach him again.

# Third Day

## 13 May

*Munich, Hofgarten, 10am*

Gabriel Tretjak did not have a secretary, an office, or any employees. He delegated nothing. He valued this exclusivity: the people who hired him could be sure that Tretjak was personally going to fix their problem, which was necessary. It was he who sent the email, wrote the letter, went on the trip. A one-man show, which ran smoothly only when it was perfectly organised. Over time he had honed the procedures. Tretjak had consulted a specialist, an Indian by the name of Rashid Manan, whose business it was to restructure the organisation of big hospitals all over the world. Manan worked in Beijing, New York, and Mumbai as well as in Paris. He had developed the method of competing priorities, which he made the core of every new plan for the hospitals. In any hospital, questions competed with one another every minute of the day: Which was the most important case and therefore had to be dealt with first? What was the second most important and therefore came next? And so on. The clinic with thousands of patients was the hardware, so to speak, which needed a software package. And Rashid Manan provided that.

Tretjak moved the same questions into the centre of his daily working routine. What had to be done at once? What could wait until tomorrow? Or a week? What could be put off for a longer time? And what had taken care of itself? He was constantly working on different timelines, which he coordinated afresh each morning.

This morning he had planned to make four telephone calls. The fourth was probably insignificant, and had nothing to do with the other important timelines. It was this call, however, which would leave him clueless and worried.

It was just after 10am when Tretjak left his flat to take a stroll in the direction of the Hofgarten. He loved to make his calls in this park, because it was so quiet and peaceful there. His favourite spot was right at the entrance, under the arcades, where you could imagine being in Italy, just without the tourists.

He called up a number in his mobile phone. He wanted to finish the job Melanie Schwarz had assigned him and which he had got underway in Colombo the day before yesterday.

'Fritzen.'

'It's Gabriel Tretjak. Good morning to you.'

'The same to you, Mr Tretjak. I don't know what to say. I guess, first of all: thank you. I've received your package with the papers and have checked everything, if that was possible in such a short time. It seems indeed to be a fact that our two directors were involved in a conspiracy. That is an extremely unsavoury business as it not only would have cost Mr Schwarz his job but it would have cost us a lot of money.'

'According to my information,' Tretjak said, 'things don't look too bleak for your firm. I guess Mr Schwarz can still get the agreement with Union Carry going.'

'I love your optimism, Mr Tretjak. We'll see. I have followed your suggestion and told Meinhardt and Busse to expect a call from you this morning. I have also allowed myself to give them a piece of my mind. Let's say: they broke into a bit of a sweat.'

The conversation between Tretjak and Joachim Fritzen, the head of the supervisory board of the company producing cooling aggregates, was uncomplicated, as the two already knew each other. They had cooperated on a previous occasion, four years ago. Whenever Tretjak accepted a new assignment, he looked for connections in his network which might be used as a leverage point. A former and, more importantly, a satisfied customer was a good starting point.

Back then Fritzen himself had given him the assignment. And everything had run smoothly, just the way Tretjak liked it: at the end there had only been winners.

Joachim Fritzen had been the head of the executive board of another company at the time. The economic situation of that company had been so perilous that its survival depended on securing a large contract from Turkey. But there had been a competitor, who seemed to have the edge. Tretjak was engaged – and Fritzen's company got the contract. Sure, Tretjak had applied pressure, maybe even used a few tricks, but he had also arranged for the other company to get a comparable deal from Azerbaijan.

That was his philosophy: sometimes things could only get fixed if somebody on the periphery assumed control.

'Oh, another question, Mr Fritzen: does your daughter still want to become a journalist?'

'Yes, I am afraid so. I can't talk her out of it.'

'Who knows,' said Tretjak, 'maybe it's not such a bad choice. I just wanted to say: I have found out that the *Augsburger Allgemeine* runs a first-class journalist training scheme. And they are looking for applicants. She could start straight away, if she'd like.'

'Mr Tretjak, you make me blush. I have to say thank you again.'

'Not at all. As you know, it's all part of the service.'

The second call was much shorter. Tretjak notified Mr Meinhardt that, one: his scheming had been exposed; two: he was going to leave the company; three: he had a meeting at Munich Airport, 8:30am, terminal 1, in the Käfer-Bistro; duration of the meeting: 15 minutes max. Tretjak was going to present him with a document he would be obliged to sign – an admission of guilt plus an agreement to transfer 50,000 euros into the private account of the injured party, Peter Schwarz.

'And what happens if I don't come to the airport?' Meinhardt finally wanted to know.

'Then we pass everything to the public prosecutor. Mr Fritzen and I are of the opinion that your dealings during the last few weeks constitute a serious case of embezzlement and criminal damage. It is up to you to save yourself and the company from this becoming public knowledge.'

'I will come,' Meinhardt had replied.

The other one, this Busse fellow, had been much more self-confident and aggressive on the phone. Tretjak did not want to waste too much time and decided after a few minutes to play his trump card, which he had held back just in case. The evidence a private detective had produced was conclusive: the man had a lover and had paid for an apartment for her – and in addition there were compromising pictures taken in a so-called sauna. Tretjak described them on the telephone and at the same time observed two boys playing badminton in the park. The wind, which had just risen, was making it easy for them. When he finally hung up, it was clear that Busse would have to make his way to the airport tomorrow morning.

The fourth call was of a more private nature. Tretjak was already walking towards the exit from the park when he dialled the number of his cleaning lady, who had not shown up yesterday. She normally came every Monday and was very reliable. He wanted to find out whether anything was wrong, but even more importantly wanted to ask whether she was going to come today instead.

Tomorrow was his next appointment with the lady from the Inland Revenue and everything should be clean when the tax inspector showed up.

The daughter of the cleaning lady picked up the phone. That was good as the cleaner spoke very little German. She was Argentinian and had arrived in Germany many years ago. Her strength had been sufficient to build a new life, but not to learn a new language. For the past five years Rosa Lanner had cleaned his apartment. They could not have a conversation, but Tretjak did not mind that, quite the contrary. He had to do a lot of talking anyhow. And the woman had something he liked. Was it a certain decency? Conscientiousness? Or was it the way she shook his hand, how she caringly grasped his in both of her hands?

'But Mr Tretjak, I don't understand. My mother is with you. She said that she was going with you to your house in the country. She was going to stay there for several days, as there was so much to do.'

'House in the country? I don't have a house in the country. And I didn't make any arrangements with your mother. You or your mother must be mistaken.'

'Mr Tretjak, my mother hasn't been home for two days. And she spoke of you, I am sure of that. For heaven's sake, what could have happened to her?' The voice on the other side of the line was breaking. She was going to call everybody and as soon as she knew anything, she would get in touch.

*

It was early afternoon when Carolina Lanner called back. Her voice glowed with excitement. Tretjak first thought she was crying.

'My mother has been in touch. Thank you, thank you so much, Mr Tretjak. My mother is overjoyed. Thank you, Mr Tretjak, we all don't know what to say.'

'I don't understand,' Tretjak replied, and for a brief moment started to get annoyed, 'what are you thanking me for?'

'What for? My mother told me everything. How a driver picked her up and took her to the airport and put her on a plane, first class. And how she flew to Buenos Aires. My mother. For the first time, back to Argentina. For the first time, back to see the family. My mother was crying with joy. And all that you made possible – and paid for it as well, Mr Tretjak. You are such a good man, such a good man!'

It was dawning on Tretjak that it was useless to try to clear up this misunderstanding. Because it had to be a misunderstanding. What else could it be? Who would come up with the idea of sending his cleaning lady half-way around the world, and in first class? Gabriel Tretjak was experiencing a wave of anxiety rising up his spine. He asked the daughter when she expected his mother to return and when she would come back to work.

'Next week, Mr Tretjak, but you know that better than anybody. Next Monday she will be with you, like always.'

*Munich, Institute of Forensic Medicine/CSI*
*(Criminal Investigation Services), 12 noon*

The pathologist was a friendly, stocky lady with the distinctive accent of the Swabian region of south-western Germany. Inspector Maler had known her for a long time, and every time he saw her he was struck by the contrast: on the one hand this MD with her pleasant femininity, and on the other hand the brutal reality of the bodies which she investigated.

In the case of the murder of Harry Kerkhoff the forensic scientist had not found any traces that would have offered up any clues about the identity of the killer. Cause of death: stabbing of the liver. There were two more knife wounds: one had hit the kidney, the other the right lung. The knife had been thrust with precision, and only a little blood had seeped out. Somebody had known what they were doing. A professional hit. The murder weapon had been a pointed, thin, extremely sharp blade, like a dagger. That was it for the moment – more details later.

Time of death: about six to ten hours before the body was discovered in the horsebox. Harry Kerkhoff had being drinking, his blood alcohol level had been 1.2 millilitres. 'That's about three glasses of wine where I come from,' the doctor added helpfully.

What made this murder particularly gruesome was the fact that the perpetrator had removed both of the eyes of the victim with a round instrument, something like a spoon. It could also have been a sort of scoop similar to the ones used in ice cream parlours to scrape the ice cream from the tubs, the pathologist explained. One could assume that the scooping had not damaged the eyes, leading to the conclusion that the murderer had taken them along as a souvenir. As the removal had been done with great precision one could further assume that this was not the first time the perpetrator had done this. Maler looked for a reaction in the face of the doctor, but could find none. Madame Doctor had herself totally under control.

An ice cream scoop. When Maler heard this word, he knew that it had started. Again. Whenever he worked on brutal murders he was plagued by day-mares, as he called them. Suddenly, in the middle of the day, these images would appear in his mind's eye. Always following the same pattern: he would see the scene he was just living but arranged as a catastrophe. The waitress in the coffee shop, for example, was suddenly covered in blood and her right arm was missing. Or he was driving along a street and saw a horrific accident with many fatalities. It always only lasted for a split second. Then the image was gone. As if a picture editor had inserted a brief clip into a scene.

Maler had always imagined that these day-mares functioned as a transformer of his over-worked police brain. All those horrible experiences which he had to live through in his line of duty were spat out as little bits so he could get rid of them. He had come up with this theory to calm himself down, so he could live with it. He had not told it to anyone. Amongst policemen there was a silent agreement: one kept quiet about one's own sensitivities, if they existed. He had not even mentioned them to Rainer Gritz, his long-time assistant. Not because he was ashamed of them. Gritz, the long, dangly Gritz, was the best policeman he knew, the most methodical and persistent. There was no one else he trusted more. But Maler was convinced that if he told Gritz about his daymares, Gritz would have dug up everything and anything there was to know about such phenomena. Gritz would have drowned him with that knowledge. And that was precisely what Maler didn't want. He didn't want information. He wanted to forget the images. As soon as possible and whenever possible.

But then, after his heart problems several years ago, Inspector Maler had found himself sitting opposite an elderly lady, the head psychologist of the clinic on Lake Lusterbach where he was convalescing. She was well over 80, but nobody would have dreamt of talking about a possible retirement age since she owned the clinic.

Dreams were her speciality. Her first question for Maler was always, 'what did you dream about last night?' And it was her that he first told about the day-mares. The woman had white hair and a pleasant, calm voice. And it was in the same calm and pleasant way that she reacted to his account. She told him about her own dreams that she had at night and about the fact that for decades she had experienced fantasies of murder. 'And I tell you, Inspector: I was feeling great while dreaming. It was only in the mornings that I was sometimes shocked by my own feelings.' They talked extensively about the nature of evil and how nobody was safe from it. Maler remembered from these conversations that he had to recognise these visionary attacks as a kind of thermometer. The more these images flashed up in front of his eyes the more urgently his soul was signalling to him that he was expecting too much of himself.

This time only three hours passed between his leaving the Forensic Science building and the start of the daymares. The first one came to Maler when he was stopping at a red light: the driver of the taxi waiting next to him was suddenly headless. The second image flashed up at the newsagent and was even shorter than usual – the whole stand was doused in blood.

Maler took a walk. He left police headquarters, located right behind the cathedral, went to the Odeonsplatz and through the Hofgarten, strolling in the direction of St-Anna-Platz, his usual route if he needed a bit of peace and quiet. He hoped that this Tretjak fellow was not leaving his flat just at this very minute and that he wouldn't bump into him. That morning Tretjak had called him. He had apologised for not telling Maler the truth the other day: he had known this Kerkhoff, in fact he had known him very well.

Maler still had the Swabian voice of the pathologist in his ear. She had said that Kerkhoff's eyes had been removed post-mortem. The victim had not been tortured. One had to assume that the perpetrator was sending out a sort of message.

# Fourth Day

## 14 May

*Munich, St-Anna-Platz, 2pm*

She came by bicycle. Tretjak had expected her to ascend the escalators from the underground. So he was surprised to hear her voice behind him.

'Somehow it doesn't look very tiring,' she said, 'your job I mean of course, Mr Tretjak.'

It was early afternoon, the sun was shining, and Tretjak was sitting at a table outside the café on St-Anna-Platz with an espresso in front of him. Fiona Neustadt pushed her bicycle next to the table, raised it on its stand and sat down opposite him. The clock of the big church struck two. And then the little one followed suit: two o'clock. The tax inspector was dead on time. She was wearing a Sixties-style knee-length white dress with black polka-dots and a denim jacket. Her feet were clad in navy blue canvas shoes and her hair was tied back in a ponytail.

'Summer must have arrived at the Inland Revenue,' he quipped. She laughed. 'And it hasn't for the management consultant? Or I beg your pardon…' she raised one eyebrow mockingly, 'for the "personal management and economic consultant". You can buy me a cup of coffee. Cappuccino, please.' She carried with her one of those ugly shoulder bags made from durable plastic and took from it one of Tretjak's ledgers which she had taken with her after the first meeting. She had been a little surprised that he was using such an old-fashioned way of keeping his books. Tretjak's cashbooks were all black A4 notebooks and followed a simple principle: on the left-hand side all the monies coming in were noted down by hand, on the right were all the expenses, and at the bottom of each page the figures in both columns were added up. These sums were carried over to the next page as the opening balances. Each entry carried the name of the client and key words such as *ticket Rome* or *fee part payment.* The receipts for each of the entries were filed in separate folders, which Tretjak, in preparation for the meeting, had lined up on the table in the kitchen.

The ledger Fiona Neustadt now opened was peppered with yellow post-it notes. Tretjak saw that each had something written on it; most of the sentences ending with a question mark. Fiona Neustadt had angular, almost male handwriting – at least that was his impression.

'You see,' she said, 'a lot of work lies ahead of us. But don't worry too much: it looks worse than it is. Most of the questions are quite harmless, sometimes I think I know the answers already and just need confirmation.'

That was how the afternoon they spent together started, with a coffee in the sun. That morning, while driving to his appointment at the airport, Tretjak had caught himself thinking that he was actually looking forward to his meeting with the tax inspector. In contrast to other people he was not worried in the least about the inspection of his books. This much had always been clear: his business was shady, legally shady, morally shady; it thrived on discretion, on action behind the scenes, hidden from view – so he couldn't afford a less than completely transparent accounting system on top of that. In his job he encountered many enemies, always new ones, always different ones. It was important to identify and to know them. Unnecessary ones should be avoided. With the Inland Revenue it was very simple: you had to pay on time. And that's what he did. Therefore he could just enjoy the company of this interesting woman. Fiona Neustadt was intelligent and good-looking – and *simpatico*. He could let her take his mind off the disturbing thoughts which kept preying on his mind. Did Kerkhoff's murder have anything to do with him? What was going on with his cleaning lady? What, and more importantly who, was behind all this? Why on earth had he given the wrong answer to the inspector? When he called Maler that morning to correct himself, he immediately realised that the guy had already found out about his connection to the brain expert. He seemed alert and suspicious, and would start sifting through Tretjak's business. And the police were nothing like the Inland Revenue.

When Tretjak opened the door to his apartment and let Ms Neustadt enter in front of him, he noticed her perfume. The scent of grapefruit, he thought. Or was it lime? Later, when they were sitting at the kitchen table working, he noticed that she was not only wearing a fine old IWC Swiss watch, the classic *Ingenieur* model, on her left wrist, but also one of those colourful, cheap fabric bands connected with a wish which one wore until it fell off by itself and the wish came true. That was new, and Tretjak asked himself what Fiona Neustadt might have wished.

Following the chime of the church clock striking every quarter of an hour, they worked through the yellow notes. Some questions dealt with expenses which were not associated with one particular client. Tretjak thought of the member of parliament and explained to Fiona Neustadt that only about one fifth of all the people who contacted him actually become clients. There were also yellow post-it notes next to entries in the account book where Tretjak had written *received in cash. Fee EURO 75,000 received in cash. Fee, first down payment, EURO 50,000 received in cash.* And another time even *EURO 500,000 received in cash.*

Tretjak presented Ms Neustadt with a copy of a receipt made out by him for each of these entries, the corresponding pay-in slip from the bank, and the correct listing of the amount in his income tax returns. What was not evident in these cases were the names of the clients – on the receipt copies the names were obscured. It was about this point Tretjak had expected more of an argument with the tax inspector. For this he would have had a well-rehearsed legal disposition ready and waiting, which protected his clients' anonymity. But Fiona Neustadt only casually remarked: 'Well, I guess we can see it as some kind of medical confidentiality.' She only compared the figures, and checked whether the entries tallied with the written receipts. For this she had donned a pair of black-rimmed spectacles over whose rims she occasionally shot him a glance. There were periods when they sat there without uttering a word, with only her pen moving systematically from column to column. Once Tretjak brewed them a fresh pot of tea, twice he got up to fetch them a fresh bottle of water from the fridge. The two pieces of American cheesecake, which he had bought at the café before they went up, stood untouched on the kitchen counter.

Sitting there in his kitchen, Tretjak slowly started to feel something, which surprised him: he envied this young woman. A real job, a regular working day with a bicycle and a shoulder bag, and with what he guessed was a small apartment. And with wishes you could tie around your wrist.

Tretjak had always seen his extraordinary memory as a gift: it had served him well. Today, now, doing this work, it seemed to take his breath away. Each entry in his books which they discussed conjured up images, stories and destinies in his mind's eye, lines of people appeared, long-passed situations played out again. While the tax inspector audited the past three years of his life from a strictly accounting perspective, he was sitting in his kitchen thrown back into the mess of human emotions and behavioural patterns. He suddenly felt unwell, felt that his pulse had started racing, that the palms of his hands had become clammy. For a short moment he thought about interrupting the appointment. Later he would think back to that moment and how things would have panned out if he had done just that. But instead he apologised and went to the bathroom. He took two Tavor and splashed cold water onto his face.

When he returned to the kitchen, Fiona Neustadt asked: 'Are you alright? You look a bit pale.'

'Yes, everything is fine,' he answered.

She closed the account book lying in front of her on the table. 'May I ask you a personal question?'

'Sure.'

She took off her glasses, leant forward, with her elbows on the table and her head resting on her cupped hands, and looked directly at Tretjak. 'I know the books of management consultants,' she said. 'I know the books of investment advisors and those of enterprise coaches... they all look different. There include project forecasts, project schedules, cost calculations. There are reverse remuneration, profit shares...' She paused. 'What exactly is your job, Mr Tretjak? For what kind of consulting are people willing to pay these kinds of sums?'

He almost told her: this has nothing to do with consulting. I am not advising my clients what they should do. I do it for them. I send them away, get them to leave their lives, and for a while step into their shoes. Only when everything is fixed do they return. Instead he said: 'Where did you get this very beautiful watch?'

She smiled, lifted her wrist up and looked at the watch. 'From my grandfather,' she said, 'I had always admired it, from when I was little. When I turned eighteen, he gave it to me. And one year later he died.'

She did not say: you didn't answer my question. She did not even say: I understand, you can't talk about that. She simply picked up the next accounts book, opened it, put on her glasses and said: 'Each month you transfer 2,000 euros into the account of a church in Niederbayern. That is done by standing order. One could assume that this is a donation, but you have not applied for tax relief for it.'

Tretjak felt the tablets working as he became calmer. 'I want to support the priest in that community. He does a great job. I don't want him to think that I am doing it just because it is tax deductable.'

She looked at him: 'Are you some kind of Robin Hood?'

The melodic tone of the doorbell chimed. The police would later record the time to have been 17.55.

'I have a delivery for Mr Tretjak,' the voice on the intercom said. A few seconds later the man connected with the voice was standing at the front door. He wore the orange jacket of a courier firm and was carrying a giant bunch of flowers in his hands, wrapped in see-through plastic. It was a distinctive bunch, exclusively roses, but in different colours. 'I am supposed to deliver this to Mr Tretjak personally,' said the guy. 'And this message.'

Tretjak took the flowers and a little white envelope. Deep in thought, he closed the door.

'Oh,' said Fiona Neustadt when he came back into the kitchen with the flowers, 'you must have left a good impression with somebody. And it seems not to have been a man.'

Tretjak saw that she was packing up her shoulder bag and making a move, wrapping up the appointment. He placed the flowers in the sink, closed the drain and turned on the tap. Still standing, he opened the envelope. It contained a card, on it a single, typed sentence: *shrouds are white*. Tretjak observed the water filling the sink. When its surface drew level with the edge, he absent-mindedly closed the tap. The church bells chimed six o'clock.

Only then did he notice Fiona Neustadt standing and ready to leave, with her bag slung over her shoulder and her jacket buttoned up, looking rather sheepish as though she had just witnessed an intimate moment. 'I'd better be going now,' she said. 'We could speak on the phone about another appointment.'

Tretjak nodded silently. He would have to inform the inspector. *Shrouds are white...* What the hell was going on here?

'I have written down another few questions for you... They are lying on the table,' Fiona Neustadt said and turned towards the hallway to go. He heard her footsteps approach the front door.

'Wait,' he said, and followed her.

She stopped, turned towards him, her hand already on the doorknob.

'Have you got any plans for tonight? Do you have a date or something?' Tretjak asked.

There was an astonished look on her face. The look of a tax inspector who is asking herself whether somebody is overstepping the line.

'I'm sorry,' Tretjak said. 'I didn't want to… I just wanted to show you something.'

Now she smiled. 'What did you want to show me?'

'Forget it,' Tretjak said.

'I'm meeting a girlfriend to play badminton at 7pm,' she said. 'But afterwards I'm free.'

Tretjak hesitated another moment, but then he smiled as well. 'Then you can exhaust yourself for a really long time,' he said. 'Because what I want to show you can be seen only when it is pitch dark.'

### *Bolzano, Italy, 5pm*

It was exceptionally hot for late spring. Maria left her apartment directly over the ice cream parlour on Waltherplatz just after 5pm. She had put on her blue woollen jacket and on top of that the navy apron. A bit too warm, but she did not mind. On foot it would take her eight minutes to get to the hotel.

The little Maria. There must have been a time when she had been pretty. But as a woman of 83 years, this was no longer a distinguishing characteristic, especially not for a woman like the little, old Maria, who had never known any affairs of the heart. No, she always said, I didn't have time for any of that. She had been married to the hotel, for all these decades. Married to the hotel Zum Blauen Mondschein in Bolzano, one of the best in town. The owner of the hotel had changed a few times, yet standards had remained the same. Breakfast was served in the beautiful garden, as was lunch and dinner. From the rooms you could look down to the garden, and from the garden up to the windows of the rooms, framed by green shutters.

Maria had been a chambermaid at the Blauen Mondschein for almost 70 years and had seen the various owners come and go. When it had become known that the new proprietor had toyed with the idea of retiring Maria, the Mayor of Bolzano had written a letter. Bolzano was a complicated town, it had said, a little bit of Austria, a little bit of Italy; living together was a somewhat fragile, sensitive affair. One was proud of the

Blauen Mondschein it said, especially because the hotel had always placed a special emphasis on tradition. And, as the mayor put it, part of that tradition was Maria Unterganzner. Italians as well as Austrians could not envisage the hotel without her. He was politely asked to consider that fact.

Maria was very slender and over the years she became more and more slender, which gave the impression that a mere puff of air could knock her down. But that impression was wrong. Maria was never sick, not even for a day. She sometimes had a fever and suffered extreme pains in her joints, but she never took time off because of it. She had a soft voice and seemed warm-hearted. Those who knew her better also knew that she did not show deep emotions. In fact, nothing daunted her, neither the big nor the small calamities. Whatever happened in the hotel over the decades, Maria would show up for work the next day.

She never talked about the old days. Especially not about what might have been the hardest time the hotel had experienced. The owner had suddenly become very ill and could not work any longer. Her husband had not been there; had abandoned her overnight. One could see that the hotel was leaderless. The crisis had ended with the death of the owner. That was now over 30 years ago. When the hotel had organised a party on the occasion of Maria's 80th birthday they had wanted to invite the little boy, who back then had lived with his sick mother in the hotel. His name was Gabriel Tretjak. Maybe Maria would have enjoyed seeing the now grown-up boy again, if he had come to the party. It had not been easy to find his address: St-Anna-Platz, Munich. Twice the invitation had been sent. But Tretjak had not reacted, had not even politely declined.

On this day, like every other day, Maria started her late shift with a short chat at the reception desk. She always asked whether any of the guests were titled, who was a doctor, a Professor X or a Magistrate Y. Or nowadays more and more often the guest was a Frau Professor or Frau Dr Z. Maria loved titles, and she loved to address the guests properly when she met them. Between 5:30 and 6pm she would turn down the beds in the rooms for the night. She liked doing this and gave it her very special touch: the crisp white linen was folded back in a sharp corner. A guest once told her that it looked a little bit like the floppy ear of a big white rabbit.

Maria knew that a professor had checked into room 242, a new guest, who had never stayed at the Blauen Mondschein before. Just before 6pm, Maria knocked on the door and entered when there was no reply. The first thing she noticed was the huge bunch of flowers standing next to the television. Different kinds of roses, and lots of them, in all sorts of colours. The flowers definitely were not compliments of the hotel, that much Maria knew. It only placed small bunches in the rooms, flowers from the garden. And in the garden, they only grew yellow roses and a few orange ones.

Only then did Maria notice that the professor was in fact in the room. He was lying on the bed, covered with a white sheet, which was not white anymore, but drenched in deep red. Maria now saw that the whole of room 242 was covered with blood, the floor, the ceiling, blood everywhere. Maria did not scream. She just left the room, closed the door, and ran down the hall to the stairs, maybe just a tiny little bit faster than normal. She flew down two flights of stairs and told the receptionist what had happened.

# Fifth Day

## 15 May

*Mörlbach, Jedlitschka Farm, 12.15am*

A man should not try to prove to others what he is worth. He should prove to himself what he is worth. That's what makes him attractive. Gabriel Tretjak had been a student when he read these sentences – in an interview with a French actress he adored. She didn't want to notice immediately, she said, that a guy was wearing an expensive suit. In the morning, after she had gone to bed with him, she wanted to *feel* the jacket, casually tossed over the chair the night before, and *feel* that he thought he was worth wearing cashmere, preferably triple ply. Tretjak remembered these sentences. And he remembered how impressed he had been as a child when he saw a single word in the papers on a Rolls Royce specifying how much horsepower the engine had: 'enough.'

Fiona Neustadt, who had only this afternoon looked into the high fees listed in Tretjak's account books, was obviously looking out for a flashy car. Tretjak drove a charcoal grey BMW without a model number or any other visible distinguishing characteristics, but with enough power under the bonnet and special additional equipment inside, which was not immediately obvious.

When he saw Fiona Neustadt standing, as arranged, outside Scarletti, the ice cream parlour on the Rotkreuz-platz, he immediately noticed that she had not followed his instructions. She was wearing jeans, trainers, a thin grey sweater and a black leather jacket. He caught her attention by honking and she got into the car.

'Where is your hat?' he said while turning the car around and taking off in the direction of the middle ring road. 'And where are your gloves? You'll be freezing. It is cold where we're going.'

'Go ahead: tell me, where are we going?'

He had already noticed this afternoon that she had an iPhone. 'Would you like to put the coordinates of our destination into your smart-phone?' he asked.

'Google Maps?' she asked and took her phone from her jacket pocket.

'No,' he said. 'Google Maps is too limited. Put M-51 into an ordinary search engine and look for pictures. Capital M and the numbers 5 and 1.'

Fiona Neustadt typed the digits onto the display. He turned off the ring road and connected with the auto-bahn in the direction of Garmisch-Partenkirchen. It was already after midnight. The roads were empty. Tretjak had only ever been alone when he had driven along this route. He had surprised himself a little, by making it different today. But recently he had surprised himself a lot. More and more often he felt the urge to change things a tad, to change his habits, his rituals, and mess up his principles a little. Like a planet wanting to leave its orbit.

'Ah,' he heard from the passenger seat. He saw the image on the display of the iPhone when he glanced over to his side.

'M-51 is the Whirlpool Galaxy. It is 25 million light-years away and part of the Hounds Constellation. This is where we are travelling tonight, if you agree.'

Tretjak had no idea whether Fiona Neustadt knew what a galaxy was, whether she was looking at the image appreciating the fact that here was a mass of billions of suns, very similar to our galaxy, the Milky Way. He did, however, sense that the picture impressed her. The arms of the spiral lunging out, the red and blue dots, which showed the age of the suns, the dark dust bands between the brilliant light sources – all this in front of the pitch dark sky of the universe.

'Do you have music in the car?' she asked when he took the exit marked Hohenschäftlarn.

'No,' Tretjak answered. 'I'm afraid you have to find a radio station you like. I practically never listen to music. But we're almost there.'

He directed his car towards Mörlbach. The road ran through hilly territory, through fields and forests. During the day one would have been able to see the Alps from here. Now, however, it was totally dark, only occasionally a light appeared, which belonged to a house. Once the car lights picked up a deer on the right side of the road. For the last few minutes they had driven in silence, and this silence was getting a bit tense.

Tretjak picked up his telephone and hit speed dial. 'Frau Jedlitschka, it's me, your tenant,' he said. 'I am going to be there in a few minutes. Could you switch off the lights on the farm? Thank you.'

How many times had he offered to have a remote control system installed so that he could switch off the lights? But the old lady had told him that she couldn't sleep because of the bad circulation in her legs and was up anyway, sitting in her kitchen. The young family was sleeping in the annex and would not be woken up by the telephone. Between Mörlbach and Bachhausen Tretjak made a sudden and sharp turn onto a dirt road. It was now almost eight years ago that Tretjak had crisscrossed this area south of Munich to find the ideal position for his telescope. He had got lost many times, had talked to the wrong people – it had been a time-consuming business. But then suddenly, from the top of a hill, he had spotted the Jedlitschka Farm. It was lying there, totally by itself, not a single neighbour anywhere close by. There was a big old farmhouse, the first floor framed with a wooden balcony decorated with flowerpots full of geraniums. Next to the old farmhouse was a small annex, almost like a bungalow, with a terrace and a round plunge pool for the children. In front of both buildings was a yard paved with concrete, with a wooden barn on the left and two wheat silos on the right of a brick-built shed for the tractors and trailers.

Tretjak had been interested in the back of this shed. From there one had unobstructed southerly views, with a deep horizon and not another house in sight, which could have produced light pollution at night. The Jedlitschka family back then was made up of the old farmer and his wife, plus their son and his wife and two small kids. Tretjak had negotiated with the old farmer, an open and friendly man with a Bavarian moustache covering a small harelip. He had gone there twice and then they had had a deal: Tretjak was allowed to construct a small observatory with a permanently installed telescope. For the space and the bit of electricity he needed he wanted to pay an annual rent. The farmer had suggested 600 euros, and Tretjak, who thought the sum embarrassingly low, had countered with 800. Laughingly, old Jedlitschka had shaken hands on 700. He did not want a contract: 'If you are quiet and don't need any light you can look up at the sky from here for another 20 years if you want.' The old man had died since then, struck down by a heart attack sitting on his Bulldog-tractor in the middle of the corn harvest, but the arrangement persisted. Once a year, just before Christmas, Tretjak visited the family and brought them small gifts. Otherwise they did not get to see him at all, because he came only when it was dark. A path circled the whole farm, leading directly to the observatory, the small white building with the rotating cupola on top of the roof.

*

Fiona Neustadt turned out to be a capable and useful companion on the way into the universe. She did not ask any questions and left it to him to explain what he thought important. The thing about the darkness, for example: there was no light whatsoever, so the pupils would dilate, only one small red flashlight was permitted. Tretjak took the tax inspector by the hand when they left the car and they trudged through the darkness in the light of the red glimmer. And the thing about the heat: no radiators near the telescope, because otherwise the air would oscillate and the images become blurred. When they entered the observatory, Tretjak opened a little closet and took out two fleece pull-overs, a fleece cap and woollen gloves which he handed to his companion, who remained standing in a corner while he got the telescope ready. Tretjak mastered each and every task as if he were sleepwalking, moving safely and quickly through the darkness.

His telescope was a Celestron C14, with a mirror measuring 35 centimetres in diameter and a black tube which was mounted on a black column in the middle of the room. A complicated mechanism with counter-weights allowed the instrument to be turned in every direction and every angle. Red spots lit up on an electronic dashboard. And then cupolas opened over their heads and with a muffled motor noise revealed a metre-wide glimpse of the star-filled sky. The fresh night air carried in the smell of the surrounding meadows.

Tretjak screwed an ocular into the telescope. 'Sit down

here on the observation chair,' he said, 'the show is about to begin.'

He had spent many a night here. Sometimes he stayed until dawn. The reliability of the universe was immensely calming, he found. With his telescope he could look up old acquaintances with wonderful names, stars like Betelgeuse, gas regions, in which new stars were born like the Orion nebula, and milky ways like the Galaxy with the Black Eye. There were remnants of supernovas and formations known as dark clouds, globular clusters and binary stars… each season was different. During the course of the night these old acquaintances crossed the whole firmament at quite a pace, so quickly in fact that one got the impression not of sitting in an observation chair, but on a carousel, and in a way that was right: the earth was a carousel, a tiny carousel in an infinitely huge fairground.

Tretjak explained to the tax inspector that everything she was seeing belonged to the past. If light needed 25 million years to reach Earth from the Whirlpool Galaxy, then the image of the galaxy was 25 million years old.

The more her eyes became accustomed to the darkness the lighter Tretjak's observatory seemed to her. In the end she could make out the contours in his face and the sparkle in his eyes. That was how they spent nearly two hours together.

At one point Tretjak had to think back to that afternoon and her question, what exactly he did for a living. And he remembered that he had sat with the farmer's wife in her kitchen and had talked with her, whose breathing became heavier from year to year and whose legs kept swelling, about exactly the same thing. Why was it, Mrs Jedlitschka had pondered, that people longed so much for somebody else to take care of matters for them. 'The more well known they are, the more money they have, the deeper is that longing,' he had responded. And he had told her a little about what his clients asked him to do, only the harmless stuff of course. In the end she had said: 'So you are a fixer...' And after a while she had added: 'You know, Mr Tretjak, in the old days you wouldn't have made a lot of money doing what you are doing. Back then people were too stingy, at least around here. Maybe also there was not so much to fix back then.' From that day onwards the old farmer's wife had called him The Fixer.

Tretjak turned the telescope in the direction of the constellation of Leo, where a particularly bright spot was visible. 'This is Jupiter,' he said and looked at his watch. 'In four minutes you will be able to observe how one of its moons passes in front of it.'

'In four minutes,' said Fiona Neustadt. 'What do we do if it is late?' She rubbed her hands together for warmth.

It was almost three o'clock when Tretjak stopped his car in front of the long-closed ice cream parlour on the Rotkreuzplatz back in Munich. Fiona Neustadt had taken off the fleece and thrown it on the back seat. He admittedly had expected her to lean over to the driver's seat to kiss him good-bye and thank him. But nothing like that happened. She seemed tired, opened the passenger's door, and had already set her foot outside the car, when she looked around at him again and said: 'That was very interesting. I have never seen something like that before. Good night.' Then the door fell shut and she disappeared through the entrance to one of the apartment buildings. When Tretjak later, back in his garage, folded the fleece to stow it in the boot, he stopped for an instant and smelt it. Grapefruit. No doubt about it.

### Brenner Pass Highway, 3am

If there is one argument amongst the people from Munich which will never be resolved conclusively it is the debate over the quickest route when driving to South Tyrol: it is either via the motorway which leads to Salzburg taking the exit to Kufstein, or one takes the motorway in the direction of Garmisch-Partenkirchen and the village of Scharnitz. Inspector Maler belonged to the Garmisch-Partenkirchen faction. In his opinion one reached the Brenner Pass Highway and, over the pass, South Tyrol much faster this way, especially in high travel season.

Although it was not the peak travel season and he was driving during the night, Maler had chosen his usual route. It was just after three in the morning and the highway was eerily empty. Above the beam of his head-lights Maler gazed into a remarkably clear starry sky. He had made good headway, the Zirler Berg and the Brenner Pass both lay behind him. He was already on the Italian motorway, clearly identifiable by the green signs ahead, and had just passed the exit to Brixen when his telephone rang.

It could only be his office in Munich. Or his colleagues from South Tyrol. One thing was certain: they were going to provide him with new information about the strange body they had discovered. Maler got the phone out of his jacket pocket and held it with his right hand to his ear. He hated car kits.

'Hello?'

'Inspector Maler?' A female voice.

'Yes.'

'We met at Gabriel Tretjak's flat,' the woman said. 'I am the tax inspector. Neustadt is my name.'

Maler took his foot off the accelerator to lower the sound level in the car. The speedometer fell to 120. On the left-hand side the illuminated silhouette of a castle appeared against the backdrop of dark slopes.

'Yes, Ms Neustadt, I remember.'

'I want to meet you, Inspector, and tell you something,' the woman said on the phone.

Maler looked at the clock in his dashboard. 'And that is so important that you are calling me at this hour?'

'I think so. Can we meet?'

A green sign scurried by. *Bolzano/Bozen 45 kilometres.*

'Now?' asked Maler. 'I fear that will be impossible. You will have to put up with the telephone for now.'

'No, I don't want to do that.'

'I am away on official business, you know,' he said. 'I don't know when I'll be back.'

There was a pause. Maler believed that he could hear the tax inspector breathing despite the engine noise. 'Maybe you could call me when you get back,' she finally said and then hung up.

Maler briefly contemplated calling her back to get her to reveal her information straight away, but then decided against it. As an investigating policeman one got these kind of calls quite often, and in the end they were often worthless, revealing more about the psyche of the caller than contributing to the solution of the case.

He wanted to concentrate on driving now. He was soon going to leave the motorway. Next to him, on the passenger seat, was the new edition of *Psychology Journal.* He had bought it at the central station before he left. The lead story was entitled: *Can the soul be reprogrammed, Professor Kufner?*

A word was nagging Maler, it had taken hold of his thoughts during the drive. The inspector from Bozen had not used that particular word when he had informed him late last night about the murder of Norbert Kufner, Professor of Psychology, in the hotel Zum blauen Mondschein. The reason the policeman from Italy had contacted his colleague in Munich had all to do with the distinctiveness of the body, was all down to the eyes of the dead man. Police forces all over Europe had been looking out for this particular feature since the day before yesterday. And it was that feature which had conjured up these words in Maler's brain. And now they were stuck there: ice cream scoop.

### *Kochel am See, 5pm*

What a beautiful picture, down there on the terrace. The beautiful mother, the pretty son. She was drinking an espresso and a glass of dark sherry, he a coke, a real one, as he said, nothing light, nada zero. They chatted and laughed, and seemed very relaxed.

He was talking about what he wanted to be when he grew up. He wanted to do something useful, maybe a development worker, he said. Maybe go to Africa. Somewhere where he could help people. He was enjoying the sound of his own voice, as he often did. He didn't want to be like the others, he wanted to do something which really made a difference. He wanted to make the world a better place. He knew, he said, that he was a very special human being, a very sensitive human being.

The way he talked, sitting on the terrace, was the same way many other young people talked as well. And on that day his mother was not in the mood to contradict him. She simply did not want to think about the advice she had received from his therapists: 'You should make sure that each conversation with your son is structured, has a beginning and an end. And most importantly, make sure that in the end it is clear how the next conversation will continue on from the one just completed. You have to construct with your son a conversational net, which holds him up.' The last therapist who had said this to her had been short and fat, with a strikingly oily complexion. At least for this one moment, the guy could take a hike as far as she was concerned. She was happy about the friendly atmosphere. She was happy that Lars was not getting on her nerves. The sherry was helping a bit as well, she liked its first, subtle effect. It made one a little more forgiving towards the rest of the world. And in a way, her son belonged to that rest of the world as well.

They remembered joint holidays, the long drives to their destinations. She had always packed a suitcase full of surprises for him, full of small presents. For the holiday, for the drive. 'My favourite holiday,' said Lars, 'was Corsica.' And the long ferry ride. 'Yes,' she said, 'that was nice.' That was how the conversation bobbed along. 'Remember?' 'Yes.' The yellow plastic penguin, which disappeared out to sea. The table tennis competition at the beach in Ravenna, which Lars won. He was nine years old then. Gosh, how time flies.

At one point Lars said: 'You are the best mama in the world.' He got up when he said that and gave her a hug. 'Mama, all will be alright. I promise.' Then he went to his room.

She had rented two apartments for herself and Lars in the holiday village in Kochel am See, 50 kilometres from Munich. It seemed exactly the right distance. It was easy and quick to get to Munich from Kochel, and it was quick and easy to get from Kochel to Munich. Wherever and whenever this Gabriel Tretjak wanted to have the first meeting with her son.

'I'm going to pick you up in two hours for dinner,' she called after him.

'OK, Mama.'

*

When Charlotte Poland knocked on the door of her son's apartment two hours later, nobody opened it. She knocked more forcefully. No reaction. She called his mobile phone. She only got the reply: 'There is nobody here to take your call at the moment.' She got a second key for his room from the receptionist. The big hold-all she had packed for him was there. The small shoulder bag was missing. She went down to reception again to ask if anybody had seen her son. Yes, she was told, her son had ordered a taxi an hour ago and had left with it. She asked whether one could enquire with the dispatcher where the taxi had taken her son. Of course, the receptionist would make that call.

She went back to her room. When she opened her handbag she already had her suspicions. Her purse was gone, together with all the money inside it, the credit cards and her papers. Lars must have stolen them when she had left the terrace to go to the ladies cloakroom. Lars knew that she would not use the purse to pay as she was going to sign for it and charge it to the room. She called her bank's service number and cancelled all her credit cards. Lars had had an hour. The previous times Lars had managed to withdraw about two thousand euros with her cards. The little fat therapist had advised her to report the next incident to the police. She was supposed to inform on her own son.

Charlotte Poland sat down on the bed in her hotel room. She was looking at herself in the mirror mounted on the door of the wardrobe. She had got a little colour. It suited her, she thought. She also liked her white dress. She was one of those women who liked to look at themselves. Her publisher had once told her that she was too beautiful to be an author. Nobody would believe that a woman with the body of a model and such huge eyes also possessed a brain. The author photographs on her books were intentionally discreet. Her face was in profile, black and white.

I am rich and beautiful, she thought. And? She undressed and lay down on the bed. It had become a habit, that was how she could best calm down, being naked and closing her eyes. She had even taken off the big Cartier panther ring from her finger. She had given it as a present to herself, the first time one of her books had hit the bestseller list.

Her novels always had the same theme: a misleadingly idyllic life with hidden depth, a magic box with a false bottom concealing a second compartment beneath the visible one. She knew all too well why she loved these stories. She loved to write about hidden depths, because hidden depths were the story of her life. A friend had once told her that she loved deception, that she only felt real in deception. She couldn't have put it better herself, this was the book jacket copy of her life.

It was quiet in the hotel room. She thought she could hear the quiet buzzing of the mini bar. The lonesome chirping of a bird entered through the open balcony door. The metaphor of the secret compartment, of another floor underneath the visible one pleased her because it implied that there was a firm grounding somewhere underneath her feet, even if it were not immediately visible. This was her make-believe; a life which looked good, which was presentable. The floor beneath – which only worked if it had a solid grounding. The appeal of this deceit lay in its contrast to respectability, to conventionality. Damn it, she wanted to scream, I need the beauty of the make-believe!

Her brain now conjured pictures of her son. Lars in the hospital, just after his birth. A quiet baby, so quiet in fact that the doctors were worried there was something wrong with him. Lars in kindergarten, the prettiest child of them all, blond, sweet, radiant. Nobody could help but fall in love with her little one. Lars on the shoulders of his father. How they had played football together in the garden of their new home. Lars with Konrad, his best friend, laughing, in front of the computer in his room. The image had always been perfect with Lars. Even now, only two hours ago, down on the terrace. Of course she should have smelled a rat, when he suddenly embraced her, and all his talk of 'Mama, Mama'. It had never been a good sign recently when he became so overly sentimental. As if this sugary sweetness was a precursor of the next bout of aggressiveness.

Lars was ten years old when his teacher first called her in for a talk. Fellow pupils were complaining that he was stealing from them, beating them up. Shortly afterwards the police showed up. He had stolen two computer games at a department store and had been caught shoplifting. Lars was eleven when he was kicked out of his school and they found him a place in a private school the same year. He was twelve when Konrad's mother called and said that they couldn't see each other any more. Certain things had happened, but she didn't want to talk about them. 'I think this would be better for both of us,' she said. 'Mrs Poland, I don't know how to put it other than to say that I am afraid of your son.'

The first therapist foisted on them by a juvy judge asked her whether she knew that her son liked inflicting cruelty on animals. The most recent doctor who had talked to her about her son had asked her whether she knew that he took drugs – that was about six weeks ago. He used everything he could lay his hands on. Hash, crack, heroin. Lars had turned fourteen four days before. In the beginning she had not believed what people were telling her about her son, but they had all been right.

It had not been easy to persuade the head of the correctional facility to let her take Lars on this trip to Kochel. He had been sent there by a judge two months ago. She had told him that she believed the journey was important for him. And: 'I'll return him to your care, I promise.'

'Mama, all will be well,' Lars had said on the terrace, 'I promise'. She now knew all too well what Konrad's mother had meant when she had said that she was afraid of him.

*

The hotel telephone next to the bed rang. Someone from reception was on the line. They had managed to talk to the taxi driver who had picked up her son. It had not been a long ride. They had stopped a couple of times at ATMs and then gone to the station. He had got out there. And something else: he had managed to persuade the driver to charge the fare to the room. 16 Euro 40. Was that OK?

'Of course,' Charlotte Poland said, 'of course.'

Lars, her son, 14 years old. White, smooth face. Blond, messy hair. One piercing in the lip. A small tattoo at the back of his neck, a blue dragon. Her son, who everybody liked at first sight. The diagnosis of the doctors was of course not visible. Lars, her son, the pathological liar.

It was a personality disorder. He was not capable of imagining what would happen tomorrow. To experience, to feel that life was more than just this single moment in time. And for Lars, the currency of the moment was lies. Mama, all will be well. Such sentences hit their target. Even when the taxi was already waiting outside. 'The word "later",' the therapist had said, 'means nothing to your son.' But a moral code without a time dimension can't function. In his therapy one had to try to build time bridges for him. This was the only way out of his amoral state.

For Lars there was no secret compartment. There were no hidden dark sides. With him there was *only* a dark side, she thought. Nothing else. She sat up and swung her legs off the bed. She looked at her naked body in the mirror. Sometimes her left breast was slightly bigger than her right one. Like it was today. My child is a monster, she thought. She did not even notice that she was talking aloud. That she was talking to the man whose idea it had been to come here. 'Paul,' she said, 'my son is a monster. One has to face the truth. Could it not be, Paul, that not only you have a son who is a monster, but I do too?'

It had been just before Christmas, about six months ago, when they had talked about their respective sons. Charlotte had only then learnt that Lars had just been indicted again for GBH. She told Paul about it and poured out her heart with her complete tale of woes. Up to this point, she had not even known that Paul also had a son. Paul, whose last name was Tretjak, said: 'Lars is still a child. He is no monster and will not become one.' He knew all about monsters. For many years he had had no contact with his son Gabriel. But one thing was certain: he deserved the attribute monster. And as Paul Tretjak had said back then, he was well aware that it was partly his fault that his son had become a monster.

She rummaged around in her bag for her mobile phone and dialled the number for Paul Tretjak. It rang three times before he answered.

'Hello, Charlotte.'

She liked to hear his voice, liked how he pronounced her first name with the emphasis on Char*lotte*. They had not switched to the informal way of addressing each other that long ago. 'Hello, Paul. Where are you?'

'Where I always am. Above the clouds, you know?'

*Above the clouds*, that meant in his little house high above the Lago Maggiore, above the village of Maccagno. The hut had three rooms, over two floors. Big windows with a direct view of the lake and the adjacent mountains. It was in the centre of a huge plot of land with palms and fruit trees and even a bit of forest on the steep slope. There was only one drawback: it could not be reached by car. One had to climb a very steep path to reach it, which took about 20 minutes from the village.

She had a mental image of Tretjak, with his mobile pressed to his ear, walking up and down in the living room, in front of the fireplace, then outside on the terrace. He was big and sturdy, and nobody would have guessed that he would turn 70 this year. She briefly pondered whether there were any similarities between father and son, the man above the clouds and the other that she had observed in the Italian restaurant in Munich. Describing people's appearances was not her strong point. One thing was sure: they were both quite good looking.

'What's the situation? What's up?' Tretjak asked.

'Lars made a run for it. With my money. The same old story again.'

'Where did he run to?'

'I only know that he took a taxi to the station.'

'Do you think he is now in Munich?' Tretjak asked.

'I have no idea. I don't know.' Both were silent for a while, then she asked: 'Anything new on your side?'

'Yes,' he answered, 'you can try again with my son.

Again in the restaurant Osteria, the day after tomorrow, from 8pm onwards.'

'May I ask you a question, Paul?'

'Sure, what?'

'You have had no contact with your son for years. How do you know where and when he dines out?'

Instead of answering, Paul Tretjak said in conclusion of their conversation: 'Charlotte, I'll get into my car tomorrow morning and will be with you in Kochel by midday.'

## Sintra, Portugal, 5pm

The dark green Rover, which had been made available for her, went well with the colour of the hedges. Coincidence or planning? Everything in this hotel was very tasteful: the colour of the carpets in the reception area, the covers of the antique furniture, the precious wallpaper. Melanie Schwarz admired how everything came together in a harmonic way, as if it had grown organically over centuries. The hotel Palacio de Seteais had been the ancestral home of the family of the Marquês de Marialva. An alley of perfectly clipped eucalyptus trees lined the drive. The view from the windows and from the terraces stretched down over the city of Sintra to the Atlantic.

It was late afternoon. Melanie Schwarz parked the Range Rover near the hotel entrance under one of the trees there and thought of her house in Potsdam. Peter Schwarz was a generous man, and they had put a lot of effort into the decoration and had had the help of an interior designer, who was a friend. But if she was honest, her house had never really radiated any warmth, any character.

How might Peter be? When she thought of him, her stomach contracted into a tight knot. She had now been here, on the Portuguese coast, for five days, for five days and five nights, and the hours had curiously merged into each other. She could not tell any more when she had sat in the magnificent dining hall, whether she had eaten at all or whether she had only picked at her food, how many times she had gone down to the pool only to get up from the sun lounger again after a short time, and how many hours she had paced up and down the stone terrace of her room at night. Since her departure from Germany she had spoken to no one. Only once had she received a message, from Gabriel Tretjak, that everything was proceeding according to the agreed plan.

Had she made a mistake? Should she not have spoken to her husband and daughter herself? What was her new life worth, if it had been built by another, a stranger? What was her old life worth, if it was destroyed by a kind of demolition firm? This Tretjak fellow had been nice enough, and when he had been sitting across from her and had talked to her in that clear, calm way, she had been so sure that it was the right thing she was doing. One accepted the help of others so often in one's life, the help of professionals, whenever one got stuck oneself, when one's own capabilities were not enough any more, to fix a dripping faucet, to sort out the children's problems with their school work, or to clear a skin rash... and she had got stuck.

But now, when Tretjak was no longer there and in her head had slowly morphed from a real person into an almost imaginary idea, he appeared to her increasingly scary. Last night she had almost got up and gone, packed her bags, left the hotel, and driven to the airport at Lisbon to check in for the next available flight to Germany. She could have begged Peter's forgiveness, she could have made it all go away... However, there were also the other emotions mixed into the cocktail which had kept her hovering for days between exhaustion, fatigue and delirious nervousness. Feelings of wild happiness, for instance, which suddenly and unexpectedly took hold of her, brought on by totally banal impressions, the smell of clean laundry, the sight of an old woman sitting outside a café. Wild happiness, looking forward to a new life, a taste of everyday life.

In most hotels known to Melanie Schwarz the reception desk dominated the entrance hall, broad, heavy and ugly. Not so in the Palacio de Seteais. Here you could almost entirely miss it, the way it hid in a tiny niche, shy, as if it did not want to disturb the harmony of the beautiful room. The package, which the receptionist handed her, was about 40 centimetres long, 20 centimetres wide and 10 centimetres high, was wrapped in brown paper, and had only a name as the sender: Gabriel Tretjak. The man at the desk was called Senhor João, and he looked like the actor Omar Sharif, whom Melanie's mother had adored. He explained to her that the package had been delivered by courier directly from the airport in Lisbon.

'Thank you,' Melanie Schwarz said, but she was not sure that the words had actually left her mouth or if they had been suffocated by the beating of her heart. She took the package and went to her room. She carefully closed the door behind her, stepped out onto her terrace, and put the package on the big, round, stone table. Then she went back into the room and poured herself a glass of the Japanese whisky standing on on the chest of drawers.

Somebody had made sure there had been a bottle of the stuff in her room when she arrived. Peter had brought this whisky back from a business trip to Japan and had claimed that real connoisseurs considered it the best in the world. Melanie did not really drink whisky, but in the following weeks it had grown on her, as she put it. It had become her companion, not just on social occasions, but also during long, lonely nights in her Potsdam home, when it made her put on her old records, made her drown in self-pity or egged on her aggressive determination, although most of the time, by the next morning, the only remnants of that determination had been discarded, like scrunched up drafts of letters.

Melanie Schwarz stepped in front of the wardrobe in her room and opened the doors. She would not have been able to say why, but she took a minidress from one of the hangers and placed it on the bed. It was light blue and the fancy tailored back revealed a delicate white lace ornament. She had bought it in a Berlin boutique; only a woman ten years younger can get away with wearing this, she had told the sales assistant. Girls that young can't afford this dress, the assistant retorted. Melanie Schwarz took off her jeans and tee-shirt and after a brief hesitation even her underwear. Then she slipped into the dress, for the first time since she had tried it on in the boutique. She climbed into white high heels, grabbed the glass of whisky she had poured herself, stepped out onto the terrace, and sat down at the stone table in front Gabriel Tretjak's package.

The brown wrapping paper revealed a box, grey carton, the lid held in place by a grey ribbon. Melanie Schwarz untied the ribbon and took off the lid. The box contained a pile of papers. On top lay a cover note on Tretjak's letterhead. *Dear Melanie Schwarz*, it read, written by hand with pen and ink. *You can rejoice, the waiting has come to an end.*

Letters on paper have a different effect on people's brains than spoken words. The brain can quite easily reinterpret spoken words, can misunderstand what is meant, can adjust it to the individual's reality in a way that makes it bearable. Words on paper are *the* reality, merciless, without any feelings. The obituary in the newspaper, the good-bye note on the kitchen table, the job dismissal, the report card, the medical test results.

She was not patient enough to read the rest of Tretjak's letter and pushed it aside to investigate the rest of the papers. A ticket in her name for a flight, Lisbon-Frankfurt, tomorrow morning at 11.15am. The details of a flat in Heidelberg, Regenstrasse 3, fourth floor, three rooms and a small roof terrace. An information pack about a shop in the centre of Heidelberg, at the moment still occupied by a shop for outdoor clothing, but with a sign in the window announcing a closing-down sale. Rental agreements in her name. Melanie emptied the whisky glass in quick gulps. Her fingers trembled while she was leafing through the papers. The letter from a stable in the Taunus... *we are delighted to provide a good home for your animals…* The legal papers regarding the settlement of her divorce, including the scheduled hearing date in Berlin. The purchase agreement of a car, Mini Cooper convertible (dealer demonstration model), colour: black, owner: Melanie Schwarz. Registration: Heidelberg… The confirmation from a removal firm. The forms necessary for voter registration, for mail redirection. She took only fleeting notice of the papers and dispersed them on the table. What she was finally holding in her hands was an envelope, on it was only her first name, written in Peter's hand, the writing she knew so well from the way he had written love letters back then, a time which now felt very close again. She took only the letter, leaving everything else behind on the table, went back inside and lay down on the bed. She ripped open the envelope and read the first and the last sentences. *I am writing these lines calmly and with great understanding. You don't have to be afraid and you don't have to worry*. That was how it started. And the letter ended with the sentences: *Mr Tretjak wanted to pick you up from the airport in Frankfurt. But I thought it would be better if I did that. If somebody should deposit you in your new life, it should be an old friend, don't you think? Yours, Peter.*

Melanie Schwarz began to cry. She kept her eyes fixed on the ceiling. The whole cocktail of despair and relief, embarrassment, joy and sadness flowed right and left over her cheeks on to the silk pillow cases.

Only later, when she appeared in the bar, where the high,

open windows revealed an always spectacular sunset over the ocean, did she read the entire contents of the box. Even Tretjak's letter, and even the one paragraph in which he wrote that he thought it right that in the near future she should take care that her soul could handle this rather rapid change. He had taken the liberty and arranged a few appointments for her. The man who she was meant to consult on this matter was an expert; his name was Norbert Kufner, Professor Dr Norbert Kufner from Vienna.

Senhor João, who because of his black eyes and his grey, parted hair, was always asked about a certain resemblance to a famous actor, and who at this hour of the day was looking after the guests in the bar, noticed two things about Melanie Schwarz. She was a changed woman since he had handed her the package – she almost appeared intoxicated. And he noticed that she was wearing no underwear beneath her light blue dress. The hotel management had, of course, forbidden members of staff to start personal relationships with any of the guests. But Senhor João was the director of the Palacio de Seteais, a fact unknown to most of the guests, and he decided to continue to watch Melanie Schwarz and, if need be, ignore his own rules.

# Sixth Day

## 16 May

*Munich, Buttermelcher Street, 10am*
The editorial offices of the magazine *Psychology Journal* were located only a stone's throw away from Munich's famous Viktualienmarkt. Great location, Inspector August Maler thought, when he entered the office block and took the lift to the third floor. The building had three floors and housed several lawyers' practices and doctors' clinics, and one editorial office. Maler was a little surprised when the editor himself opened the door. The short, young man shook his hand. 'Stefan Treysa, how do you do. Please come in, Inspector.'

The editorial offices had two rooms, both filled with heaps of paper and journals. Treysa led him into one of them and sat down at a desk; Maler took the place opposite him. The walls, the desk, the chairs, everything was white.

'In case you were wondering,' Treysa said, 'there is nobody else here except me. We have a few people working for the magazine, but they are all freelancers.' He closed his laptop, equally white, and asked whether the inspector wanted something to drink. Water? Coffee?

'A glass of water would be very nice,' said Maler. It was really warm outside now. Summer had taken over early this year.

Suddenly there was a loud noise, which came from the second room. When it came again, Maler recognised it as a high-pitched thin voice, which said something like 'woof'.

Treysa said: 'Oh yes, in case you are wondering: that sound in there is a parrot, my only colleague. He only says this one word, all day long. But you get used to it, believe me.'

'Do you know why the parrot says "woof"?' Maler asked, and had to laugh. Treysa smiled. 'One can only guess. Maybe he had a traumatic experience in his childhood, which involved dogs. But the psychology of parrots is a relatively new discipline. Would you like to meet him?'

'Not really,' said Maler, 'to hear him is enough.'

'Well, inspector, what can I do for you?'

'It has to do with the lead article of your journal,' said Maler. 'I mentioned to you on the telephone that I need all the information I can get about the murder victim, this Professor Norbert Kufner.'

'Dreadful business. I have seen the news on television. They hyped it up, of course. Famous psychiatrist, murdered in luxury hotel. Three networks have already contacted me, asked me to make a statement about Kufner. But I won't, too tabloid for me. Do you know more about the murder now?'

'No. I hope you understand that I can't divulge any details.'

'Of course,' said Treysa and refilled the inspector's glass. Then he took two copies of the latest issue of *Psychology Journal* from his drawer, gave one to Maler and put one on the table in front of him. 'One thing is for sure: Kufner was a very impressive man, really charismatic. Interviewing him was very exciting.'

Maler looked at the cover photograph. It was meant to look diabolical to suit the headline: *Can one reprogramme the soul?* But one could still see the fine, sensitive features. And for a moment Maler fused this image with the other ones of this face, such as the one he had seen in the pathologist's in Bozen. The face without eyes. The autopsy report had indicated that Kufner, like Professor Kerkhoff, had been killed with one precisely aimed stab of the liver. And again the eyes had been scooped out post mortem. There was no doubt: Kerkhoff and Kufner had been murdered by the same person.

Treysa said that he would have to elaborate a bit in order to explain Kufner's significance and the vehement criticism that went with that territory. In the Nineties a group of US therapists had tried out a new way of treating severely depressed patients who were at risk of killing themselves: they hypnotised these patients – mainly women – and persuaded them in this state that they as children had been sexually abused by their fathers. Which in most cases was not true. Of course the fathers were up in arms against the therapists. Successfully: some went to jail, all lost their professional accreditations. None was allowed to continue to work as a therapist.

'Serves them right,' said Maler. 'It's not right to just make such dramatically wrong claims, which are totally unfounded.'

'You are right, of course,' said Maler. 'Let me, however, add two points. First: the patients believed the stories to be true, even after the therapists were convicted. They were convinced their fathers had abused them. In other words, they had been reprogrammed under hypnosis. And second: the patients were feeling much better than before. There was no doubt about it. The women felt really good to have found somebody responsible for their suffering. Even if that somebody was not really responsible.'

'And how did Professor Kufner judge the work of the American therapists?' Maler asked.

'Outwardly he condemned them, of course, and also in our interview. But I didn't really believe him. Because deep down Kufner followed a philosophy which many modern psychotherapists believe in: there is no one truth, only the construct of many personal truths. And that particularly applies to the soul. Let me put it differently: if a patient has panic attacks and receives a plausible explanation for why these attacks occur then this explanation helps him. Is the explanation the truth? Doesn't matter, the main thing is it works.' That had been Professor Kufner's area of research, Treysa said. Kufner had talked about new constructs, which patient and therapist should build together. Kufner, according to Treysa, always talked about *clients*, he didn't like the word patients.

Maler wanted to say something just when the parrot from next door interrupted. Two or three times the word 'woof' was clearly audible.

Treysa told the story of a dinner with Kufner in Vienna. Kufner's wife had joined them, herself a psychologist. It had been a really nice evening. A beautiful restaurant, wonderful food, *Tafelspitz* (boiled beef, the local speciality) and the superb fluffy desert, *Salzburger Nockerln*. 'Well, we all had a bit too much to drink. And at one point Mrs Kufner told the story of how her husband had once pacified a particularly irritating friend over coffee and cake.'

'Pacified?' asked Maler.

'Sounds odd, doesn't it? But he simply put this exhausting and always much too noisy friend into some kind of trance over coffee. I followed up, of course, and Mrs Kufner said her husband had used certain code words, which he repeated again and again in his conversation with the woman. In a way he reprogrammed a loud woman into a quiet one. If you ask me, Inspector, a commercial winner.' Treysa laughed.

Maler also laughed and then finished his water. 'Tell me, in your article you are talking about the *extremely controversial* professor of psychiatry. Why was he so controversial? I guess not because of these coffee and cake experiences.'

'I've already said that Kufner was very charismatic. And he was prone to acting out the genius who changes the world. He once told me: "just imagine you could re-programme all the sick souls in the world…"'

Maler repeated his question: 'That's why he was so controversial? A new version of the Frankenstein-theme? Only now in psychology?'

'That's about it. Many of the so-called serious scientists don't like megalomania, especially in others. In addition to that there were always those rumours which circulated about Kufner. Some people said Kufner was very rich. He himself didn't talk about it. But there were persistent rumours that he made his services available to influential bosses of industry. There was even talk of involvement with some secret service or other. There was never any proof. Kufner only laughed when you spoke to him about it.'

The conversation had come to an end, and Treysa accompanied the inspector to the door.

Maler asked: 'Do you think it possible that somebody murdered/killed Kufner because of his work?

'You are asking the wrong person there. I'm only the little editor of an even smaller psychology magazine.'

'How did you become the editor, by the way?'

'In my case, it was the fact that I was a therapist myself once upon a time, not even a bad one, but nobody liked me. I was too negative for them somehow. That's why I became editor of my own magazine.'

*

When Inspector Maler had disappeared into the lift, Treysa went back into his office. He had not yet sat down before he picked up his mobile phone and dialled Gabriel Tretjak's number.

'Hi. The inspector was here just now. He asked me lots of questions about Kufner.'

'Did he ask you about me?' asked Tretjak.

'No,' said Treysa.

*Oberronnberg, Lower Bavaria, 11am*

Father Joseph Lichtinger unlocked the little church in Oberronnberg with mixed feelings. It was just after 11 o'clock in the morning and he was almost an hour early for the appointment. But he wanted to collect his thoughts a little bit. He had been to the hospital this morning to visit the old farmer's wife Sigl whose eyes were dimmed by glaucoma, and the mechanic Staiger, who had just had an operation on his gall bladder. And he'd had to administer the final sacraments to a nine-year-old girl. She had been knocked off her bicycle last night at the nasty corner near the station in Neufahrn, where so many accidents had happened already because everybody collided there; the pedestrians coming out of the underpass, the cyclists from the Marktberg, and the lorry drivers using the old commercial road. And little Jacqueline, called Jackie. Lord, be good to her.

In the little church of Oberronnberg regular mass had not been held for a long time. The church had been incorporated into Joseph Lichtinger's congregation of Grisbach and was only opened for special occasions like baptisms, memorial services and now and again an intimate wedding. It was situated at a distance on a hill, with big cornfields in front and the forest behind it. Inside there were ten rows of wooden benches on either side of the aisle and a simple altar at the front. On the wall behind the altar hung the gem of the church: a relatively big, hand-carved oak cross, which was quite famous around here because its Jesus did not appear to be suffering but angry. The little steeple was directly above the altar and the bell rope was wrapped around a brass hook on the wall beside it.

Lichtinger sat down in the front row and lifted his eyes towards the cross. He was of medium height and had an athletic figure, which even the badly-cut black priest's outfit could not obscure completely. In his youth, he had been an active gymnast. Horizontal bar. And he still played football, as a member of the senior team of Grisbach. His most striking feature was his straw blond hair and bright blue eyes, which had always been the cause of much ridicule here at the place of his birth. Joseph Lichtinger was one of four brothers, the youngest, and they all had these eyes and this hair, despite the fact that both their father and mother had brown hair and dark eyes. A good-looking Swede must have passed through the area once upon a time, so the joke went when the four boys entered elementary school in Grisbach. His brothers had been dispersed all over the world. He had initially gone abroad as well, but then he had come back wearing a black suit and white collar. The nickname 'Swede' had stuck, priest or not.

He had not heard from Gabriel Tretjak for two years and had not seen him… How long ago must that have been? Tretjak had called last night, and the sound of his voice had unsettled Lichtinger.

'What's up?' he had asked, 'is there anything wrong… in our affairs?'

'Maybe,' Tretjak had answered. 'Possibly. We've got to talk.'

He could come over straight away, Lichtinger had proposed. But Tretjak had declined. He wanted to go stargazing first. At least in that respect nothing had changed. A clear sky had always put an appointment with Tretjak at risk.

Oberronnberg was not a well-lit church, the windows were on the small side and colourfully painted with scenes from the New Testament. They did not let in a lot of light. Maybe it was because of this strange twilight at midday that Father Joseph Lichtinger – the Swede – suddenly became very calm and let his thoughts wander back a long way into his own past. His memories were connected with warm feelings as if he were not remembering himself but another person he had once known well and liked, but now did not know what had become of him. That person had been a physics student back then, and for a brief moment now in the little church he thought he could solve a differential calculus without difficulty despite the fact that this had been over 20 years ago. The lectures had taken place in the southern wing of Munich's Technical University, a concrete building which had been razed in the meantime. At that point he had owned a dark blue racing bike, a *Montarino* with ten gears, a Dunlop Maxplay squash racket, and he had inhabited a student pad in Freimann. He had a girl-friend at the time, Helen, an English girl from Bristol – and a best friend. Gabriel, a guy who had showed up at a lecture on theoretical physics one day, who looked foreign somehow – you would not be surprised to see him at a PKK rally – but who had opened his mouth and spoken with a broad South Tyrolean accent.

He was not a student of the Technical University, but was reading psychology and philosophy at the other Munich university, the Ludwig-Maximilians-Universität. But he was interested in the theory of relativity–the expansion of time, the curvature of space – and quantum mechanics. At some point they happened to be sitting next to each other and immediately started arguing. 'If I move much faster than you,' Tretjak had said, alluding to the phenomenon of the theory of relativity, 'then my time passes more slowly than yours and you age faster. Does that also apply if I think faster than you?' It was now clear to Joseph Lichtinger that this particular discussion had never ended: throughout the following two years, it had continued during lectures, in cafes, at nightly parties, while walking along the Isar river... it had not even been interrupted when the two had not been together because they had only used the breaks to gather new ammunition: questions, phenomena, theses. Fundamentally, it had all been about two questions. Can one predict the future if one knows all the facts, the premises? And on the other side of the same coin: how fundamentally can one alter the course of matters, redirect them, if one alters these facts?

They had incorporated every discipline of science into their discussions: like junkies constantly needing a new fix they had read biochemistry, the newest discoveries

about the brain, research into human communication…
They had placed bets. Can we succeed in manipulating the couple at the window over there into having a flaming row? In most cases it was Tretjak who bet on something like that, carefully observing them first and then taking action. For example, he knocked over a glass of wine, which emptied itself over the dress of an already fidgety woman. Another time he pressured a shy man into a conversation, which annoyed the woman… Then they just sat back and watched.

They had played games. At one point Tretjak had hired a private detective to have him, Lichtinger, watched. They had such fun watching the guy despair because they stage-managed the whole thing, mixing in a bit of quantum mechanics. Tretjak donned a blond wig and the appropriate clothes, turning himself into a copy of Lichtinger, and he arranged for the detective to observe Lichtinger getting off his bike and walking towards the entrance of a building. But at the same time the exact opposite would take place as well: Lichtinger leaving the building and getting on his bike. Tretjak was mainly interested in the end of the game, namely the report of the detective. He was fascinated by how the human brain could rearrange what it had perceived until it appeared logical, until it fitted its own way of looking at the world.

'You can challenge anything,' Lichtinger had once said, 'except the laws of physics.'

'That's what Newton said as well,' Tretjak had laughed,

'and along came Einstein. And then Einstein said the same thing. But then Heisenberg shows up.'

Following a sudden impulse, Lichtinger got up, stepped behind the altar and took a book of matches and two big, white altar candles from a wooden box. He placed them on the altar and lit them. Two candles for the two young men they had been. And it was as if the white wax was taking over the warm, forgiving memories, as if they were only continuing to glow in their flames. The warmth had faded from Lichtinger's mind. He thought of where the boisterous games had eventually taken them. He thought of the old grey cardboard suitcase, which was lying amongst the junk in his attic, seemingly carelessly tossed there by mistake. Inside the suitcase was a steel strongbox with a number lock. And inside the strongbox was money, lots of money, in orderly bundles. What was sitting in the attic of the vicarage in Grisbach was 50 million dollars.

The road up to the little church in Oberronnberg had no tarmac surface. Even before noticing the sounds of a car engine, one could hear the wheels on the rough gravel. Joseph Lichtinger went to the entrance to the church, opened the door and stepped outside. He saw the charcoal-grey BMW approach. The sunlight made it impossible to recognise Tretjak's face behind the windscreen, but the headlights of the car flashed a greeting.

'I once asked you a question,' Tretjak said, 'a long time

ago. I wanted to know what I would have to envisage when it is said that physicists are searching for a global formula. Do you remember?'

Lichtinger looked at him and only shook his head in a tired way. Tretjak was wearing blue jeans, black loafers and a lightweight black pullover. He was sitting on the altar step, on the floor, next to his open laptop. Lichtinger was sitting opposite him, in the first row of wooden benches. He had locked the door of the church behind them. The first thing Tretjak had done was to extinguish the two candles. 'Permit me...'

One couldn't really say that he had indulged in small talk. He had started up his computer and had rapidly filled Lichtinger in on everything that had happened in the past few days. The message in the hotel in Sri Lanka, the murder of Kerkhoff, the curious occurrence with his cleaning lady, the floral missive and now the murder of Kufner. Tretjak had documented everything on his computer; even a picture of the racehorse Nu Pagadi had appeared on the screen. As in the past he was eager to be precise and did not leave out any detail – they sat there for over an hour. Just to complete the picture, as he put it, Tretjak had told him finally about his client Melanie Schwarz and the disgusting politician.

Tretjak rubbed his forehead. 'Back then you replied to my question by saying that I should imagine a couple in love having dinner together, man and woman, a beautiful, candle-lit meal with champagne, fitting music from the CD player – maybe he had invited her and had cooked the food. Finally they end up in the bedroom, leaving the empty plates on the table.'

Tretjak looked at him again. 'Now you remember. You said I should imagine scientists from another world, from a different part of the universe, where they know nothing about us humans. They investigate the dinner table, because that's the only thing they've got. They measure everything, analyse everything, every particle is sent to the lab to be checked: the remainder of the sauce, the lipstick on the glass, the traces of sweat on the napkins. They put forward their theses, then reject them. And then they go on analysing, even more precisely. At one point they realise that there were living beings present, beings who need to eat and drink – maybe they even realise that these beings had a language, because the music gave that away. You explained to me that the scientists found out a lot about what happened that evening. But there was one fundamental realisation missing, and only that realisation completed the picture.' Tretjak paused. It was very quiet now. 'Only when they discover love, this phenomenon which is not made out of anything, only then will they fully comprehend us humans and what went on that evening. That's how you explained it to me back then. The global formula is that all encompassing idea – the physicists are not just looking for some numbers, but for the big idea that explains our world.'

Lichtinger nodded. Yes, he remembered. That's how he saw it back then. Today, however, he wasn't so sure anymore where they were, those theoretical physicists. He saw Tretjak get up, with arms akimbo, and look down at his laptop, which was standing on the stone step in front of him. 'I don't know what's happening here, Joseph. I am standing in front of it like your extra terrestrials in front of the dinner table.'

Lichtinger thought of the name somebody had supposedly given Tretjak. 'The Fixer is at a complete loss?'

Tretjak looked up. 'And the man of God? Does he know what to do?'

Lichtinger had now got up as well. 'You are not really at a loss, Gabriel, are you? You know exactly what is happening here. Nu Pagadi. A bill is being presented, in Russian. Why did you come? Do you finally want to tell me exactly what happened back then? What exactly you...' he stressed this word, repeated it, 'what *exactly* you did back then?'

'Do you want to hear my confession, Father? Are you kidding?' Tretjak's voice turned cold. 'You know exactly what happened back then. You were there, you know what we did and what we wanted to do.' He looked up to the ceiling. 'And your Almighty knows it as well.'

'I only know your version of the story, don't forget that,' Lichtinger said. 'Your version of the story and the money, that was all you served up to me. And if your version is the truth then what's happening right now shouldn't be puzzling. Somebody wants their money back. And that somebody is pretty angry that you got it off him back then.'

'Somebody…' Tretjak shook his head. 'That some-body doesn't exist anymore.' He rummaged around in his trouser pockets. 'Do you have a toilet here?' he asked.

Lichtinger immediately noticed the South Tyrolean accent and he almost smiled. 'No,' he said, 'I'm sorry.'

'And water?'

'We've got water. Just behind the screen you'll find the tap.'

Tretjak took a few steps, moved the screen away, opened the tap over the little basin and didn't even try to conceal that he was taking some pills.

'Aren't you afraid?' he asked when he turned around.

'Fear… No, not anymore. Of all the emotions inside me connected to that effing suitcase, there is only one left over now: I am ashamed.'

'Oh, yes,' said Tretjak, 'Saint Joseph.'

'Maybe nobody knows about me…'

'I want to tell you something,' Tretjak interrupted him, 'whoever is behind this knows a hell of a lot, he knows my life inside out, he knows much too much. We can therefore assume that he also knows about you.'

'Isn't that your doctrine,' said Lichtinger. 'Know eve-rything about the key person. Maybe you said so to these guys back then.' Lichtinger remembered how Tretjak had drawn diagrams on pieces of paper, like spider webs. In the middle was the most important person. Now he asked himself whether Tretjak had mapped out such a diagram for him, his former friend. How much did Tretjak know about him? Everything? This thought unnerved him.

Lichtinger stepped in front of the altar, placed the two candles back in the wooden box and moved the screen back in front of the basin. He saw that Tretjak had closed his laptop. They walked along the aisle in the direction of the exit, stopped halfway and sat down next to each other in one of the pews.

'I hear of your great success putting on "Science-Slams",' Tretjak said. 'What's that all about?'

'We always hold them in big barns or toolsheds,' Lichtinger said. 'The stage is normally a tractor-trailer. And then people stand up and explain a scientific topic. Everybody has five minutes and when their time is up the audience screams "Stop!" or "Continue!" depending how good that particular performer is. And at the end of the evening there is a vote for who is the winner.'

'What topics?' asked Tretjak.

'Totally open, marine biology, oral surgery, research into aggression, all is possible. Pupils perform, also students, we even had two real professors. It's fun, you should come.'

Tretjak nodded and smiled. And if he hasn't changed completely, Pastor Lichtinger thought, then this thought really appealed to him, at least in that very moment.

*Munich, East Station, 9pm*

Dimitri Steiner stood next to his motorcycle and pondered, maybe for the hundredth time, whether he should get himself a windscreen. The advantages were clear: when it rained one stayed dry behind it, and also on the motorway at higher speed, it promised a more relaxed ride. On the other hand on hotter days one missed the cooling airstream, and above all Dimitri was a great believer in the pure motorcycle experience. Machines with sound systems, GPS, seat or handle heating were not for him, he called them 'fitted kitchens'. Dimitri looked at his rear-view mirrors. They were drop-shaped, and he thought about exchanging them for circular ones, the ones he had spotted in the Harley-Davidson catalogue a while ago.

Dimitri Steiner was completely happy when he pondered these kind of questions. He could spend hours doing just that, inspecting every detail of his motorcycle: should he replace all the screws with chrome ones? Attach a small oil pressure metre down near the engine block? Pad the seat a little more softly? He didn't have to account to anybody for these mind games, they could be interrupted at any time, they didn't have to go anywhere, and above all: he didn't ever have to do anything about them, there were no consequences for either himself or somebody else. Ever since Dimitri Steiner had renounced his profession, had retired so to speak, these harmless mind games were his hobby.

It was just after nine o'clock in the evening. Steiner was

standing with his motorcycle at Munich's East Station at the loading ramp for the motorail train to Hamburg. He stood there in amongst other riders who had all attached a white piece of paper with sticky tape to the tanks of their machines: on it was written, *Hamburg-Altona.* Dimitri and his motorcycle stood out in the crowd. His Harley Roadking was sprayed in two colours, an antique off-white and a sunny yellow. Dimitri's helmet, which was hanging on the handlebar, was also white, and he himself was wearing a bright red, massive leather jacket. He was a strangely square man, a bit too short, with a bit of a belly, but quite a broad, muscular back for a man in his late fifties. His icy-grey hair was cropped in a crew cut, and his face was tanned after his 14-day tour through the Alps. Dimitri Steiner knew that he looked funny somehow, and that would be reflected in the face of the inspector whom he had been told to meet.

It had been four years since he had last received a message from his former life. And then one had arrived today in the form of a telephone call, not a long one, a rather clipped one, a bit too short for his taste. The man on the other end was obviously still young and did not quite appreciate who he was dealing with. Even without the lecture, Dimitri would have known what information he could reveal to the police inspector – and what he could not. He had taken the call standing in the parking lot outside the motorway restaurant at the Zirler Berg. Afterwards he had gone inside and ordered himself a large portion of warm apple strudel with vanilla ice cream and extra cream. He loved this apple strudel that you could find everywhere around here.

The boarding was beginning, and the motorcycles were first up. One had to mind one's head when driving into the wagons as the steel girders supporting the levels above hung deep. Dimitri knew that, he had taken the motorail many times before. He was well practised in moving his Roadking into the position assigned to him by the guys in the orange vests. He turned the alarm to transport mode, took his black leather bag from the carrier – and threw it on the bed in his compartment a short while later. Dimitri Steiner travelled the most luxurious way when he took the motorail, a single bunk compartment with private shower and toilet. A small bottle of red wine already stood next to the bed. Tomorrow morning, an hour before his arrival, he would be served breakfast here. He hung up his leather jacket, took off his tee-shirt and took a fresh, red and blue checkered shirt from his bag.

He had only had got along well with policemen all his life. No matter what country, policemen were sensible, nice guys. Clueless about what really went on, but you had no problems with them. Inspector Maler, who was already expecting him in the dining car, was cast in that same mould. Maler was wearing a pale beige shirt, a grey jacket and had grey skin. Dimitri was reminded of his childhood in Rostow, a grey city of a million-odd grey inhabitants in the middle of nowhere in the former

Soviet Union. There everything had been as colourless as the inspector; the houses, the streets, the people. They had three quarters of an hour to talk, then the inspector would have to get off and the train would leave the station. Dimitri would have forgotten the man before the train reached its ultimate travelling speed.

'I have to confess, Mr Steiner,' Maler opened the conversation, 'that I am at a loss as to what our meeting is all about. Maybe you can enlighten me.' He was sitting in front of an alcohol-free beer and a black coffee. Dimitri had ordered a yeast beer. 'I am investigating a murder, two as a matter of fact,' Maler continued. 'In these cases there is a person of interest on whom I require additional information. Gabriel Tretjak. Our police computer supplies almost as much data as the telephone book. But today I received a somewhat strange call from the Federal Criminal Police Office.' He looked at Dimitri. 'I was told that a certain Dieter Steiner could assist me in my investigations. A meeting had already been set up. Not much more was revealed by that colleague, who talked about a discreet affair, something which lay outside the normal police remit. The information which you could give me would be the only information I would get on this matter.' Maler reached for his cup and waited for the man sitting opposite to say something.

Dimitri was always a bit surprised when somebody used the name Dieter, especially if nobody had addressed him that way for a while – like in the past few days. He had never had a problem with Steiner, but Dieter he simply couldn't get used to. Dieter Steiner, Grosser Elbberg 27, 22767 Hamburg, German citizen. Sometimes, when he awoke in this flat on the ninth floor overlooking the harbour, he pondered what turns life could take. Who would have known that the little Dimitri Tschernokov would morph into a Dieter Steiner, a man without any financial worries, secured by the German state, a man who looked out onto cranes, cruise ships and oil tankers like a king from his castle turret, living in a flat which cost almost 3000 euro in rent a month. Every day he was greeted by a friendly doorman, and he had private health insurance which meant he could consult the best doctors. Although there was nothing wrong with him, blood pressure a bit on the high side, that was all.

Dimitri realised that he had to let the inspector in on who was sitting in front of him. So he began to talk about two worlds: there was one in which a normal life was lived by people who had normal jobs, whose children attended normal schools, who ordered normal cars and who were protected by the police while doing all that. And then he spoke of the other, the world of shadows, the world of the secret services, the world of the investigation bureaus, of agents and of contacts, but also the world of organised crime, of the mafia, with all that is connected to it like drug and human trafficking. 'In that world,' he said, 'laws have a different meaning. I was active in that world all my life.'

The expression on the inspector's face told him that he

did not have to be too explicit at this point. It was obviously not the first time that Maler had been confronted in his work with state activities belonging to a more shadowy world. 'It is a cold, somewhat more technocratic world,' Dimitri added. 'To the secret service you are a file, sometimes only a number. As far as organised crime is concerned, you are just a name, often only a first name. Loyalties change all the time, people you deal with disappear, power lines shift. You don't have a guilty conscience if you change sides, like I did.'

Further back in the dining car a five-strong Danish family had sat down, all of them blond, all of them tanned, all of them in good spirits.

'When the Iron Curtain came down, a chance presented itself and I took it,' Dimitri said.

For a moment he thought back to the arrogant behaviour of his German handlers. Now that your empire is collapsing turncoats are not worth anything anymore, their behaviour implied... Nobody was interested in his skills, in his networks, which spanned the world, his know-how. He was paid a modest sum to get him started and was used as a shabby little agent, as a courier, security guard, things like that. If his former contacts hadn't passed the occasional job his way he wouldn't have been able to live off the meagre salary from the German Intelligence Agency.

And then, after 9/11, everything changed. Suddenly they got off their high horses, suddenly he was picked up by limousines and brought to meetings where he wasn't bossed around by simple bureaucrats, but nice men in well-cut suits offered him espresso and smoked salmon sandwiches. Suddenly they were not rubbing his face in morals, human rights and the rule of law, which he was supposed to learn first. Instead, everything was reduced to the all-important question: what methods did the Soviet Union deploy – and Russia still deploy – to prevent its citizens becoming the victims of terrorist kidnappers? Americans, Germans, Italians, Japanese – citizens from all these countries ended up in the hands of terrorists, ransoms were demanded from companies, from governments, from private individuals. Only the Russians were spared. Why? They knew that this had been his special field. In these weeks after 11 September 2001, Dimitri Tschernokov, already called Dieter Steiner, his new code name, but without his German citizenship yet, understood that his knowledge was worth a lot of money. And the German authorities understood a few things as well: the man was no show-off, his information was correct, most of it checked out. And the man was dangerous. For years he had organised targeted assassinations – in many cases he had carried them out himself. Not that the officers were afraid for their own lives. The danger was inherent in getting involved with him. Dimitri Tschernokov had worked in the Arab world, where a German secret agent had once called him 'a Blitzkrieger against terrorists', and he was known in terrorist circles, still was, which was undoubtedly part of his strategy: whoever kidnapped a Russian never saw any money but got to know Tschernokov's troops. But who said that the terrorists from back then were the terrorists of today? They had continuously voiced that worry: was their cooperation with Tschernokov going to attract the attention of terrorists to Germany and make German citizens targets?

Finally came the conversation that clinched the deal. It took place in a small conference room in a business hotel near Münster. There, Dimitri, who at that point was still a master of external inconspicuousness, met an equally inconspicuous man, who had nothing to say and was only there to make a telephone connection. The important part was the voice on the phone. Dimitri knew it belonged to the head of the German Federal Investigation Bureau although no mention was made of any names. The voice was soft and matter-of-fact. 'We reject the methods you applied,' the voice said. 'We don't want you to work for the German state or German organisations or companies. We just want your knowledge, your information.'

In the dining car of the stationary motorail train in Munich it took Dimitri only a few seconds to remember this decisive point in his life, only a pensive look down onto the top of the table.

Inspector Maler ordered another coffee – 'decaffeinated again, please' – and said: 'Mr Steiner, we will probably never meet again. You couldn't care less, nor could I, what I think about you, what you did or how you made a living. I was informed that you could tell me something about Tretjak which might help me in my investigations.'

Dimitri nodded in the direction of the drinks on the table and said: 'Alcohol-free, decaffeinated... you like to take risks, eh?' He saw a fine line of irony crease the corner of the inspector's mouth, but he otherwise didn't remark on his nod. 'Tretjak, Gabriel Tretjak...' murmured Dimitri. 'You know Inspector, in my business it is like in every other one. There are some first rate people, some mediocre ones and a lot of completely useless ones. And like in every profession, outstanding ones are noticed very quickly.'

'That's what happened with Tretjak?'

Dimitri nodded. 'Let's say, it's like in ice hockey. Suddenly there is this young guy. He is playing at some God-forsaken provincial club, but he is dancing with the puck completely differently from all the others. It doesn't take long before a certain buzz, an excitement surrounds this youngster. And then suddenly powerful people are standing at the barrier and want to take him away.' He explained that the young Gabriel Tretjak had stood out because he'd carried out unusual jobs in an unusual way. He was somebody who pulled strings and changed things that way. Although it was not clear at first where the assignments came from, or who this Tretjak was. Was that really his name? 'In my world,' Dimitri said, 'you see secrets everywhere.'

'What kind of jobs were they?' Maler asked.

'Harmless stuff, you could say,' Dimitri answered.

'Once he arranged for the smashing of a newly founded sect in Cologne. Dealing with sects is not easy. Tretjak initiated simultaneous actions against the founders. One was arrested for drug trafficking, the other, an editor at the *Westdeutscher Rundfunk*, got into trouble when it was made public that he belonged to a sect. Tretjak skilfully juggled the information. After just about three weeks the sect didn't exist anymore.'

'And why did he do it?'

'There was no other explanation than that he got the assignment from an industrialist whose daughter had lost her way and had ended up joining the sect.'

'And you had noticed that?'

'I personally hadn't noticed it yet. But a short time later he tried to extricate a German industrialist from an Algerian detention centre. He needed my help for this job. And this was proof of his abilities. He shouldn't have even known that I existed.'

Dimitri reached for the menu and scanned it quickly. He was hungry, signalled to the waiter, and pointed at the photo with the large cheese platter. 'I of course started to investigate,' he said. 'None of us could imagine that Tretjak was working for himself. Everybody thought that he had an organisation, a secret service, some company or another or the mafia behind him...'

'But that was not the case, was it?' Maler asked.

'No, it wasn't.' Dimitri answered. 'But now he was getting offers from every quarter.'

Maler looked at him. 'The powerful people showed

up at the barrier… Were you one of those who wanted to whisk him away?'

'Maybe.' Dimitri felt his mobile vibrate in his trouser pocket. A message. He knew full well who it was from.

'And who, in the end, bought him?'

Dimitri took his time with the answer, chose every word carefully. 'Nobody bought him. He was paid for his work, yes. But as far as I know he didn't join forces with anybody.'

Maler now leafed through a little notebook. 'Tretjak is being investigated at the moment by the Inland Revenue,' he said. 'The tax inspector told me…'

'Ms Neustadt,' Dimitri interrupted. 'Ms Fiona Neustadt.'

Surprised, Maler looked up.

Dimitri smiled and raised his arms in his defence. 'Sorry, Inspector, information was my business for too long, my drug. Sometimes you have relapses.' He liked this policeman, who was now closing his notebook with an irritated expression. 'So what did this Ms Neustadt tell you?'

'That Tretjak meddles in the lives of a lot people by profession,' Maler said after a short break. 'And that this probably conjures up a certain degree of enmity. That's what she said. I believe she wanted to protect him somehow…'

That was the start of the sort of policeman's questions Dimitri had been expecting. Who were Tretjak's enemies? Was there somebody in particular who wanted

to settle a score? When was the last time Dimitri had
seen Tretjak? Did the names Kufner and Kerkhoff mean
anything to him?

Dimitri had, in the meantime, devoured the German
Rail cheese platter, which had made it possible for him
to fob off the inspector's questions with monosyllabic
answers or the occasional shrug. But at the end of the
conversation Dimitri tore off a piece of the menu and
with the inspector's pen scribbled a few words and a few
numbers on an empty space on it.

Darkness had fallen outside; the inspector had paid
for his drinks and stood up. Dimitri rose too and handed
him the piece of paper. 'There is a man in room 324,
ward F of the Munich University Hospital in Großhad-
ern who you should go and see,' Dimitri said. 'He is
going to die and this is going to happen soon. Pancreatic
cancer, terminal phase.' Maler looked at him, unmoved,
but Dimitri had the feeling that the mention of the
clinic – or the illness – made him feel uncomfortable.
'The man's name is Krabbe and he is a doctor himself,'
Dimitri continued, 'Dr Martin Krabbe. Your records
will show him to be an ear, nose and throat specialist
with a practice at the Tegernsee. Forget that. Just show
him this piece of paper and then talk to him about his
pupils. Because he was also a kind of teacher.'

Dimitri saw that Maler only looked at the paper when
he was already outside on the platform. It had the ward
and room number noted on it – and a term, which didn't
mean anything to Maler, which was meant exclusively

for Martin Krabbe. *Liver a la Veneziana*, Dimitri had written there. This was not only the name of Dr Martin Krabbe's favourite dish in any Italian restaurant, but also a sophisticated method that he had developed to kill somebody. Dimitri asked himself whether the inspector was placing enough value on this clue.

When the train had left the station he took out the mobile from his pocket. He wanted to read the message from Gabriel Tretjak. He had received a message from him at lunchtime: *Don't care where you are. Have to meet you immediately. GT.* In the afternoon they had spoken on the phone. Now Tretjak had sent a suggestion. *The day after tomorrow. Café Paris, 10am.*

Dimitri typed the reply, which consisted of a small correction. *10.30am.* He was retired after all; he wanted to sleep in.

# Seventh Day

## 17 May

*Bolzano, Hotel Zum Blauen Mondschein, 6am*
It had been three days since she'd made the gruesome discovery in room 242. Maria was scheduled to do the early shift and showed up for work as if nothing had happened. She had been asked whether she needed psychological support. She had only shaken her slender head.

Maria entered the hotel Blauen Mondschein through the trade entrance in the courtyard at the back. Like every other day she first went to reception to enquire whether there were any special tasks to be carried out that day. Max was on duty. Maria and Max had known each other for almost 40 years. For her he was and would always be Little Max, the pageboy she had trained back then. Little Max was almost 65 years old now, soon to retire, and weighed 120 kilos because he loved every kind of pasta there was. But that didn't change her image of him. 83-year-old Maria still saw the Max he had once been.

'Maria,' Max said, 'you've got some mail. Special mail, I think.'

He handed her a large envelope, big and padded. In

beautifully formed letters it said: *For Mrs Maria Unter-ganzner.* The envelope had no return address. Maria took and opened it. As if she received letters like that every day. And she didn't mind that Max was watching her. What could be in there anyway? She had no secrets from her hotel.

It was indeed a rather special kind of letter. At first the content seemed to be some sort of certificate. A sheet of paper, but not really paper, finer, thinner, like parchment. Decorated on all sides in colour. Yellow and red lines, heads of animals, a coat of arms. And in the middle stood a number and a few words. *Room 242*, it said, and: *Dear Maria, please tell the police the story of Gabriel Tretjak.* No signature, nothing else. The letters seemed to have been written with a fountain pen, sweeping, almost a bit over the top, somehow antique.

A few minutes later Max called the police. First the local station, which knew them, as it was the one they often called when tourists blocked their entrance without being guests of the hotel. The man there connected Max with the police headquarters. When the connection was made between the strange letter and the murder of the scientist, everything moved very fast. Maria was supposed to come to the headquarters as soon as possible. The inspector himself wanted to talk to her.

Maria quickly went home first. She changed from the dark navy-blue dress with the blue apron into the black dress she wore at funerals. That seemed appropriate to her for a visit to an inspector. Black dress and the topic of death, that's only right and proper, she thought.

Inspector Fritz Innerhofer was on his fifth cup of coffee of the morning. His secretary knew that this was an indication of how the current investigation was progressing. The more coffee, the worse it was. Five cups this early in the morning could mean only one thing: it was going very badly. The conversations with the family had not led to anything, nor had the forensic examination of the hotel room, except for the realisation that this was the work of a professional killer – the room had been cleaned of evidence perfectly, leaving only the large amount of blood everywhere. There was no decent clue so far, no suspect. There was only this name: Tretjak.

They had very quickly connected the murder on the Bavarian motorway to the one in the hotel room in Bolzano. The inspector from Munich had mentioned a dubious businessman called Tretjak, who played some role in the case, but he was still completely in the dark as to how he was involved. Innerhofer remembered the name – he was an ice hockey fan, and there had been a legendary Soviet goalkeeper with the name Wladislaw Tretjak. He had mentioned that straight away in his conversation with Maler, but his colleague knew nothing about ice hockey and said only: 'My Tretjak's first name is Gabriel. A very odd man.'

And then he had received the call this morning. When his secretary popped her head through the door and announced that Mrs Unterganzner was here now, Innerhofer said: 'Good, she should come in straight away.'

Maid was probably not really the right term for her, he thought, when the small, petite, old Maria took her seat opposite him. She handed him the envelope. Innerhofer opened it and carefully took out the page of parchment. He read the text and then said: 'Well, Mrs Unterganzner...'

'Please, Inspector, call me Maria. Everybody calls me Maria. I never hear my last name, it makes me nervous.'

'With pleasure. Well, Maria, tell me the story of this Gabriel Tretjak.'

'There is nothing to tell. I haven't seen him in 30 years. I know nothing about him now.'

In these moments Innerhofer hated his job. First his expectations were raised, and then dashed. Outwardly he didn't show any reaction, he just looked at Maria.

She said: 'I only knew him when he was still a child.'

It took another three cups of coffee for the inspector from Bolzano – Maria didn't drink anything – to get the full story Maria had to tell about Tretjak. It was not always very easy to follow; the old lady was not a natural story teller. The sentence she repeated most often was: 'Gabriel, he was such a lovely boy!'

Gabriel Tretjak's mother was a capable Turkish woman who with her husband took over the management of the hotel Zum Blauen Mondschein back in the Seventies. She was intelligent and hard working, in contrast to her husband Paul, who was a good-for-nothing, always chasing after skirts. There was also a son from Paul's first marriage. Must have been a nasty character, causing trouble every time he came to stay. He was about 10 years older than Gabriel, and Gabriel had always been afraid of him. Maria didn't remember his name.

Then the mother got sick, cancer of the brain, the illness worsening very quickly. And Gabriel's father, the shifty Paul, cleared out of there very abruptly. He deserted his family, the dying wife and the little Gabriel. The mother had to ask her family in Turkey to help out. Her two sisters arrived with their entourage. All of them only spoke Turkish.

This was the story Maria Unterganzner had to tell about Gabriel Tretjak: the development of a horrible childhood. She remembered two scenes in particular. Once little Gabriel had fallen down the stairs and hurt his knee and was crying. Gabriel was about 10 years old back then. His knee was bleeding, and he cried and cried, and then suddenly he called for his father, 'Daddy, Daddy, where is my Daddy?' And the only one who was there was one of his aunts. She was nice, for sure, tried to calm him, comfort him, and she also said something like 'Daddy later, Daddy later'. But the maid Maria, who was observing the scene, had the feeling, a feeling she remembered over 30 years later: The boy was afraid of his aunt, the woman with a headscarf, who he didn't understand.

The second memory wasn't much better. Little Gabriel was sitting on his bed in his room, totally motionless, unresponsive, with his stuffed animal in his lap, a white tiger. Maria shook him, took him in her arms. No reaction. Outside you could hear his mother scream, in such great pain that no medicine could ease it. This time it took hours before the morphine finally worked. When his mother eventually fell asleep Gabriel was still sitting on his bed, totally frozen. Maria remembered calling the paediatrician. He gave the boy an injection, and then finally things returned to normal.

Horror stories, absolute horror stories. And then Maria told another story, a beautiful one, actually. After the mother had died, there was nobody who could take care of little Gabriel. The Turkish family he didn't really understand? The father, who had taken off? No. So the hotel and the city took over the responsibility, if you like. The mayor back then became his guardian. One of his relatives had a farm in the hills above Bolzano, with a big family who took Gabriel in. After school every day at noon he came to the hotel, where Maria cooked him lunch. Thus he was a son of Bolzano, and people were of course a bit disappointed, as Maria put it, that he didn't keep in touch with anybody after he left school. But she, said Maria, she had understood him. 'He had to go and start a new life for himself.'

Inspector Innerhofer thanked Maria for her statement and took her to the door.

One thing was clear now: somebody wanted the story of this childhood to be known. *Please tell all this to the police*, this somebody had written on the parchment. And this somebody could be a double murderer. Innerhofer stood at the window in his office and looked at the dirty-brown wall of the building opposite where the plaster was coming off. He was convinced that this was the ugliest view in the whole of Bolzano. But for a moment he didn't mind all that. The solution to the murder of the professor had moved closer through the evidence the maid had just given, which established that the killing had some definite connection to Bolzano. The hope that it would be a case of a murder of a traveller just passing through town, killed here by strange coincidence, that hope had been dashed.

What was the purpose of the message to Maria? For a brief moment the inspector wondered whether the old lady was somehow in danger, whether he had to do anything. But then he thought not. Why would anybody want to hurt a little wizened lady?

Innerhofer had the switchboard connect him with the man Maria had mentioned: Gabriel Tretjak's paediatrician who had been called out to treat the distraught boy. 'He was also called Innerhofer.'

Innerhofer was a common name in Bolzano. When Innerhofers talked to one another, they had a certain routine. 'Well,' said the paediatrician on the phone, 'in this case it's simple, you are Inspector and I am Doctor.'

Doctor Innerhofer was a young man back then; today he was old, but still practising. He remembered poor little Gabriel well. 'What ever happened to him?' he asked.

'Businessman in Munich, apparently quite successful.'

'What do you want to know, Inspector?'

Innerhofer didn't really know himself. The doctor said that he had been impressed how the child had set himself against the difficult reality. Gabriel, in a way, had turned inward. What fitted into that picture was also the fact that the little one had started to be interested in the stars. 'He looked inwards and upwards, but definitely away from the life that he saw day by day.'

The inspector asked whether this kind of childhood could somehow be significant in any way. The doctor laughed and replied: 'Certainly. This childhood could be a definite explanation for anything that happened later.'

Inspector Innerhofer placed two calls after this one. He left a message on Inspector Maler's voicemail, informing him about the evidence the maid had given. And he called his colleague in the art theft division, who he had passed the envelope with the parchment to. Yes, said this expert, it hadn't been very difficult to recognise: it was a page from a medieval illuminated manuscript from the city of Udine from the 16th Century. The complete manuscript, some 100 pages, was of immeasurable value. This page alone was probably worth 10,000 euros. He had already contacted Udine to find out where the manuscript was at the moment.

### *Kochel am See, 11am*

In the end, it had been easier than she had thought. In the end, it is always easy. Charlotte Poland decided to remember that sentence. Maybe she could use it in her next novel.

Shortly after 10am, still from her hotel room, she had called her husband and had ended her marriage. It had lasted seventeen years, three months and eleven days. She had done that calculation just before pressing the call button on her mobile. 'Markus,' she said, 'I want a divorce. It's the best thing for both of us. I know it and you know it, too. In fact we have both known it for a long time.'

Markus replied, rather quickly: 'Maybe you are right.' And then he attempted to jest, as he so often tried to make light of a depressing situation with a joke: 'At least we don't have to fight about the custody of Lars.'

Celebrity couples often named as a reason for their separation the fact that they had drifted apart over the past few years. Charlotte Poland thought this was not a bad description: two people go separate ways, though at the beginning they are always close by, within shouting distance and clearly visible by the other. So they don't notice at first that through forks in the road the distance between their paths becomes ever bigger, so big in fact that they end up in different worlds. Charlotte was 25 when she met Markus, who at that time was approaching his 50th birthday. She was a student who wanted to be a writer or a journalist or something that had to do with writing. He was an IT entrepreneur and had just sold his company for an eight-digit figure. They had met by chance in a hotel in Düsseldorf. He had slipped a note under her door in the middle of the night. He had written two short romantic poems for her. Maybe that was the moment that they had been closest in all those years.

Charlotte liked his generous nature, his distant character. He never quizzed her, never pestered her. Then she noticed that he treated everybody the same way, friendly, vague, like a charming host of a television show. She suddenly realised that in truth he was not interested in anybody, not even in their son Lars, who was born three years after their marriage. Markus had a few hobbies: he renovated Tuscan villas, bred French bulldogs, and somehow his family was a kind of hobby as well. He kept his distance emotionally, neither cold nor warm. But he was always friendly and tried to fulfil all Charlotte's and Lars's wishes. Charlotte was too clever to want to change Markus. She chose a different route: in his way Markus was the perfect husband to equip her with a structure for her life. It was now up to her to live within that structure the way she wanted.

Her first affair was with her publisher. She had published a few racy articles in some magazines and now wanted to try her hand at writing a novel. She wrote 30 pages, the beginning of a psychological take on a relationship, and sent the manuscript to the most famous publisher in Munich. He liked the pages, and liked

Charlotte Poland even better. He met her for dinner and told her after the second grappa that he was going to publish her book if she went to bed with him. She sat there thinking this was a bit too much like a scene from a trashy novel, but on the other hand she was old enough to know that life sometimes is like a trashy novel. So she looked at the publisher, who was a bit portly but still rather good-looking, and said: 'OK, where shall we go?'

They went to the big hotel at the airport, and kept up that routine even after Charlotte Poland's books met with success after success. Every two months, they met at the Munich airport and spent an afternoon together.

Other affairs followed, numerous and quite varied. Sometimes it felt good, sometimes not. Sometimes cheap, sometimes less so. She believed she was happy. This was exactly how she had imagined her life, a life of many shades. She was aware that sometimes it appeared that she was mistaking her stories for her real life. But why not? She even saw a psychotherapist and in many a session internally examined her life. And if she had to take personal stock of these sessions she would say: yes, she needed the play with lies to round off her life. It was not really evil; it suited her.

But then there was that little boy, who was growing up, and with him grew the problems he created – yet she loved him so much. No matter how much she suffered for it, how angry he made her, and how she hated him for brief moments. Soon after the problems with Lars began, she started to imagine that he had turned out the way he had because of her, that he had in effect become the metaphor for her life. Her son, the monstrous liar, presented her with the reckoning for her own hypo-critical and deceitful life. This thought took hold of her more and more. Not only was she responsible for Lars's fate, it was also up to her to save him. For that, she was prepared to completely change her ways. She wanted her son back. The termination of her marriage was the first step. She was determined to act, at all costs.

She was waiting downstairs in the lobby, and ordered another coffee, black, without anything, as always. She was wearing her white summer dress and flesh-coloured bra, which she sometimes left off when she wanted to make a man nervous. Paul Tretjak didn't belong to that group. He had become a friend in the last few weeks, a companion for what was to come. She looked at her watch. Paul had to be here soon. He was going to send a message when he approached the hotel. They didn't have a lot of time; they had to quickly drive on to Munich. Paul had made three appointments for her, which she had to keep. First, two guys from the drug world and then, this evening, the meeting with his son Gabriel in the Osteria.

A while ago Paul had given her a text by Sigmund Freud, from his early years, in which he explained why he had turned to psychology. Essentially it dealt with the question of whether the soul punishes a life gone wrong. Why do childhood fears, for example, from which a man has run away all his life, eventually catch up with him?

Or why does a woman, who all her life has had to put on an act of being strong and perfect, but who in fact was the complete opposite, eventually commit suicide? Freud asked the question: who was the authority who determines which life is the right one and which one is wrong? And who decides to take revenge, so to speak, if the person insists on sticking to the wrong course? Freud, at the end of the text, called this authority the soul, and announced that he would devote his life to the study of this authority. And this also meant, as he put it, that he was determined to do battle with this avenging angel, the soul.

Charlotte had read the text and then asked Paul why he had given it to her. 'Don't ask me why,' he had said curtly. '"Why" lost its meaning for me a long time ago.'

Her mobile buzzed. *I am here. Paul.*

Charlotte left the lobby and got into his car, an old blue Volvo, always pretty dirty and messy. This time he had at least cleared the passenger seat.

'You look nice,' Paul said.

'Thanks,' she said, 'so do you.' Which was not the case. As always, he was wearing old jeans and a washed-out denim shirt. His eyes were bloodshot and puffy. He obviously hadn't had a good night.

If you wanted you could indeed find parallels between their family histories. Charlotte Poland and Paul Tretjak both felt they were the offenders: their failures in the upbringing of their sons had made them into what they were now. And they both felt that they were victims too: their sons had taken revenge. The way the sons had taken revenge, however, could not be more different. The little Lars had cast his mother into a psychological hell by developing into a totally immoral and at the same time extremely dangerous human being. He had turned into a constant accusation. Gabriel Tretjak had chosen a more direct version of revenge: he had destroyed his father's life. One could not really put it any other way.

One evening at the Lago Maggiore, in a pretty village called Maccagno, he had told her the story. They sat in the garden of a restaurant, ate pasta and drank wine – a lot of wine. Paul called the restaurant 'The Evil', not for any metaphysical reason but merely because he had not been served there once, when it had been closed for a private party or something like that. He loved that restaurant, and Charlotte Poland had come to love it too. 'The Evil' was the perfect place to experience the particular atmosphere resulting from the special, idiosyncratic clientele that frequented the joint.

A few years after Paul Tretjak had left his family in Bolzano he had settled in the Bavarian town of Bad Tölz, about 80 kilometres from Munich. He had opened an inn with a few rooms, its own trout lake and a wonderful view of the mountains. Next to it, he built a miniature golf course and a tennis court. He got involved in local politics in Bad Tölz, and was even elected to the town council. Not that he was particularly interested in politics, but he realised that you could only prosper in the hotel trade if you knew exactly what was happening when and where. In Bolzano he had not been engaged enough. And it worked, business was booming. Paul Tretjak had a new capable partner – and a lover besides her, of course.

This idyllic situation, however, was shattered one day when on 15 September 1990 the following headline appeared in a Munich tabloid: *Hotelier From Tölz Abuses Six-Year-Old! Innkeeper Paul T. sexually abused the innocent little Julia, who was staying in his hotel with her parents.* In addition, it had been ascertained that he had several bank accounts, which showed six-figure transactions, allegedly from arms deals with Serbia, the country of his birth. Sex with children and dealing in weapons – Paul Tretjak had to close his hotel immediately. The media and several curious onlookers were camping outside the inn. The mayor came by personally to suggest that he should step aside from his council duties for the time being. Most of the others didn't speak to him at all. The report also named his lover. His partner had immediately moved out.

Two days after the publication of the tabloid article his son Gabriel showed up. Paul hadn't seen him for years – he looked very elegant in his suit and shiny polished leather shoes. 'I have come to make a proposal,' Gabriel Tretjak said. He placed an envelope on the table. 'In here is the DNA proof that you indeed abused the child. And evidence that you are up to your neck in the arms deals. You can study everything.'

In that moment, Paul told Charlotte, he lost it, he was furious. 'What are you talking about, what evidence? I never had sex with a six-year-old, madness, all of it! Arms deals, what arms deals?'

His son reacted very coolly: he could be sure that the case was absolutely watertight. And then Gabriel added: 'If I remember correctly, the truth never played any particular role in your life. What is true and what is not, that doesn't matter to you, does it?'

And then came his offer: here are the keys to a small house on the Lago Maggiore, beautifully situated, it can be reached on foot, 'you'll like it.' The rent is paid until the end of your life. And here is a deposit account with a little money. Gabriel Tretjak made it very clear for him: if he accepted, the case in Germany would be dismissed, the accusation found to be untenable. 'If, however, you ever decide to leave this house for a long period of time and try to live somewhere else, I will pass this evidence on to the police and the press. You have until tomorrow morning to think about my offer.'

Gabriel Tretjak went to the door without saying goodbye. Paul Tretjak had remained seated and had said: 'Can you please explain to me why you are doing this?'

'Yes,' his son answered without turning around, 'I can. I want to make sure that you disappear from my life forever. And it gives me a good feeling that this time I will know where you are.' That had been the last time they had seen each other. Or to be precise: the last time he had seen his son's back, and then the door closing behind him.

When Paul Tretjak had finished his story, he ordered two more grappas, a double for himself. 'Now you know what kind of a man I really am. I have been dead for a long time. A puppet, hanging on strings pulled by my vengeful son. I am an impotent puppet.'

From that moment on Charlotte Poland felt a great connection with Tretjak. She knew how it felt to be a puppet, to hang on the strings pulled by her son. And she liked this new perspective on Paul Tretjak. Up until then, she had seen him mainly as a slightly aged flirt: now there was this sense of tragedy about him, a depth to his demeanor which bore the inevitable hopelessness.

They drove into Munich on the Garmischer motorway. On the final approach one could see the steeples of the Church of Our Lady grow bigger and bigger. The motorway headed directly towards this Munich landmark, a nice touch of the motorway planners. Approaching something: maybe that was what was getting to Charlotte Poland. The situation had some of the feeling of a Hollywood Western, she thought. They were letting their two sons approach each other, until they came to a showdown. Alright, she thought, maybe that is a little exaggerated, the comparison was almost embarrassing. But who cared, she liked this kind of dramatic situation.

They didn't talk much as they drove on the motorway. Once Charlotte asked Paul about his new girlfriend. Very young, not even 30. He had talked about her before. 'How is it going with your young princess?' 'Good,' he said. 'I think she loves me. It is just beautiful when we are together.' And then he became emotional: 'She is immensely intense and somehow…'

'Don't say: somehow vulnerable,' she interrupted him.

'… like a deer…'

They both had to laugh, and then they were quiet.

The first appointment was at a bank, the Sendlinger Strasse branch. It once had been a long-established Munich financial institution, which merged with another and in the end was swallowed up by an Italian mega-bank. Charlotte Poland's appointment was at 4pm, a meeting with a financial advisor called Borbely. Mr Borbely had no idea that this was going to be a special kind of conversation: he had been told to expect a wealthy woman who wanted to invest some of her money. Mr Borbely was small and pudgy, and his handshake was spongy. They sat down in a small meeting room.

'What can I do for you, Mrs Poland?'

'I want to get straight to the point. I am here because of my son. You know him, he is 14 and his name is Lars. He has disappeared and I want him back. And fast.'

Mr Borbely cleared his throat. 'I have no idea what you're talking about. Please excuse me, but there has to be a mistake.'

'Mr Borbely, I am very worried and not interested in playing any games. I will make a deal with you. If my son stands in front of me by midday tomorrow I will pay you 10,000 euros. If not I will inform your bank about your extra-curricular activities.'

'I think, Mrs Poland, we should end this conversation right here.' The pudgy man tried to sound very hard. 'I don't understand a single word you are talking about.'

'Alright, Mr Borbely. If that's the case, then I would like to see your manager to talk about account 678678678.'

The pudgy man turned soft again. 'Please, Mrs Poland, I didn't mean to appear unfriendly. Where can I reach you tomorrow morning?'

When she was back outside in the Volvo she said to Paul: 'What on earth has this guy to do with my son?'

'There are people who claim that 50 percent of the drug trade in this town involves this man. I too would also prefer if Lars had nothing to do with him.'

She looked at him: 'Who learned from whom? Your son from you or you from your son?'

He did not answer. They drove on. They crossed the Isar, passed the pretty façade of the public baths and the Gasteig, the ugly, brick cultural centre. Somewhere close by Paul stopped his Volvo in front of an apartment block.

'You have to go in here, then cross through to the courtyard. There are several entrances. Take Number 11c, the third staircase, up to the third floor. There is a grey metal door there, with nothing written on it. That's a club. *Nadraj Temple*. Pretty hip, supposed to be the top place to be at the moment. I have no idea, I've not been in there.' Paul smiled. She got out. 'It will take 10 minutes, max. Do it the same way as with the guy in the bank.'

*

The man was already waiting for her at the iron door. He had about 10 piercings in both ears; the lobes were heavily hanging down. 'Hello,' he said, 'I am Kurt Meyer. This joint belongs to me. Do come in.'

It was just gone 6pm, and the *Nadraj Temple* would only open in a few hours. Just two sparse lights illuminated the room, there were no staff to be seen anywhere. They were standing at a dark bar.

'Would you like something to drink?'

'No,' said Charlotte Poland, 'I want to be very quick.' She repeated her offer of 10,000 euros that Meyer would receive if Lars was back with her by the day after tomorrow. He was given an extra day's grace. She didn't threaten him with anything. She did add that she had spoken with Mr Borbely, the man at the bank.

It was difficult to guess Kurt Meyer's age – somewhere around 50. He was very thin, and kept his eyes closed during almost the entire conversation. She was not quite sure whether he was on drugs. Only once did he open his eyes and utter a few words: 'So, you are Lars's mother. I had imagined you totally differently.'

*Mörlbach, Jedlitschka Farm, 12 noon*

Information turns into knowledge. Knowledge becomes power. Maybe the three suitcases, which Gabriel Tretjak unloaded from his BMW, contained all of his power. They were sturdy flight cases, custom-made by a specialist firm appropriately named *Don't Panic*. Coasters, extendable handles, inside different special compartments, outside massive locks. He had them built for exactly this kind of occasion, for the moment when he had to take all of his knowledge to safety. All the papers from his office, the hard drives, the big computer, plus the media of the past, magnetic tape, audiocassettes, all that was stowed in these three trunk-like suitcases, which he placed side-by-side on the concrete courtyard of the Jedlitschka Farm. He briefly contemplated that his knowledge mainly concerned people. That it consisted of dossiers about their lives, their careers, their passions, about things they had done which nobody else should know about.

It was just after noon, the sun was shining, and an incredibly blue sky spanned over the landscape. In Munich he had had the feeling that he was being followed by a car. Police? He had lost that car with an abrupt turn at an amber light. The old Mrs Jedlitschka was slowly coming across the courtyard. As she walked, she swayed like a ship, maybe because of her swollen legs. She was wearing a blue dress with a placket in the front, which made it look a little like overalls, and she had a dishcloth in her hand, with which she was wiping the sweat off her brow.

'My, what a month of May,' she said, halfway across the courtyard, 'it's like at the height of summer… are these all your tax files?'

On the telephone, Tretjak had put forward the tax inspection as a pretext and asked whether he could deposit some files temporarily at the farm, 'just to be on the safe side.' The Inland Revenue didn't have to know everything, did they? Mrs Jedlitschka had immediately mentioned a chamber at the back of the tool shed, and her voice had exuded pride. In this case she was obviously happy to be his ally. Farmers didn't like the Inland Revenue.

She had now reached Tretjak, shook his hand, and said with an eye on the suitcases: 'Quite a bit of stuff that you have to hide here.'

The chamber was a wooden crate behind the big Ferguson tractor. To the right there was a stack of tyres of different sizes. To the left, long poles were leaning against the wall, extensions for tools, propeller shafts for machines, a whiffletree for a trailer. The Fixer's suitcases found their place in the corner behind the pile of tyres and were covered up with an old black silo sheet. 'I still have to do some work, Mrs Jedlitschka, may I…'

'Of course,' the farmer's wife smiled. 'Go ahead, I'll bring the apple juice.'

Minutes later Tretjak was sitting at the wooden table in the shadow of his observatory at the back of the tool shed, his laptop in front of him, as well as a pile of white paper, a pen and a carafe of homemade apple juice. It was completely quiet. To a stranger the scene might have appeared peaceful, but this word was totally inappropriate to describe Tretjak's state of mind. He was in fact very unsettled, and had the feeling of being faced with something ominous that was brewing up, that he was running out of time. He knew he had to do something. He had to shake off this strange paralysis which had taken hold of him. Hadn't that been his strength all along? To act faster than the others? To always be one step ahead of them? Somehow he had fallen behind, which he had to change, and fast.

He took a piece of paper from the pile and placed it horizontally in front of him. On it he wrote four words next to each other: *money-box, father, Kerkhoff* and *Kufner*. From each of these words he drew an arrow downwards. At the end of the arrow underneath *money-box* he noted: *Dimitri*. Tomorrow morning he was going to meet him in Hamburg. And he was going to lean on him: was everything that was happening around Tretjak somehow connected to their mutual past? Was it connected with the suitcase full of money, which was now being stored in the attic of the vicarage? One could only get to Dimitri one of two ways: with money or with violence. Tretjak was going to take money with him to the meeting, stacks of money, in neat bundles. Dimitri was one of these people who could be seduced with cash. The other card, violence, Tretjak had to play in a different way. He had to make it crystal clear how far his

connections reached, which circles he could access. That
had already been taken care of. When Dimitri awoke
tomorrow morning in his flat overlooking the harbour,
he would find, to his surprise, a nicely-wrapped little
parcel on his living room table. It would contain a piece
of cake, his favourite: apple strudel. And a card with the
message: *To be enjoyed with care. Cordially, GT.* Dimitri
was going to poke around in the cake and find a few
nails; big, shiny builders' nails. He was a professional, he
would understand what the message meant: I can gain
access to your flat at night without you noticing. I know
what you like. And I can turn nasty.

Below the name *Dimitri* Tretjak wrote tomorrow's
date and *Hamburg, 10.30am.* And he added another
name with a question mark: *Lichtinger?* Then he drew a
circle around these words.

Underneath the arrow below *father* he wrote: *Today,
8pm, Osteria, Mrs X.* His father was up to something,
that much was clear. But his father was a miserable
worm, who was no match for the Fixer. He had to be
taught that lesson. He was not behind the murder of the
scientists. But maybe he was being used by somebody,
was part of that somebody's plan. Which meant that
somebody knew about their past. Who was that somebody? Was that somebody part of that past? Yesterday
he had sent his father a curt message: *Make sure that this
woman is at the* Osteria *tomorrow night. And supply her
with good answers to my questions.* He had only written
these two sentences, not even really written but typed as

a text message on his mobile – and still he had felt sick to the stomach. The same way he had felt when he had to write to his father as a child.

Twice his mother had made him write such a letter. He had sat at the table, and he had not wanted nor been able to write, and the tears had run down his cheeks onto the paper. Angry tears about his mother, who had good reasons to hate this man; his mother, who was ill and still tried to make excuses for this man by saying: 'He is going to be so happy to hear from you. He is not so well himself. He only behaved this way because couldn't help himself, you know...' Both times Tretjak had eventually squeezed a few sentences from his brain, and both times he had afterwards gone to the bathroom and thrown up.

He now drew a circle around the notes about the meeting tonight. Following an instinct, he reached for two new pieces of white paper. As before, he turned them horizontally and wrote one word on each of them. Then he placed them next to each other on the table, above the one he had been working on before. *Inspector Maler* was written on one. And *hell* on the other.

In the meantime, the sun had passed the dome of the observatory and shone onto the table. Tretjak opened an umbrella. Back in the shade, he turned on his laptop. Last night, while packing, he had transferred the most important data from the big computer to the laptop. He now forced himself to gather everything he had filed in the past under the names *Kerkhoff* and *Kufner* and integrated the information into a single designated folder, to make it easier to find any possible clues. He did so reluctantly, as he was actually too nervous, but he was so used to precise working practices that he quickly got into the task. More and more windows opened on the screen, words were highlighted, paragraphs copied and pasted.

The discussion about the value of knowledge was an old one. From Socrates – 'I know that I know nothing' – to Heisenberg, who discovered that knowledge about a certain course of events inevitably leads to ignorance about another. Tretjak had always been convinced that the blind accumulation of ever more knowledge eventually caused one to lose one's direction, to become confused and disorientated. Some physicists were already working on the concept of anti-knowledge, along the lines of antimatter. Surrounded by the quiet of the Jedlitschka farm, rummaging through endless files on the internet, Tretjak suddenly felt his chest tightening again, felt as if he couldn't breathe. He was wondering whether he was actually already accumulating anti-knowledge, this dangerous stuff which would take him deeper and deeper into the darkness instead of leading him towards the light. Not only in this particular case, but in general. Maybe it would be better to remove the cover from his suitcases and to sink them in the nearby Mörlbacher pond.

He got up and started some breathing exercises. Two years ago, when the panic attacks had started, Stefan

Treysa had sent him to see a specialist. The breathing technique which he had been taught there essentially consisted of imagining that the air needed to breathe was not all around you but in an open barrel a few meters away. One had to suck it in by inhaling powerfully, if possible in a constant stream. And it was the same in the other direction: one had to imagine 'watering' a tree that was standing a few meters away, with the air one was breathing out.

He wasn't doing too well with concentrating. And then Mrs Jedlitschka came around the corner to ask whether he wanted a cup of coffee. He declined rather gruffly, broke off the exercises and, when the farmer's wife had disappeared, popped two of his tablets in his mouth and washed them down with the remainder of the apple juice. Stefan Treysa had said that he should take care that these tablets didn't become his constant companions.

Tretjak's eyes came to rest on his papers. *Inspector Maler.* He is going to focus on me, he has nothing else – so he thought, maybe he is going to search the apartment. What could he do to keep him away, to use him for his own ends? The Fixer never gave in. Of course, he had accumulated information about Maler in the past few days, all collected in a file on his laptop named *Jack of Hearts.* Standing up, he leant over the table and wrote the words on the piece of paper. He quickly added the name of the minister of the interior and the district commissioner. A wasp was circling the apple juice and then landed on the piece of paper.

Suddenly Tretjak had to smile. The police... the police were really harmless, why was he getting nervous about them? He was starting to display the behaviour he normally induced in others. Tretjak took the piece of paper, shooed away the wasp and scrunched it up. He would play with the Jack of Hearts when the time was right. Maybe he hadn't had enough sleep last night, he thought. He should have never let himself get drawn into a long discussion with Lichtinger. It might have been 20 emails which had gone back and forth, the exchange ending long after midnight. And Tretjak had poured himself a couple of vodkas to go with it, two for sure, maybe even three.

From early on, they had carried on their most important discussions in writing, back then of course on real paper, handed over in envelopes. Like the moves in correspondence chess.

His friend, the sceptic; his friend, the hesitant; his friend, the more fearful of the two of them. But Lichtinger had also been the more original thinker – the newer, more unashamed, more unexpected thoughts had usually come from him.

Last night he had started very carefully, had felt his way forwards rather slowly. The question which Lichtinger had pondered was: how much had Tretjak trespassed in his life through what he did? Tretjak had pursued a false lead for a while. He had assumed that Lichtinger was searching for a motive, revenge, for example. Suddenly he understood: Lichtinger was introducing a new thought. For him the guild of this world was not what concerned him. His friend, the priest. And then the question appeared on his computer screen in digital flashes of light:

*Have you ever considered that you might be dealing with a power which has no name, no address, no form?*

And even while he was thinking of a mocking reply the next mail arrived: *It is like the global formula, that the physicists are desperately searching for.*

*What an honour. You think I have picked an argument with God?* Tretjak typed.

*No,* came the answer. *Not with God. With Evil.*

Tretjak had sat in his office, on the packed suitcases, the laptop and the vodka in front of him. He had suddenly known exactly what he wanted to answer. And that's what he wrote.

*End of discussion, Joseph. I don't have time for this. Good night.*

Lichtinger had still sent him another two long messages. He had written about cases of people being possessed, of attempts at exorcism, of crimes which could never be solved, and he pointed to the conspicuous role of blood in both the murder of Kerkhoff and Kufner – in the first case there had been almost a complete absence of blood and in the other an abundance. He knew Tretjak was reading the mails. And when he didn't get an answer he wrote one final one.

*Gabriel, I know that in your world all this doesn't exist. But let your old friend tell you something, and I am deadly*

*serious: for the Church this is not a question of faith. We
know that Hell exists. I pray for you.*

Tretjak scrunched up the paper, on which he had
written *hell.* When this matter had been sorted out, he
was going to have another lengthy conversation about
this point with Lichtinger.

The manufacturer of Tavor had vaguely mentioned
the possibility of losing touch with reality as a possible
side effect of taking the medication over long periods
of time. Much later Tretjak would ask himself whether
it had been the fault of the tablets that his instinct for
seeking out the really important points had left him so
completely, and that he had instead lost himself in so
many thoughts – without seeing the essential questions.

Tretjak looked at his watch. He still had time for a cup
of coffee with Mrs Jedlitschka in her parlour. Then he
would get going. He had a date. He smiled when he felt
below the belt of his jeans to make sure his swimming
trunks were there. He had received a text message from
Ms Neustadt yesterday:

*Can you let go of the controls for once? I too want to
show you something. For that I need only one star: the sun.
And four hours of your time, in the afternoon. What do you
think?*

He had suggested this afternoon and she had agreed
promptly: *2pm. Parking lot of the Icking Riding School.
Wear your swimming trunks underneath your clothes.*

Icking was not far from the Jedlitschka Farm. The

route led from Lake Starnberg to the Isar Valley in an almost straight line on small roads over gentle hills. Tretjak was in a good mood, and nervous again, but for a much more pleasant reason. When he entered the village from the hill above he got a message on his mobile. He assumed it was from Ms Neustadt, maybe saying she was late. He decided he would turn off the phone later. For now he looked at the display. To his surprise, he had received only a photograph. Sender unknown. What he saw in the picture, however, was familiar to him. It was an image of his own office, taken from inside it, obviously today. The computer had already been removed, that could be seen clearly. On the Van Eek table stood the vase with the many-coloured roses, which had been sent under such mysterious circumstances.

Tretjak became annoyed, following the instructions of this navigational system. Icking stretched over a long hill. Beautiful villas, old farmhouses, two schools, one church. At the bottom, already in the forest and near the Isar dam, was the riding school. In the parking lot stood a big Mercedes, a parked horse box – and an older green Golf, with a fairly big, military-grey dinghy balancing on its roof. Ms Neustadt was leaning against this vehicle. Brown Bermuda shorts, white tee-shirt, straw hat. When she saw Tretjak's car, she waved.

## County of Bad Tölz-Wolfrathshausen,
## Upper reaches of the Isar River, 3pm

She let her fingers wander down his spine. And up again. Step by step, from one vertebra to the next, until they reached the neck. It was not a determined movement, but a hesitant one, a tender one. He was lying on his stomach, his arms folded under his head, his face turned away from her. She lay on her side beside him, resting on her elbow. His swimming trunks were black, his hair was black, his skin tanned, the colour of a Southern European, she thought.

Just now she had kissed him, in the middle of a sentence on the power of water, and how it could grind stones... It had been one of these sentences, which you utter just to say something, anything, sometimes simply in order not to say something else. Her first boyfriend had once described her accordingly: 'You wrap yourself in words, you hide behind sentences.' She had been 15 at the time and had become very angry. But from that day forward, she realised that she had an instinct for such sentences. The kiss had been soft, very soft. And now there was only the sound of the flowing water. The Isar in its upper reaches was a rapid river and could flow really noisily.

Fiona Neustadt had brought along two towels, with big red and white stripes, which she had spread out on the gravel not ten metres from the water's edge – this nice gravel of round and flat polished stones. The dinghy with the two paddles and the bag with the bottles inside it were pulled up beside them, and their clothes lay on the big air hose facing the sun. The green water with the white caps was still far too cold to swim in at this time of year. It never really reached a very pleasant temperature, but now it was 14 degrees Celsius max. They had only freshened up and cooled their feet in the water.

She had already told Gabriel Tretjak a lot about herself as they had paddled the dinghy on the river. It had been a pretty picture she had painted, like an old picture postcard. She had spoken of herself as a little girl who goes down the river in exactly the same dinghy with her father, who leads the dinghy to water at the same spot near the Tattenkofer bridge. And exactly here, in the great bend and before the tributary of the Loisach channel, they stop for a break and the little girl jumps on shore. The mother appears in the picture, in her flowery dress, and their white bungalow at the edge of the forest, and a dog named Aki, a salt-and-pepper-coloured schnauzer, who later gets run over by a truck. It's these kind of paintings, Fiona Neustadt thought, always these kind of paintings one shares, when one is about to fall in love.

The man who had sat opposite her in the dinghy for an hour had been a patient listener. Or at least he had mastered the art of appearing to listen. Sometimes she got the impression that his perspective turned inward. After all that was not surprising since the man had quite a few problems. She wondered how she would have interpreted this inward look if she hadn't known about these problems. Maybe it would have made her suspicious.

Her hand was now stroking his neck. He turned on his back to face her, squinting against the sun. She kissed him again. Again the kiss was soft, but this time it lingered longer, and his hands were soft as well, so soft in fact that she hardly noticed how they were progressing underneath the material of her white bikini. The beach they were lying on was a great wide shingle bank which could be seen from all around, especially from across the river. She felt her nipples harden, and she felt something hard in his trunks. But she also felt that something was taking hold of her, which she hated: her body was beginning to contract as if it had been thrown into ice-cold water, her pulse had shifted entirely into her wrist, where it was hammering from the inside against the walls of her veins, and the air she breathed tasted of iron. She knew that state from her childhood, and it always came when she had suppressed a wish – another run on the merry-go-round for example – later simply when she was particularly excited. Twice in her life she had fainted in this state.

She let go of him, got up and walked with well-practiced steps barefoot over the stones towards the river. She bent down, and held her wrist under the flowing water for a while. Then she turned around. Tretjak had sat up. A good-looking man on a red-and-white striped towel.

'I am not going to tell my friends about you,' she shouted against the roar. 'They're going to tell me off. A successful businessman with a BMW, 15 years older, that's not on!'

He laughed and shouted back: 'But I'm a good badminton player!'

'That's what you say!'

Later, when they had pulled the dinghy out of the water near the dam in Icking and were letting out the air by stamping on the tubes, she asked him about his parents, his childhood. She was interested to see what pictures he was going to paint. But he didn't do her that favour. 'It's not the stuff for so beautiful a moment,' he only said. Then he kissed her and shouldered the heavy wet pile of plastic. It had to be carried at least another kilometre, steeply uphill through the forest to the parking lot of the riding school. She had told him that when she was a child her family had only had one car and that therefore her mother had waited for them there.

In the car he asked her: 'Do you have any plans for tomorrow evening? We could grab a bite to eat.'

'Tomorrow? Oh, I thought, we might do that now… I am hungry…'

'I'm sorry,' he said. 'I am busy tonight. There is something… I have to…'

'Don't worry,' she interrupted. 'Osteria?'

For a moment he was surprised, then he smiled.

She said: 'I checked off the monthly bills. So many cheques.'

At the beginning of their little excursion, she had revealed that the tax inspection was complete, everything was in order, and that he was going to receive a report in the next few weeks. She found the timing of this statement to be perfect, because it added to the relaxation. Not only for him but for her as well. Tretjak was a man with all sorts of connections after all, and if he felt pressured he might begin to think about poking around in the affairs of the Inland Revenue to take control of his inspection. That would have made everything unnecessarily difficult.

'I want to go to another restaurant tomorrow, not to the Osteria,' she said, while Tretjak turned onto Highway Number Eleven. She pulled her straw hat low over her face.

### *Munich, St-Anna-Platz, 6pm*

The message on her voicemail this morning was the last thing she needed right now. It was the electronic female voice of a messaging service: the message it conveyed was from Gabriel Tretjak, and it asked whether it would be at all possible for her to make an exception and stand in for her mother, who was still away, and come to clean the flat. It had become rather dirty due to a small accident. The key to the flat could be picked up at the Italian restaurant at the St-Anna-Platz. Of course everything would be paid for generously and in addition to the normal remuneration. A sincere request, warm greetings, Mr Tretjak.

Carolina Lanner had a small café in Agnes Street, a good location, in the middle of Schwabing. Ten tables inside, three small ones outside. She served homemade cakes, fresh sandwiches and a soup of the day she prepared herself at home. 'Homemade' meant that Carolina baked, prepared, cooked. The café opened at 8am and closed at 6pm. Carolina arrived at six in the morning and never left before nine at night for six days a week; they only closed on Sundays. In a good month, she made 2,000 euros, in a bad one only 500. She had a student, who occasionally helped out for a couple of hours, but she couldn't afford more staff.

Only her mother helped out, whenever she could. Her mother was always there when she needed her. A life without her mother? Unthinkable. She was not the type to ponder what kind of relationship she had with her mother. She also didn't mind that she was starting to look like her mother. Mother was Mother and she was her daughter. That's it. And she couldn't imagine not drinking her first cup of coffee of the day with her mother in her café. And with that cup they ate a piece of homemade cake, one piece each, sometimes two.

It was now almost a week since her mother had left for Argentina. The first time she had called, her mother had seemed blissfully happy. Her cup had literally over-flowed, and she had said again and again: 'Carolina, I'm at home.' And then her mother had started to cry, at least that's what Carolina thought, and she had started to cry as well, of that she was sure. In the end they had agreed that they wouldn't speak again on the phone because it was much too expensive. And that Carolina was going to meet her at the airport, when her mother returned on Sunday.

Just after 6pm she locked the door of her café. She walked down the Agnes Street towards the under-ground. It had not been a bad day, she had sold 22 pieces of blackcurrent cake, 24 bacon sandwiches and 12 cheese rolls. She changed trains once to get to St-Anna-Platz. As arranged, the key to Tretjak's flat was waiting for her in an envelope at the bar of the Italian restaurant. Her brown coat was much too warm. She was sweating. The sun was still powerful on this early evening in Munich.

Carolina Lanner was not the kind of woman who pondered where her life was leading her. *Que sera, sera.* But tonight there were a few thoughts swirling through her head. Maybe she should also go to Argentina one of these days. It was, after all, her native country, even though she had no recollection of it. She only spoke Spanish with her mother. She was definitely looking forward to the stories her mother would have to tell. The most important thing now, however, was not to run into this man, this Gabriel Tretjak. He had been so strange on the phone. First he organises this trip, and then he seems so cold. Hopefully I'll be gone quickly, Carolina thought, when she unlocked Gabriel Tretjak's flat at 6.22pm.

### *Munich, Restaurant Osteria, 8pm*

When the Volvo turned into Schelling Street, the image of the puppet flashed up in her mind's eye again. She was hanging on Paul Tretjak's strings. Nothing more, nothing less. She didn't mind. She was happy to follow a script.

Gabriel Tretjak was sitting at the same table as the first time. But this time she sat down at that same table, directly opposite him. She was suddenly very excited, surprisingly excited. Her heart was pounding. She thought of his father waiting in the car outside in the street, only a few metres away. This thought didn't really calm her down.

There were two bottles of mineral water on the table, one sparkling, one still. He had a glass of champagne in front of him.

'Would you like a glass as well?'

'Yes,' she answered, 'that would be nice.'

That was the end of the friendly part of the conversation.

'Let's not waste any time, Mrs Poland,' Gabriel Tretjak said, 'I have two questions. You are going to answer them and then I will leave. I will contact you again one more time tomorrow by telephone.'

She nodded and remained silent.

'First question: why did you want to talk to me several days ago? What was your concern?'

Charlotte Poland began to tell the story of her son, of all the problems, of Paul Tretjak's idea that his son, 'meaning you', could help. 'I know you are not a Samaritan. Far from it. But I have a high opinion of your father, and if he says that you are really good at what you do, then I believe him. I want to believe him, because I am afraid for my son. It would be nice if you could help. I will pay, of course, I am a wealthy woman. But beyond that I am also willing to do what ever you say in this matter.'

Gabriel Tretjak listened without uttering a word. He didn't take any notes, didn't type anything into his mobile lying in front of him. He appeared to be concentrated, interested. She didn't feel that she was talking too much. He was a good listener, she thought.

'Second question,' Gabriel Tretjak said. 'Back then you said that I was making a mistake not talking to you. That sounded like a threat. What did you mean by that? Why were you threatening me?'

'It wasn't a threat,' she said. 'By "mistake" I meant that this might be a chance for a rapprochement between you and your father. I like your father, he is a great support for me.'

He looked at her but remained silent. Did he believe her? Just then, his mobile phone lit up briefly; he had received a message. And now she saw a reaction – he appeared terrified. She noticed that he was briefly deliberating. He called the waiter, and ordered another glass of champagne. He didn't ask whether she wanted another one.

Maybe this was the moment she was supposed to have

waited for. Paul had imagined a pause in the conversation, this way the sense of drama was more intense. 'Mr Tretjak,' she said. 'Now I have a question, a question about your father: what really happened ten years ago, on the evening of 11 May?'

She got up, excused herself by saying that she had to powder her nose. That, however, was a ruse. She didn't turn left towards the toilets, but right to the exit. She left, got into the Volvo and they drove off.

## *Munich, Osteria, 9pm*

Gabriel Tretjak sat at the table and was still trying to come to terms with the image on his mobile, which had just been sent to him. He wondered what was keeping Charlotte Poland and looked searchingly in the direction of the toilets. Exactly at that moment, Inspector Maler entered the restaurant, with two policemen in uniform behind him. He stepped up to Tretjak's table and said: 'Mr Tretjak, you are under arrest. Please come with us.'

Gabriel Tretjak sensed the unease spreading in the restaurant, the worried looks of the waiters. He looked at Maler and asked: 'Am I allowed to know why you are arresting me?'

Maler nodded. 'A few minutes ago, the body of a woman was discovered in your flat. And you are the prime suspect in her murder.'

Tretjak got up. 'Can I settle my bill before we leave?'

Maler said: 'You don't seem to be surprised.'

Tretjak noticed that he was shaking his head nervously as he showed the inspector his mobile phone. 'I received this image a few minutes ago,' he said. The image showed Tretjak's flat, like the one he had been sent that afternoon. But this time there was blood everywhere, on the walls, the floor, the table.

They went outside. The two officers went ahead, then Tretjak, then the inspector directly behind him. Maler said: 'You've got something there on your neck.'

Tretjak reached for the back of his neck. He felt the leaf of a willow tree. From the banks of the Isar. From this afternoon.

## *Munich, Hotel Splendid, midnight*

He was unashamedly horny. His hands were already between her legs before they had properly said hello. And, as always, Fiona Neustadt attended to his desire. Downstairs, in the hotel lobby, she had briefly gone to the cloakroom to take off her knickers. And she had dug a small bottle of massage oil out of her handbag. She rubbed the liquid into all the places which now fell victim to his fingers.

There were only about four metres from the door of the room to the bed. Over this distance, he had managed to take off her blouse, to roll up her skirt around her hips and to ram himself into her. She was thinking back to this afternoon, to the murmuring of the river. To Tretjak's tenderness. What a difference! Was it because of his age? His experience? Fucking. This word would have not fitted this afternoon. But now it fitted perfectly. Fucking. That's what this guy was doing here. Up and down, in and out. Sweat was appearing on his skin and on hers. She felt her orgasm building, like a thunderstorm in the mountains, quick and intense.

He had ordered her to come to a hotel called Splendid, a cheap little pension on Müller Street. Poor artists, penniless gays stayed here. He had brought along a bottle of red wine, Primitivo; the name fitted the sex they were having. She didn't know anything about red wine, but she liked the taste. Surely it cost one tenth of what Gabriel Tretjak was going to dish out that evening for the wine in the Osteria. How many souls did she have? Fiona Neustadt asked herself later, when they were lying next to each other drinking the red wine. She heard his voice, his pleasant voice, but she was not listening to it. The voice was talking about some book he had read. How many souls? Did she have to take care of them all? Or should she let some wither, on purpose? None of her friends could get to grips with these questions. Most of them had several affairs going on simultaneously, and the others none at all.

Alcohol sometimes made her feel sorry for herself. She had to be careful there. Don't start blubbering now. The sound of the tram reached up to the window from the street below. When she was a child Fiona Neustadt had been quite chubby. The reason for that was that every time she had felt unhappy she had eaten something. She had even been called 'Little Hamster', because she had stored food in her cheeks before swallowing. Now she sat up and leant over the prick of the man lying beside her talking about some book or other. She took the cock into her mouth and kept it there until he ejaculated.

# Eighth Day

## 18 May

*Hamburg, Café Paris, 10.45am*

On the last day of his rather intense life, Dimitri Steiner was sitting in the Café Paris, regularly looking at his watch with increasing impatience. The café consisted of one single tiled room, domed by an elaborately renovated Art Nouveau ceiling. In former times this had been a butcher's shop. The menu was famous for a number of specialties – steak tartare, for example, prepared to order at the table, lukewarm *salade niçoise*, spicy lamb sausages – but also for its tarts. Today it featured a pear tart.

Dimitri Steiner was already on his second double espresso and had eaten a croissant; in front of him on the table lay the unread newspaper. Gabriel Tretjak was never late, but now it was almost 11 o'clock. This morning he had found Tretjak's greeting in his flat, a cake with nails baked into it. He had put his old gun in his pocket, a Tokarev TT-33, and even strapped his knife-belt around his calf. Just in case. In the course of his life he had met many dangerous people, mad terrorists drugged up to their eyeballs brandishing machine guns, professional killers who looked more like accountants, relaxed and friendly wine-swigging *bon vivants* who could decide people's fates with the snap of a finger. Overall, Dimitri had always known how to take on each of them. But with this Gabriel Tretjak it was different. He could never really make head nor tail of this guy. He lived an urbane kind of life, and had built up a flourishing business. He fixed the lives of rich people, who were too stupid, too timid or too lazy to do that themselves. And the one time when he had got involved with other more powerful forces – at least the one time that Steiner knew about – when he had accepted a commission of a very different kind, this one time Tretjak not only had got away with it, but had also pocketed 50 million US dollars at the same time. Dimitri himself had handed over the suitcase with the money.

He was sitting at the back of the restaurant, leaning on the backrest of the bench, his usual seat – when he reserved a table, they always gave him this one. Just to order something, he decided to ask for a fizzy grape juice and thought of the teetotal inspector from Munich. Because of him, he had slept badly. Had he made a mistake telling him to talk with Krabbe? Was he getting too talkative in his old age? But what could go wrong there? Krabbe was dying. The people he had trained as killers were spread all over the world. And Tretjak knew nothing about what he had written on the menu in the train. Or had the inspector been stupid enough to tell him? He didn't take him to be that stupid.

Dimitri Steiner now reached for his telephone.

'Senator Service. What can I do for you, Mr Steiner?'

'I need some information. Could you check whether a Mr Gabriel Tretjak flew this morning from Munich to Hamburg? I am expecting him, but can't reach him and I am a bit worried.'

'One moment, please, Mr Steiner.'

A pretty young woman in a short black leather skirt crossed the restaurant, passing Dimitri's table on her way to the toilet. While listening to the music in the holding loop, he looked at her ass until she had disappeared through the door.

'Mr Steiner, are you there? Our records show that Mr Tretjak was booked on LH 051 this morning, but didn't take this flight. Or any other, for that matter. I hope that information is of some help to you.'

The voice of the man on the other end of the Lufthansa special client line sounded young and well-trained. He probably uttered these sentences a hundred times a day. But for Dimitri Steiner, it was the last sentence he heard in his life. Just then, the young woman in the leather skirt was standing right next to his table. With a quick, almost unseen movement, she took from her handbag a stiletto, which looked like a knitting needle, and rammed it directly into Dimitri's heart. Seconds later she had left the beautiful Café Paris through the open glass door.

Dimitri Steiner remained seated upright, leaning against the backrest of the bench, looking into the restaurant. He didn't blink anymore. But nobody noticed that for a while. It was a good 40 minutes before the Hamburg homicide cops closed the café for the day.

## *Munich, Police Headquarters, morning*

The first night in a police cell. Cell No. 226 in Munich's Police Headquarters. Shortly after 9pm, the officer had locked him in. Bed, chair, toilet, sink. Nothing to read, no mobile phone, no computer, no television. At 10pm the ceiling light had gone out, the only light in the room. Suddenly it had been dark. Tretjak had studied in depth how people are affected by sudden and absolute silence. How a person reacts when he is abruptly and totally isolated. Inspector Maler had not spoken a single word to him in the car on the way to the Police HQ. When they arrived, the officer had already been waiting for him. And Maler had just disappeared, without a word, a gesture, nothing.

There are people who crumble in that kind of isolation after only a few hours. They experience a nervous breakdown. It happens more often to people who have spent a lot of strength on controlling their lives and reality. Gabriel Tretjak knew that the police were counting on this effect. And he knew that this was not going to happen to him. Hadn't he always used his strength to fix all aspects of his clients' lives? This time he was, in effect, his own client. Could anybody believe that he would not be able to follow his normal practices in his own case? Of course he was going to stay calm, keep his nerve, of course he would keep to his chosen path even if the end was bitter. He would keep control, especially of himself. This was precisely his profession, his destiny.

He was sensing the doubt, like little bursts of

electricity, growing in intensity. What was important now was to resist this sense of unease, this fear. The tablets, which he could normally depend on to take care of that, were not in the cell with him, as he had been ordered to empty all his pockets. He had to find the switch within himself, by which he could turn off the fear. He felt his skin becoming moist – it was cold sweat, dangerous sweat as a doctor had once explained it. He tried to do the breathing exercises Treysa's colleague had taught him. But he noticed straight away that they didn't work this time. The fear was stronger.

Gabriel Tretjak closed his eyes. Norbert Kufner, the professor found murdered in Bolzano, his teacher, had once explained to him the route to internal calmness in situations of total isolation. Kufner had told him about it during one of their special weekends. There had been ten such weekends, just the two of them, and Tretjak had paid a lot of money for them. Kufner had been very expensive.

They had once sat in a windowless room for two whole days. In front of six recording devices simultaneously emitting all sorts of different voices. Kufner wanted to show him that it was possible to hear only what you wanted to hear. And if you didn't want to hear anything, that was possible as well. And he wanted to demonstrate what a particular voice had to say to stand out from the others. What words had to be chosen to instill a certain message.

Now Tretjak was sitting with closed eyes in a darkened

room, and trying to remember what Kufner had said about the term 'double silence'. It had been a long-term investigation undertaken by Russian psychologists, which had posed the question of how certain prisoners had come through decades-long banishment to Siberia without noticeable damage, and how they had managed to find some sort of inner peace. The determining factor had been their ability to reach a sort of 'double silence'. Their ability to leave the outer, silent, still place and look inwards in search of an inner peace. To cut oneself off from the outside quietness one meditated into the outer silence, so to speak, and thereby became invulnerable. Build yourself a wall, Kufner had said, stone upon stone, until the inner core is totally encased and protected…

Kufner had divided the Self into different 'Ego-States': there is the Ego of good feelings, and one of bad feelings. There is an Ego of embarrassment. And another of weakness. There is the Ego of decisiveness and there is one of indecision. There is the ego of memories, and those of order and of disorder. All these Egos live together like nation-states, sometimes in harmony, at other times at war with each other. Kufner had explained it all to him in great detail and stressed that everyone was free to decide to which of the states was handed the leadership of the individual's life.

During that night in the cell, Gabriel Tretjak tried to build that wall. He noticed how with each moment that passed it worked better and better, how he became calmer, how his pulse stopped racing. The sweat began to dry. The wall grew higher.

But then another Ego suddenly appeared. A nervous Ego, but also a very lively one. The afternoon at the banks of the Isar. Fiona Neustadt's skin. The question, who was she really thinking about when she kissed him? The question of what he had actually felt when he was with her. An Ego of romantic feelings? Gabriel Tretjak sat on his bed in the cell and thought that he didn't really know. He knew only that this Ego was somehow trying to take hold of him.

At one point Tretjak had fallen asleep. When he woke, shortly after 6am, the ceiling light in his cell was already on. He had had a dream. He remembered it, unfortunately. He had never managed to develop a technique for erasing his own dreams. He could happily have done without them. Why were dreams so important, and so unsettling? This time it had been the hospital dream again. In this dream, he was walking along a long corridor in a clinic until he finally reached the ward he was searching for. There was noone to be seen. He knocked on a door and entered. A big room full of beds, eight or ten of them. In them lay very old people, almost corpses. Since he didn't know who he was looking for, he looked into each of the faces. Did any one of them ring a bell? Four or five faces, nothing. But then he stood in front of somebody who he did recognise. He was frightened to his core. That was the central feeling in this dream. The dream never revealed who that person was, lying in the bed, not even whether it was a man or a woman. But the face spoke to him. 'You have forgotten me. You believe I am dead, but no, as you see, I am not dead,' it seemed to be saying.

Tretjak drank a bit of the tea, but didn't eat any of the brown bread with sausage which an officer had brought on a tray. The fear was back, he sensed it, it flickered. But it was not as intense, which was good.

At 9.02am Tretjak entered the interrogation room. Inspector Maler was already there. Maler walked towards him and shook his hand.

'Good morning, Mr Tretjak.'

'Good morning, Inspector.'

'Would you like a cup of coffee?'

'No, thank you.'

Tretjak sat down on a plastic chair with a scratched backrest. He sat on a red cushion. The thought of all the people who had sat here before him was not a comfortable one. He could have touched the inspector, that's how narrow the table was which separated them. Tretjak knew that it was important that he asked the first question. The question: what had happened in his flat yesterday? In his mind, he was working on how to put it. The question had to have the right tone.

Tretjak did not know that Maler was, in the meantime, seeing him in a different light. Whoever he had spoken to about Gabriel Tretjak, whatever he found out about him, the gist of it was always the same: Tretjak is somebody who manipulates, and he is good at it, perfect, in fact. A master of his profession. Only now did Maler realise that Tretjak was also trying to manipulate him. How had it been in the beginning? Tretjak had denied knowing the murdered Professor Kerkhoff, only to then admit contritely that he hadn't spoken the truth, that he had known him after all, in fact he had known him well. Had he not been taught in some course or other about police interrogation techniques, that the admission of a small weakness creates an atmosphere of trust? And it had worked, he had believed him. Maler, you are getting old, he thought to himself.

Then came the excited call from the tax inspector. Had Tretjak organised that as well? And the messages. First the strange mobile phone found near the racehorse. Then the flowers with the hint pointing to bloody linen. Now the photograph showing the blood-soaked flat. And again the great unknown, which was behind it all. What kind of game did this Tretjak play? He created a distance between himself and each crime, all right, that much Maler understood. But what were the other rules of the game? And how was the game going to continue?

After the horrible act that had been committed in Tretjak's flat, the images had returned to Maler's head. When he had bought a buttered pretzel from the bakery early that morning, the old sales assistant had suddenly had blood spewing out of her eyes. He had looked away and then turned back, but the blood was still running down her face. It was only as he left, and turned around at the door one last time, that the assistant had stood there unharmed. Maler had driven to Police Headquarters and had decided to go back to see his psychologist as soon as possible.

'Inspector,' Gabriel Tretjak said, 'what happened in my flat? Please tell me, at once.'

'But you know what happened, Mr Tretjak,' the inspector answered.

Tretjak remained silent. For a very long moment. He just looked at Maler. Finally he shook his head, a contemptuous, almost furious shaking of his head.

'We'll get back to your flat and what happened there, that much I guarantee you. But first I want to play something to you.' Maler took a small, black recording device from the side pocket of his beige jacket and pressed the play button. It was a short excerpt from the witness statement of the old maid from the hotel in Bolzano, which his colleague had sent him. 'Gabriel was such a lovely boy,' a female voice with a strong South Tyrolean accent said. 'Gabriel had to suffer a lot. His mother was in such a lot of pain that she often screamed. Then Gabriel sat in a corner of his room, on the floor. He cowered there for hours and was silent. Nobody could do anything.' Then one could hear the old lady sigh. 'It was not a nice childhood, definitely not, poor Gabriel, it was an awful life.' Maler pressed the stop button.

Tretjak's face showed no emotion. 'And?' he asked.

'What was that all about? What do you want to hear from me?'

'The maid found the body of Professor Kufner,' Maler said. 'And one day later she receives a letter from an unknown sender who asks her to tell her story about a certain Gabriel Tretjak. Do you have any idea who might have sent this letter?'

'No, none at all.'

'Do you have any idea why this letter was sent? What could be behind it?'

'I haven't got a clue.'

Maler poured himself a cup of coffee from the thermos. 'Maybe I can help you a little in the search for a motive. Could it be that somebody wants to draw attention to your unhappy childhood? Because this somebody wants to imply that you were a victim then, and now you are the perpetrator. This Tretjak fellow has experienced something horrible and there is an open score to be settled somewhere. Could that be the message of the letter? Or is this interpretation totally off, in your opinion?'

'Inspector,' Tretjak answered, 'I want to tell you a few basic facts about my life. As you just heard yourself, I wasn't particularly lucky with my childhood. Consequently, I have taken the appropriate steps. I have expunged the first years of my life, including the family members involved. I have decided that my life starts with me, in fact with me as a young person. I have decided not to carry this shit around with me for the rest of my life.'

'And that has worked for you?' asked Maler.

'Yes, that has worked perfectly well. And in a sense I have turned it into my business model. I don't believe that one has to be a helpless victim of one's fate. I am convinced that one can do something about it. One can always give one's life a new direction, one only has to give this change certain rules, which need to be followed strictly.' Tretjak reached for the thermos. 'May I?' Maler briefly nodded. Tretjak continued: 'And now back to your question as to whether I have any explanation for why this letter was sent to poor Maria. No, I have no explanation. And I also don't think about it, not for a single moment. I don't deal with my past, I never do. That's my principle.'

'Your principle, I see.' Maler got up and walked around the desk until he stood directly behind Tretjak's back. 'You don't deal with the past. That's indeed interesting.' Maler paused and leant on the backrest of Tretjak's chair, almost touching his back. 'What kind of a man are you?' Maler's voice became loud. 'Three people have been murdered in the most gruesome fashion in less than a week. Three people who you knew well. And you are sitting here and telling me something about new rules, which you draw up to shape the world the way you want to. Please, that is ridiculous!'

'Three people?' Tretjak asked and his voice cut as sharp as a knife as well: 'Inspector, tell me what happened yesterday!'

'I will do just that.' Maler leant forward, closer to

Tretjak's right ear. 'The daughter of your cleaning lady received a call from you, asking her whether she could step in for her mother and clean the flat.'

'Nonsense,' Tretjak said. 'I didn't call her.'

'A telephone service called the daughter in your name, she said. In any case, she went to your flat, as you had deposited a key to the flat in the restaurant at the corner.'

'I didn't deposit anything,' Tretjak said.

'The daughter of your cleaning lady unlocked your flat and started cleaning. The perpetrator had invented a special kind of game. She first cleaned the kitchen, where there was blood everywhere. She was frightened, the woman said, no, she didn't say it, she screamed it, shaking all over, crying when I talked to her. She thought perhaps some kind of animal had been slaughtered.' Maler became very soft. 'But, Mr Tretjak, the woman was wrong, it wasn't an animal. It was her mother. She found the naked body in the bathtub, your bathtub, covered with countless stab wounds. And without eyes, Mr Tretjak. Who thinks up something like that?'

Tretjak got up abruptly. 'My God, Mrs Lanner, the good Mrs Lanner… yes, indeed, who thinks up something like that?'

'Where were you yesterday between 2 and 5pm?' asked Maler.

'I was at the Isar River the whole of yesterday afternoon. With a woman.'

'Does this woman have a name and can she attest to this fact?'

'Yes,' Tretjak answered, 'but I have to ask her first, before I can give you her name.' Tretjak sat down again. 'What motive should I have, if you please, Inspector, to kill my cleaning lady, and in this fashion?'

'What motive did you have,' Maler asked, 'to send old Mrs Lanner to Argentina, all expenses paid?'

'I didn't send her to Argentina. That's complete rubbish. I have already told Mrs Lanner's daughter that.'

'But she didn't believe you. Your method of answering my questions, Mr Tretjak, is getting monotonous: I don't know, it wasn't like that, I have nothing to do with that.'

'I can't say anything else,' Tretjak said.

'Why didn't you tell me about this trip of your cleaning lady which you supposedly paid for? If all this seemed so absurd to you, why on earth didn't you tell us about it?'

'I don't know why I should have told you about it.'

'Really? Two people were murdered, in mysterious circumstances – and then something else, something inexplicable happens and you don't think that you should tell the police all about that?'

'That was probably a mistake, I must admit.'

'I would put it differently, Mr Tretjak. Mrs Lanner might still be alive if you had changed your strange information policy.'

There was a moment of silence. Maler looked at Tretjak but couldn't make out any emotion, any shock.

Tretjak said: 'There is a crazy game being played out here, Inspector. But I'm not the one playing this game. I have nothing to do with it. At least not directly.'

'Of course,' Maler said, 'this is the impression you have wanted to give ever since the first day, when I stood at your door. But you can forget about it. You are not standing on the sidelines, you are right in the middle of it, you are deep in it, you can't get any deeper.'

'Give me one reason,' said Tretjak, 'why this game should be my game.'

'We are talking about three murders, three human beings. I think the word game is rather inappropriate in these circumstances.'

'Call it what you will,' Tretjak said, 'but can you tell me whether you can make any sense of it all?'

'Let's assume that you have an enemy out there who wants to destroy you. Who could that be? Who hates you that much?'

'I have no idea,' said Tretjak.

'Mr Tretjak, I have only an inkling of your particular business. But one thing seems clear to me: you break into other people's lives. That means trouble, that creates enemies. You are a professional creator of enemies, so to speak. And you want to tell me that you have no idea who wants to do you harm?'

'No, I truly have no idea.'

'I expect a list of names from you,' Maler said, 'lots of names, of people who have become the victims of your business in different ways.'

'Forget it. That kind of list will not be drawn up.'

Maler had sat down on his side of the desk again and was pouring himself another cup of coffee. Surprisingly, it was still hot. Maler had lost all sense of time. How long had Tretjak's interrogation taken? It seemed like hours. 'Three murders. An old woman, who cleans for you, is butchered. And all this leaves you cold.'

Tretjak remained silent.

'What kind of man are you, Mr Tretjak?'

Tretjak responded notably coolly. 'I am a man who is rather well informed. Inspector Maler, does the name Laura Müller mean anything to you?'

'No,' Maler said.

'A girl, 22 years old, must have been pretty. A tragic story. It was an accident with her bicycle. A drunk driver didn't see her when he turned around a corner. She died of head wounds.'

'What's all this?' Maler asked. 'What are you talking about?'

'I am talking about the woman whose heart you received,' said Tretjak. 'I am talking about the woman whose death was necessary for your survival. What does it feel like, Inspector, to hear somebody else's heart beat inside you?'

Maler felt like he had been struck by lightning. He felt the way he had felt when the doctor stood in front of him, back then when he had come into the room and said: 'We have a heart.' And explained to him that he would not be told who the heart had belonged to, that was the rule in heart transplantation cases. No information about the donor. It had been another six hours until they had prepped him for the operation and rolled him into the operating theatre on his hospital bed, the bed he had lain in for 14 weeks, each day a bit more miserable. In the last 10 days he hadn't even managed the short walk to the toilet. He needed oxygen around the clock, his heart was too weak for anything. An acute inflammation of the heart muscle, that's what the diagnosis had been, with the illness taking a particularly dramatic course. The doctor had given him only days. And then he stood in the doorway with the message: 'We have a heart.'

'What are you talking about?' Maler repeated almost in a trance. 'Nobody is allowed to know whose heart he receives.'

'It's my business to know what people are not allowed to know.'

Maler got up and walked around the room. Once around Tretjak, and then one more time. Then he sat down again. 'My heart is not the topic of this conversation, Mr Tretjak. We will not continue to talk about it. Our topic is three murders. And your role in them, to put it precisely.'

'You asked me what kind of man I am, Inspector. That's why I permitted myself to mention your heart transplantation. You would not be alive today if you hadn't corrected your fate. I thought somebody with your experience would appreciate my life's philosophy. I firmly believe that one can successfully change the path of somebody's life. I firmly believe that I can correct the path of my own life, whenever that is necessary. That's the kind of man I am.'

Maler stood up again. 'What really happened on 11 May ten years ago, Mr Tretjak?'

'I don't know what you mean,' said Tretjak.

'You've heard this question before, haven't you?'

'I know the question, but I don't know what to do with it.'

'You were sitting in the Osteria restaurant last night with a woman. When we arrived, she had gone. Why?'

'You'll have to ask the woman. She went to the toilet and didn't come back. Why that was I couldn't find out because you then arrested me.'

'Mrs Poland said that the conversation with you had become uncomfortable. That's why she left.'

'That's what she said?' Tretjak asked.

'Why did you meet Charlotte Poland?' Maler asked.

'It concerned her son, who is causing her a few problems. She was convinced that I could help her.'

'She has told me about her son. But Mrs Poland is a friend of your father. She said that that was her real reason for meeting you. She also said that you and your father are bitter enemies.'

'My father is not my enemy. I have expunged him from my life. There's a difference,' said Tretjak.

'Why then did you meet with Mrs Poland, who is a friend of your father?'

Tretjak was silent for a moment. 'Let me put it this way, Inspector: I am upset by what is happening out there. I don't understand it. I am trying to get closer to a solution and I am pursuing several leads.'

'You believe that your father has something to do with it?'

'I don't know,' said Tretjak.

'What is the question regarding 11 May ten years ago all about? What happened on that day?' Maler asked.

'No idea. You'll have to ask my father.'

'Don't worry,' Maler said, 'I will. Your father called me yesterday. He wants to meet me and tell me something important about you. We are meeting this afternoon.' Maler paused. Then he said: 'There are a number of people who want to tell me something about you.'

There was a knock on the door. A woman entered. Irritated, August Maler looked up.

'Sorry,' she said, 'but it's important. A call for you.' She held out a phone to him. 'Do you want to take it in here?'

Maler shook his head and left the room with her. He closed the door behind him.

Tretjak stayed behind alone. He got up and walked around, his eyes on the door.

Three minutes later it opened again and Maler returned. He sat down again, and so did Tretjak.

'There is a fourth body,' Maler said. 'Dimitri Steiner, you know him. He was stabbed a few minutes ago in a café in Hamburg. There is not very much more we know now except that he was supposed to meet you there.'

'That's correct,' Tretjak said. 'We wanted to talk about old times.'

'That's no longer going to be possible,' Maler said.

'At least you don't have to ask me about my alibi for this one,' Gabriel Tretjak said.

## *Mörlbach, Jedlitschka Farm, midnight*

The black sky was lit up by stars. He parked the car in a small bend in the road on the edge of the forest so it could not be seen from the Jedlitschka Farm. When he got out, the light inside the car shone briefly onto a newspaper, which was lying on the passenger seat. The headline, in fat black letters underlined in red, shouted: *Cleaner Murdered: Munich Businessman Arrested!* He locked the little Peugeot with the remote key and trudged through the darkness, first following the road at the edge of the forest for about 100 metres, then turning onto a small path to the left into an open field and across the meadow directly towards the farm. His eyes had already become used to the darkness. The Jedlitschka Farm lay peaceful and grey in the pale starlight. Step by step, Joseph Lichtinger got closer and for a moment his brain played a trick on him well known to children. For an instant, he did not see in the outline of the farm the familiar image of a human habitation, but instead recognised, in the mountain of shadows and lines and surfaces, the contours of a large animal. Lichtinger left the path and, following an invisible bend, approached the farm from the back. The key to the observatory was under a brick next to the entrance.

He had been to the observatory only once before, when Tretjak had shown him his new telescope. How many nights had they spent together when they were young, somewhere in the mountains, with ever more sophisticated binoculars and ever more daring conversations and plans…?

*Cleaner Murdered: Munich Businessman Arrested!* The sight of that headline had shaken Lichtinger to the core. The sense of shock had not left him all day, it kept reassembling in his thoughts, quickening his pulse. The layout of the *Abendzeitung* newspaper had been revised several times over the years. Typography, column width, the handling of photographs, all that had changed repeatedly. A modern, digital image recognition system, which compared the front page to one from 20 years ago, pixel by pixel, point by point, would not have found one single similarity. But Lichtinger's brain was not a computer. *Bomb Explosion: Bank Manager Dies In His Car!* In Lichtinger's brain, the headline from back then pushed itself in front of the one from today, though the logo of the newspaper was still bright red, the letters still black. In Lichtinger's brain the two headlines combined, danced with each other.

In the beam of the red flashlight, Lichtinger started up the telescope, opened the cupola, took the protective cap off the glass, and switched on the steering mechanism. Then he turned the apparatus to face the region of the Swan Formation, which was already standing high in the sky. He chose the wide lens and a fog filter, and searched the region until a soft object pushed itself into view. Long, thin, white streaks, which looked like fog or mist over a moist meadow. They spread over a huge area. The Veil Nebula, the remnants of a supernova, 1,700 light years away from Earth.

*Bomb Explosion: Bank Manager Dies In His Car!* It had

been in the time before mobile phones, before emails. The physics student Joseph Lichtinger had lived in the Türkenstrasse, renting a room in the flat of an old man. The knock of Mr Schmidt on his door had woken him, and then Tretjak had stood in front of him in his room, pale, with this newspaper in his hand. Even now, Lichtinger still saw the look in his eyes, his flickering eyes.

'You did it? You really did it?' he had asked Tretjak. They had sat across from each other, he on his bed and Tretjak on the old camel stool.

Again and again Tretjak had shaken his head. 'No, I haven't done anything. But they think I did it.' And then he had looked at him. 'Our plan was almost exactly like the way it actually happened.'

'Our plan, our plan…' Lichtinger was practically paralysed with fear. Yes, they had watched the man, spied on him, observed his life, his habits. Gabriel had repeatedly drawn all kinds of diagrams. Yes, they had talked about a bomb, and yes, Gabriel had found somebody who could build it, but all this was not really serious, it was only… 'Our plan… Was that really a plan, wasn't it only… Was it?' The eyes of his friend Gabriel had been very black in that moment. And they became blacker by the second – at least that's how it had appeared to him.

From the window of his room, one could see the billboard of a cinema. That night it was showing an ancient Yves Montand movie called *The Payment of Fear*. Lichtinger had stared the whole time at the box of Lindt chocolates which was lying on the floor next to his bed. A present from his mother. That can't be the payment, he thought, over and over, like a broken record, that can't be the payment for fear.

The remnants of a supernova are what is left over when a star dies. The death of a star is a pretty brutal affair. It fights this death, rebels, escalates, a glowing fireball getting bigger and bigger while running out of fuel. It devours everything it can get hold of in the universe, but there is not enough, and in the end it collapses. And in one last gigantic explosion, the supernova, as its last breath, exhales or rather spits out bits of matter and dust clouds, which travel through the black nothing, glimmering faintly in memory of its long and bright past.

It was totally silent in the observatory, and the night smelt like summer already. Lichtinger's right eye hovered over the lens, and his hand held the small electronic guidance system with which he moved the telescope slightly backwards and forwards to increase the contrast of the image.

In the days after the headline, Lichtinger had practically not left his room, and had told Mr Schmidt that he was ill. Now and again he had turned on his little transistor radio. The assassination had created an uproar throughout the whole country. He immediately turned it off again. He had felt he was burning up in a fever. He still remembered the smell and the pattern of the blanket under which he had crawled. Tretjak went outside, had gone into town, sleepless, getting more and more nervous, and had shown up almost every hour in Lichtinger's room to report. Lichtinger, however, hadn't been able to take anything in, almost as if he was in shock. Finally the moment had come when Tretjak had deposited the suitcase in the room. Fifty million, he had said, US dollars. The Russians have paid up. If they think we've done it, they might as well pay us for it. Fifty million, Sepp. They belong to us, he had said. You have to hide them, Sepp.

Lichtinger knew that the suitcase no longer contained exactly fifty million and had to smile. He had left $350 behind in the room for Mr Schmidt. And a note that he should sell the rest of his things. And $8,000 he had put in the pocket of his leather jacket, just like that. He had put the suitcase into a storage locker at the train station, and its key into a padded envelope addressed and mailed to Tretjak. Then he had taken the bus to the airport. Munich-Riem it had been back then, almost in the middle of town by comparison. Today's new big airport in the Erdinger Moos was still a building site back then. He took a flight to Atlanta, in the US, because that was the next one available, and from there he flew to Venezuela.

When people go on long trips, they tell stories about them afterwards, they show their photographs, share tips, tell of their experiences. Of the long journey on which the physics student Joseph Lichtinger had embarked that November day more than 20 years ago, no records exist. No letters, no photographs, no tickets, no diary. And he never talked to anybody about it.

The dangerous mountain path in the Andes in Peru, the even more dangerous drug parties in Colombia, the jobs as a drug mule, as a nurse in a clinic, as a bouncer in a brothel… nothing, so it seemed later, had been hard enough or risky enough to push him to his breaking point. Twice he had found himself in a prison cell, once in Lima and the other time in Caracas. Each day he survived, each kilometre he travelled, put more distance between the Joseph Lichtinger from Lower Bavaria he once had been and the person he was now becoming. There was no proof that this year of his life had even happened. Only for the end of that journey was there a witness. Maybe this witness was the one human being he knew best or should know best, but who tonight of all nights, in the observatory at the Jedlitschka Farm, seemed to slip away, and he had the uncomfortable feeling that he did not have the faintest clue who he was really dealing with.

Lichtinger screwed the ocular out of the telescope and stowed it away carefully in the correct box. The cupola closed and obscured the view of the sky. He thought of Tretjak, who was in jail. Would he be able to sleep?

Back then, Tretjak had suddenly appeared, sitting on his bed in a hut in Haiti. Lichtinger had been lying there for days, drugged up to his eyeballs, high on mushrooms of some sort. One put a few drops of the stuff on your tongue and sank into a fog, comparable to the misty remnants of a supernova. There was a big fiesta going on in the little town, with dancing, ritual slaughter, voodoo songs. Lichtinger had no idea how long Tretjak had been sitting there before he had noticed him, or how long he had had to stay there before Lichtinger could actually recognise him.

'How did you find me?'

'Pack your things.'

Lichtinger saw that Tretjak was slipping the owner of the hut some money.

Two days later, they were back in Munich. Tretjak took him to a small apartment in the Olympic Village, which he had rented for him.

'And?' he had asked Lichtinger in the taxi on the way to there. 'Did you manage to get rid of the bad spirits?'

Lichtinger had taken only a brief look at the apartment and then shaken his head. 'I don't want to stay here. I am going home.'

'Home?' Tretjak had asked.

'To the country. To my parents.'

'You do that. They were worried sick about you.'

The padded envelope Tretjak had handed him then had been the same one that he had sent Tretjak, and it was still unopened. One could feel the key inside. Back then they didn't routinely open and empty storage lockers after a while.

'This belongs to us, Sepp. You have to look after it.'

Lichtinger remembered this scene like it was yesterday. This had been the fork in the road. From then on, their paths had diverged. Soon after that Lichtinger started to study theology, and his friend's visits had become less frequent. Their debates about the manipulation of reality had lost their attraction. And the money in the suitcase was never spoken of again. And now, thinking back to the scene, he tried – so many years later – to read one more time Tretjak's face, which he clearly saw in front of him. But he didn't succeed.

He took out a little flask from his jacket pocket and switched on the red flashlight. The liquid contained in the flask appeared to be almost black. He had bought the rabbit from Farmer Sigl. It hadn't been difficult for him to cut the animal's throat. And the blood had immediately flowed with no problem. He had been surprised only at how warm it had been. He opened the flask, looked around the observatory, and then carefully let individual drops of the blood fall to the floor in different spots he had specifically chosen.

*PART 2*

# ALIENATION

# 1

It was a warm, almost hot September day, which was drawing to a close, and the funeral cortège with Paul Tretjak's coffin at its head looked decidedly strange. That was partly due to the vehicle that was transporting that coffin. It was in fact a tiny two-wheel tractor pulling a small wagon. On the front edge of the wagon sat a young fellow who was steering the tractor with what looked like a bicycle. The coffin was sticking out over the back edge of the wagon platform and was held in place with several belts. There were two plain, scarlet red ribbons for decoration. No floral bouquet, presumably because it would have been difficult to attach.

The people who lived in the mountains above the Lago Maggiore were used to whatever they did being done the hard way. As gay and easy as life appeared at the lakeshore, with its slim beach strips, *ristoranti* and boat charterers, it was completely different if one climbed only a few metres up the hill. Many roads and paths were not accessible by car, they were too narrow, too stony, too steep. They constantly had to be patched up, the encroaching thorny bushes cut back. The houses stood on the mountain like small boulders. The delivery of a new oven could take two men all day. In former times they had used donkeys to transport loads – and nowadays the small two-wheeled tractors, which could be used for practically anything.

The small church of Santo Stefano and its cemetery lay above the town of Maccagno and were accessible only on foot. The fit ones took 20 minutes to reach it, but for those in slightly worse condition it might take up to three quarters of an hour. In the summer, funerals took place early in the morning or late in the afternoon.

The small funeral cortège, which had gathered behind Paul Tretjak's coffin and which set off slowly, split into two groups. There was a small group of locals, identifiable by their dress. They wore lightweight black trousers and short-sleeved dark shirts on top. The mourners who had come from further afield all were dressed much too warmly, wearing suits and ties, even some hats. The Munich police officer Rainer Gritz belonged to this group.

Rainer Gritz was 33 years old, tall and thin. He had earned his nickname 'Croco' not so much because of his appearance but because of the tenacity with which he grabbed hold of the files and details of a case and wouldn't let go. Wasn't it strange how life played out sometimes? He had joined the Homicide Squad in Munich just at the time when Inspector Maler came back after his heart transplant. Slowly of course, tentatively, only for a few hours at first, then for half days. Maler had to take things easy, the police had to take care of him. So that became Rainer Gritz's job. Long-winded research, tiresome report-writing, extensive sifting through files – this part of the work became the responsibility of the young officer. And this is how they became an interesting team, the inspector with a new heart, a man with intuition and experience, and the tall thin guy who developed into some sort of super-assistant, working in the background, checking hypotheses, filling in official applications, gathering evidence and buying train tickets. By now Maler was back full-time and there was no mention of taking it easy anymore. But the division of labour had remained in place somehow.

They had meant to go to the funeral together, in a way to pay their respects to an unusual case. But Maler had been taken ill yesterday morning, and they had quickly diagnosed that his body was rejecting the new heart. Maler had had to go into the hospital in Grosshadern. It was not a serious rejection, only a Category 1b. By now Rainer Gritz had become a bit of an expert and knew that as long as there was a 1 in front, the rejection was not yet life-threatening. But he had driven to the Lago Maggiore alone, via Lindau on Lake Constance and the San Bernadino Pass.

He had taken his place in the cortège behind the locals and caught himself thinking that one day in the not too distant future he would have to walk at the very front, at the funeral of his mother or father. He loved his parents and hated this thought. Here it was the priest who led the procession, directly behind the tractor, which was huffing and puffing in a not very pious fashion. He also had come from afar, a man whom Gritz had interviewed as part of this case. His name was Joseph Lichtinger. He was wearing his simple black cassock and carried a wooden crosier with a plain brass cross on top. Gabriel Tretjak walked behind the priest. The Fixer, as they had called him in police headquarters ever since Gritz had interviewed the farmer's wife, and had seized the suit-cases with Tretjak's data files from the tool shed of the Jedlitschka Farm. Walking beside Gabriel Tretjak was his girlfriend, the tax inspector Fiona Neustadt.

Just before the path led into the forest, which was already showing autumn colours, it reached a difficult spot, a sharp corner, at which the tractor got stuck and the whole vehicle had to backtrack. In the end Gabriel Tretjak himself had to lend a hand and push the wagon to get his father's body around the bend. His face was completely unmoved.

This facial expression had been described by every-body Rainer Gritz had interviewed. Concentrated but not engaged. The manager Peter Schwarz had said that he had met the man only once personally, in a hotel in Sri Lanka. His whole expression had been: you have a problem. You. Not me. 'Throughout dinner I looked into this face – and at the end of the meal my life was changed completely.' Rainer Gritz could not shake the thought that Peter Schwarz was still trying to come to terms with what had really happened that evening. He had also visited Schwarz's wife Melanie, a former starlet, in her flat in Heidelberg. What kind of a man was this

Tretjak? 'Mainly a man who showed understanding,' was her answer. 'An attractive man, one who knows what has to be done and then actually does it. He gives one the feeling of being well taken care of.' But then she told him how quickly Tretjak had withdrawn after the job was completed. That had been somehow hard to take. She had written him two more, very personal letters, detailed letters, written by hand. There had been a rather curt response, three lines, *wish you all the best...* 'Well... I needed a while to comprehend that for him, it was only business. That it hadn't been a friend who had done all this for me, but a professional.' Gritz remembered this Melanie Schwarz well, how she had stood in the door when he left, still a bit unsure in the new town and in her new life.

Even the woman Tretjak was now seeing, who had been his tax inspector at the time, had stated in a long conversation they had had at police headquarters that this was in a way the fundamental principle of his work: stay detached – then interfere. She had said that he had not considered how deep these intrusions were and what feelings they would bring about. She was convinced that he had no appreciation as to what he was creating, a situation that in the end could turn on him.

Your problem. Not mine. That, it was clear, could not apply to the scene unfolding here on the steep path uphill to Santo Stefano. The lives of the man in the coffin and the man who was helping to push the coffin were intertwined, in a way which could only be described as ominous.

Tretjak did what had to be done: identified his father's body in the morgue. Acknowledged the body of evidence. Obtained permission to have him buried in the little cemetery up on the hill. Organised the priest, the tractor. Pushed the coffin when it got stuck. Gabriel Tretjak, Rainer Gritz knew, was not only burying his father. He was burying an enemy. And he was burying – probably for the umpteenth time in his life – his childhood. He was doing this in a very determined fashion, seemingly not looking right or left. The only thing he hadn't done yet was to deliver a eulogy. And somehow Rainer Gritz had the feeling that he wasn't going to do that at all.

The small cortège went around another bend and came out of the forest. In front of it, an almost unreal scene unfolded. Gritz looked at a gently sloping meadow with freshly cut grass framed by hydrangea bushes. Below, the dark blue of the lake with the ruin of a castle on an island, and at the horizon the snow-capped mountains. To the left was the stone wall of the church, which one could have mistaken for the wall of a farmhouse if it hadn't been for the church bell which started ringing in that very moment above the heads of the mourners. It was hanging in a small open tower, which consisted of four columns and a flat rectangular roof. The whole thing was not higher than two metres, directly above the entrance of the church, which the cortège had now reached. In front of the entrance, a semi-circle was paved with granite slabs. The young man turned off the motor of the tractor. Somebody cleared his throat in the ensuing silence. Gritz was puzzled that one couldn't see the cemetery. Four men stepped forward and loosened the belts around the coffin, and as if following a silent command, lifted it from the wagon onto a wooden trestle, which had been erected in front of the church entrance. To the left and right of the trestle stood two stone vases with bunches of dark purple aconite. Gritz saw a big gecko dash from one of the arrangements over to and then up the church wall. Just below the window sill, it paused to observe what was happening below. And now Gritz noticed Mrs Poland standing at the edge of the semi-circle, next to a stone tub with a rosebush inside it. Obviously she had not followed the cortège but had come up here earlier. She was wearing dark blue cotton trousers, a simple black blouse and a string of pearls. Big black sunglasses shielded her eyes.

Rainer Gritz had been 18, just about to sit his high school graduation exams, when he had decided to join the police force. When he had announced his decision, his family and friends had all given him the same warning: it's not like in the movies, you have the wrong impression, it is a boring agency full of boring people and dusty offices and dreadful forms and reports. You really couldn't say that about this case, he thought, looking at the well-known writer Charlotte Poland standing over there, a little bit apart from the others in the light of the setting sun. The four thick folders standing on his desk in Munich's police HQ, all properly labelled and now closed, contained so many stories, twists, characters and plots, that there was enough material for a movie.

The affairs of Professor Kufner, for example. During the investigations into his life, the search for motives for his murder in the Hotel Blauer Mondschein in Bolzano, the police had quickly become aware of the questionable way in which the renowned psychologist had looked after his students and patients. One could put it this way: the younger and the prettier the women, the more intensive the training and the therapy. Not an entirely safe passion. In an essay, Kufner had once described the power of sexuality this way: *When two people sleep with one another, they walk through a door into a new room in their lives. And they have no idea, not the faintest, what will happen there.* From Tretjak's confiscated archive files, which he had hidden at the Jedlitschka Farm, one could relatively effortlessly deduce that the Fixer had become involved with Kufner on several occasions, in fact every time that the Professor had got into trouble in yet another new room in his life. The most serious case Gritz had added to the files was the attempted-suicide letter of a 21-year-old patient, with its rounded, child-like handwriting, and words like 'transcendent love, which was not of this world', 'fulfilment which was only possible in another world'. Tretjak had started with the parents, a lot of money had changed hands, and in the end the young woman had been dispatched to the United States, to a two-year programme, with a job and therapy in Seattle.

And then there was another letter in the files. This one was in a totally different kind of writing: letters from newspapers, cut out, pasted on. Claiming responsibility for an act of terror, which had killed a bank director called Ernst Kindermann 20 years ago. Sender: Commando Red Star of June. Gritz thought back in horror to the extremely complicated dialogue with the Federal Criminal Investigation Office, the Secret Service and the Office for the Protection of the Constitution. It had taken quite some time and used up three kilometres of his nerves until finally at least part of the reports of a certain agent called Dieter 'Dimitri' Steiner had landed on his desk at police headquarters. This agent had pursued a second lead. There had been another theory which the Federal Criminal Investigation Office had put forward, namely that the letter claiming responsibility had been a fake, a clever hoax. That in truth there was no terror cell behind the planting of the bomb under the armoured Mercedes, rather it was a kind of commercial consortium, which had paid a lot of money for Kindermann's assassination. This consortium consisted of Russians who were busy building up their empire amidst the chaos created by the collapse of the Soviet Union. Kindermann saw a huge opportunity for expansion for his bank's business in the East. Behind the scenes he was forging political alliances for this expansion, but outwardly he was talking about 'the necessity to end the lawless state within Russia.' Agent Steiner, who had switched sides, was supposed to use his old contacts and informants to find out whether there was anything to this lead. In his reports, the name Gabriel Tretjak had shown up, but only on the periphery and fleetingly. The consortium had reportedly made contact with him once. Back then Tretjak was a young student, maybe too harmless to have been involved. In any case, the investigation had not been carried on any further in that direction.

Rainer Gritz had also filed separately the papers containing the notes Maler had made about his conversation with Dieter Steiner, in which Steiner had discussed Tretjak, but only with regard to the past. Then this Steiner had been murdered just before a planned meeting with Tretjak. But apart from this missed appointment, there had been no more recent connection that could be established between Steiner and Tretjak, and there was nothing linking either of them with the murders in Munich and Bolzano. And furthermore, one secret service agent had explained in an informal conversation with Gritz – the only informal conversation that had taken place between the various authorities in this matter – that the past quite often catches up with turncoats like Steiner. Some score or another, the agent had said, always stayed open and had to be settled, often by death. These murders were difficult to solve. After all, this was the work of professionals.

Father Joseph Lichtinger had started saying Mass, which he was holding outdoors, in front of the entrance to the church. If you could call it Mass. This was not Rainer Gritz's thing. His parents had left the Church before he was born, so he hadn't been baptised, and had had no Holy Communion, no Confirmation, nothing of the sort.

There was no music in front of the church of Santo Stefano, no candles, no sweet smell of incense in the air. The sun stood so low that it was almost blinding the priest. Lichtinger spoke in Latin and in German. He extemporised, there was no book in front of him. The life of the deceased was drawn with broad brush strokes, as he talked about the new home Paul Tretjak had found here on the Lago Maggiore, about the peace he seemed to have found here, with a special emphasis on the 'seemed'.

'But the ways of the Lord are mysterious...' – these were the phrases in which Lichtinger cloaked the fact that they were burying a murderer today. He spoke about death being the end of all enmity on earth, about there being only the One left to pronounce a final judgement now. At intervals, those present murmured two prayers, one in German and another, which always repeated the same phrases, in Latin. With a glance to the son, the priest spoke of the heavy burden which sometimes rested on the shoulders of the relatives, and Rainer Gritz had to think of the third letter which he had filed about this case, and which in a way had closed it. Paul Tretjak's letter to his son, which ended with the words: *What do you think, Gabriel?*

Everything had been explained in that letter. The letter and the body on the train. Both had been delivered free-freight, so to speak. What had been the name of the sleeping car conductor again? Something like some foot-baller or other… Labadia, that's it. He wanted to deliver breakfast, this Mr Labadia, to Cabin 17, first class, Car 5 of the overnight train from Milan to Munich. Nobody had opened when he knocked, so he used his master key to unlock the door. And called the police a minute later. Maler and Gritz were already waiting on the platform when the train reached Munich's main station.

It had been a peaceful scene, inside Cabin 17. At least at first. Paul Tretjak lay on the bed on his back, face up to the ceiling, eyes closed. The white sheet had been pulled up to his chin. On it lay a big sheet of paper, with blue felt pen writing on it. *I AM DEAD. PLEASE INFORM CID IN MUNICH, INSPECTOR MALER.* On the collapsible night table were the sleeping tablets, Rohypnol, an empty bottle of water, and an envelope, addressed with the same felt pen: *For Gabriel.* Under-neath the table, on the floor, stood a white shoebox with no writing on it. When a forensic officer opened it, he flinched. There were several small items in that box. What made the officer jump was the contents of the small jam jar: six eyes were floating in a transpar-ent liquid. Vodka, as the laboratory confirmed later. The other items in the box were: an ice cream scoop, a large kitchen knife, a transparent little bag containing some hair, and a small stack of receipts held together with a paperclip, including one from a petrol station from a lay-by on the motorway near Munich from the 11th

May and the copy of an order to a florist for a bouquet of roses delivered to St-Anna-Street. There was also an Ericsson mobile phone, with the images of Tretjak's flat stored on it, the bloody walls, the dead cleaning lady in the bathtub.

In front of the church of Santo Stefano, the four men picked up the coffin and shouldered it. The priest went ahead of them, beside a wall, which started to the right of the church. There was an opening in the stone wall, and an open gate. Behind it, steps led downhill about 20 metres to the cemetery. It had been invisible from above, but from here again one had the view across the lake. The men worked up a sweat, carrying the coffin carefully downhill. Finally they stopped at an open grave and placed the coffin on wooden planks laid across the hole. On both sides the belts were in place with which the coffin, at the end of the ceremony, was going to be lowered into the ground.

Paul Tretjak's last journey. He had boarded the train in Milan with the box of evidence under his arm, two packets of sleeping tablets in his pocket – and the letter to his son, typed and printed in his house in Maccagno. That was how he had delivered himself to Munich's CID. The lab confirmed that his DNA was identical with that found on the skin of the three victims. The hair belonged to Mrs Lanner, the ice cream scoop and the knife were the murder weapons. Rainer Gritz was sure that this arrest would be recorded somewhere in criminal history.

Now Paul Tretjak's body lay in a wooden box on some planks above the Lago Maggiore, and the priest uttered for him the unavoidable words: 'earth to earth, ashes to ashes, dust to dust.'

The son he had hated so much and whom he had damaged so much stood beside it like a stone. His business, his strange market niche in the service sector, was no longer. Discretion had been at the core of it, action behind the scenes. The moment when Gabriel Tretjak had hit the headlines had marked its end: his arrest, the search of his flat, the confiscation of his files. But Rainer Gritz got the impression that the whole story had affected the Fixer in other ways as well, exactly as his father had planned it. Gritz, after all, had read the father's letter often enough and knew that it represented a perpetual thorn in an old wound which maybe otherwise, with the father's death, might have started to heal.

*Gabriel,* that's how it had started, one word at the head of the letter, no date, nothing else. *Gabriel, when your mother discovered that she was pregnant, pregnant with you, there was a scene which has haunted me all my life. We sat in an ice cream parlour at the Walterplatz in Bolzano, your mother and I, and we talked about whether the pregnancy should be terminated. There was already one child, as you know...* And then, the father explained to his son that he had regretted for his entire life the decision to bring him into this world. He did that in great detail and in a rather verbose fashion, and while reading it you could sense the sick state of mind of the one who had penned it. *Doghouse,* that's what he had called the house above the lake, and then he wrote that he had thought of nothing but revenge the entire time he had spent there. *But how can you hurt somebody who has no feelings? Or should I rather say, how can you hurt somebody who only knows one emotion, fear? There is nothing that scares you more than to lose control. Certain events, which you can't dominate...*

They had had the letter examined by a psychologist. With rather meagre results. The report had spoken of an 'emotionally agitated state', of 'a sort of neglected soul', and in the long passages about the crimes committed, the meticulous description of the planning, the expert detected a 'narcissistically exaggerated sense of self' which was looking for a way to express itself. Rainer Gritz thought of the end of the letter, the last paragraph, which had been added after a slightly bigger break. *This letter, however, uninteresting for the police, and of significance only to you, also contains the doubt as to whether my revenge is truly complete with my death. What do you think, Gabriel?* No signature, nothing else.

At the very beginning of their cooperation, Inspector Maler had told Gritz that one day he was going to experience what many criminal investigators knew: when a case was closed, one was sometimes hit by a strange sensation of loss, and one had to let go of the case internally. 'It's a little bit like breaking up,' Maler had said. 'And depending what kind of case it has been, that can be tough.' All those leads they had followed in this case.

And the mind games they had played. The sheer number of senseless interrogations they had conducted and written reports on. Gritz thought of the three attempts they had made to talk to a terminally ill man, who was heavily sedated. Doctor Martin Krabbe. That lead had been followed because of something Dimitri Steiner had said. Krabbe had allegedly developed a special method of killing, which had been deployed in this case. Gritz had actually discovered something in Krabbe's research. It was obviously a silent method. With a carefully aimed stab to the liver, inflicted from behind, which was so painful that it led to a state of shock and an interruption of breathing, the murderer was given the chance to take his time to complete the crime, for example with a stab to the heart, this time from the front. Kerkhoff as well as Kufner had displayed these stabs to the liver. When Rainer Gritz had asked him about it, however, Krabbe had only occasionally and slowly opened his eyes, like a turtle, only to close them again. Only once had he whispered something and forced Gritz to bend down to get his ear very close to Krabbe's mouth. But he had not understood anything.

The coffin had been lowered into the grave and the people were filing past it, using a little shovel to throw handfuls of earth on top of it. After this they nodded in Gabriel Tretjak's direction, and some shook his hand. Rainer Gritz caught himself empathising with Tretjak. What would he do now? There was surely enough money put away. Would he withdraw to somewhere and just watch the stars from now on? Would he empty his father's house up here in the mountains himself, and pick up every item with his own hands? Or would he hire somebody to clean out the place?

These were the thoughts going through his mind. And it was probably because of these thoughts that Rainer Gritz saw what happened when Charlotte Poland passed by Tretjak, but also why it didn't really register with him at the time. Poland had not thrown earth onto the coffin, but a rose. And when she paused in front of Gabriel Tretjak, she placed her hand on his upper arm. It was this gesture which was unusual, and which Gritz would remember later on. It was a gesture of familiarity, which should have amazed Gritz, knowing about the relationships between Charlotte Poland, Paul Tretjak and Gabriel Tretjak. It was an almost tender gesture. It was not returned.

Again the bell of the clock tower tolled. The priest blessed the grave and the people present. Then it was over. When Gritz, like the others slightly unsure what to do next, headed up the steps and walked around the church, he noticed that the tractor was gone and that the wooden trestle had been removed from the entrance. The aconite branches were now standing against the wall. At the bend, where the path came out of the forest, Rainer Gritz paused on his way back and observed how the mourners dispersed. He saw that Gabriel Tretjak and Fiona Neustadt did not take the same way as everybody else, but turned behind the church onto a smaller path, which led not downhill but further up. Gritz watched them until they disappeared in the forest. He assumed that this was the most direct route to the father's house. Then the young police officer turned around and looked at his watch. It was just before seven. He wondered whether he should eat some pasta in the village. When he drove here, he had called Maler in the hospital and Maler had given him a recommendation. He recalled that Paul Tretjak had mentioned a restaurant in a conversation, which supposedly served the best ravioli in the world, a small *trattoria* directly on the lake. 'Who knows,' Maler had said on the phone, 'maybe he told us about it because he knew that we would have to come back to this place one day…' No, Maler didn't recall the name of the place, Tretjak didn't even know it, he said. He had always called it only by its nickname, 'the nasty restaurant' or something like that. But you couldn't miss it. Rainer Gritz set off and noticed that he was really hungry.

# 2

Professor Determination entered the room – that's what he called him. Maler had never met a person who seemed more determined. There was no doubt, no hesitation, only: this is how it's going to be done. Even their first meeting seven years ago had been like that. The professor had sat opposite, had leafed through his medical records, had asked a few questions, and then firmly stated: 'You are my patient.'

Being his patient meant: you are the man whose old heart I am going to rip out and then transplant a new one in its place. You are the man whose life I am going to save. You only have to do what I tell you. The professor was one of the best heart surgeons in the world. And nothing about him gave the impression that he didn't know this to be a fact.

The professor did not knock before entering. Cowboys don't knock, he always said. Maler had once accompanied him on a cold day to a pub, which was only a few hundred metres away from the hospital. When he asked the professor why he was not wearing a coat, he could have guessed the professor's answer: 'A cowboy doesn't need a coat.'

Now he was standing at his bedside. Rejection, 1b. The first, lowest category. From 2a on up, it would be grave, the professor said. No reason to worry now, but one had to watch out. And to ask why it was happening now. He had consulted a colleague, the professor said, and they had decided to change the medication. He pulled a small box from the pocket of his white coat and handed it to Maler. 'Cellcept inhibits immune defence even more. Take this one for the time being.'

'No,' said Maler, 'I won't take this.' He knew full well how little the professor appreciated the word 'no' from the mouth of a patient, and that's why he quickly added: 'I know Cellcept, I can't tolerate it. The last time I took it, it induced stomach bleeding and I ended up in intensive care. That was two years ago. When I discontinued the medication, I felt better very quickly.'

The professor put the little box back into his pocket. 'Why don't my colleagues know about that? Sloppiness. I will bring this up at our next meeting. And you are of course not going to take this medication.'

Maler would have loved to be present at such a meeting. The arrogance of the professor towards his medical colleagues was considerable, as Maler had witnessed many times. The surgeon always came first, and then nothing came next for a long, long time.

'Are you under special pressure at the moment?' the professor asked.

'I had to catch a serial killer,' said Maler, 'nothing else.'

'But that's your job, isn't it?' said the professor. 'Catching murderers. I mean, is there something else, something out of the ordinary?' He was not a great believer in the psyche. 'You can't really operate on the psyche, you know.' There was a hint of a smile around his mouth. 'But there are a variety of studies which prove that in transplant patients there is a connection between extraordinarily stressful situations and the body rejecting the transplanted organ. So, is something up with you?'

'No, there is nothing,' Maler said. But he knew that this was not the case. He had actually quickly put a slim file into his bag, together with his underpants and his bathrobe, when he got the news that because of the rejection he had to immediately go to the hospital for a few days. The file was on Laura Müller. The woman whose heart he was carrying inside him. After Tretjak had surprised him with the name of the donor, he had gathered information about her. Just a few calls to colleagues, who had logged the accident back then and who had informed the family. The most shattering document was one that Maler had found on the Internet. In a newspaper produced by her school, fellow pupils had remembered Laura Müller. Everyone had written something about Laura, who liked to dance, to listen to jazz, who quite coolly rejected some suitors, who wanted to go abroad, to South America, who wanted children and lots of men, who always laughed and had a boyfriend, the fat but extremely clever Max, whom she loved a lot.

'No stress. I see,' said the professor. 'Of course. I had forgotten, Inspector. You are not one for feelings. You like to play the tough guy, I know. And like you, I prefer clear colours, black is black and white is white. And that's exactly why I want you to think again: is there something? There has to be something.'

Maler didn't mention Laura Müller. But he asked the professor what the heart meant for him. Was it something mystical, or just an organ, which powered everything?

'The heart,' the professor said, 'holds no mystical meaning for me. None. It isn't complicated, the heart is something totally simple. The heart is a muscle, full stop, nothing more and nothing less. I know what I'm talking about. I have operated on thousands of hearts. A muscle, nothing more. There is no deeper meaning that one should read into it. '

August Maler liked the professor. Every day for two weeks back then, seven years ago, he had stood by his bed in the ICU, and Maler had recognised him, and known that this was the doctor, this was the professor. The transplantation had been a success, the new heart was inside his body and it was beating. The body was not causing any problems. But Maler had slipped into a post-operative state of paranoia, in which he lived a seemingly never-ending nightmare. Part dream, part reality. He was lying in his hospital bed, hooked up to all sorts of tubes, and his imagination turned everything into a completely different story: He dreamed, day-dreamed in fact, that he was caught in a cage at an airport. He was cold, and his wife and his family passed the box and did not hear his cries for help. He felt betrayed and tried to escape the cage – which led in reality to his flailing wildly about in the ICU, talking gibberish, and therefore being tied to the bed, restrained as they put it. Maler could not remember any details of his nightmares, but he could remember the deep sense of fear and loneliness he had experienced, the feeling that he was surrounded by gruesome torturers.

The only reality in these weeks had not been his family, who could only helplessly watch his delusional state. It had been the professor, with whom he could talk and who had been able to explain what was happening: patients in intensive care often slipped into such worlds of fantasy, it was nothing unusual, it was like being high on LSD, caused by the illness and a potent drug cocktail. We doctors, the professor said, call this the transit. It is similar to entering a room of madness. Some stay in it longer, some more briefly, but all come out of it again. 'Can you hear what I'm saying, Maler?' the professor had called out to him every day. 'You are going to come out of this, for sure. You have to believe me.'

August Maler had been caught in this limbo for a long time, in these worlds between reality and madness. What was real, what was imagined? That had been the central question of his life for many weeks. Only very slowly did he come to recognise the boundaries between these worlds, and to be able to decide what belonged in this and what in that world. The thought that he could not get rid of, and which he had been aware of ever since, was: this other world did exist, and it could switch itself on whenever it wanted to. Sometimes Maler thought that it wasn't so bad having this other, expanded dimension. Then again, he cursed this weak and frightening feeling that the ground could start to shift under his feet at any time.

Once, Maler had told the professor about his 'daymares', the horrible images which recurred from time to time, such as the petrol station attendant who suddenly had blood pouring out of his mouth, and how he, August Maler, had to close his eyes several times and open them again before the horror disappeared from the face of the attendant. No reason to worry, the professor had said, those are just the final stages of the horror trips he had suffered in the ICU, chemical leftovers which clouded his consciousness. No reason to worry, it will pass. Here the professor was mistaken. It was now seven years since his heart operation, but the images continued, and sometimes they occurred more often, sometimes less. The other night Maler had happened upon some TV science programme when he was zapping through the channels. A brain expert had been explaining that, unfortunately for many patients, the brain could remember pain, even though whatever had caused it was no longer present. The brain recreated the pain without any physiological reason. My brain, Maler thought, remembers the madness.

He had now been back in the Grosshadern hospital for three days. He had always been treated in this hospital, right from the very first examinations, because the professor was the head of its cardiovascular surgical unit. And for three days now, the images of the other world had returned with a vengeance. Maler wondered whether his brain had this particular place engraved on it, this colossus of a hospital with the ICU, where everything had begun, and therefore felt compelled to produce an extra dose of madness whenever he was in a hospital room here. This time, however, the madness had a new dimension. The images still changed the faces of the people around him, in this case the male nurses, but this time there was no blood, no catastrophes. Nurse Marco, a friendly guy, entered the room to check his temperature and blood pressure, but then suddenly it wasn't Marco looking at him, but Gabriel Tretjak, with a strange expression on his face as if he was saying: 'See, Inspector, wherever you go, I can be there too.' With the doctors in charge of the ward, the same thing happened. Gabriel Tretjak forced himself into view. What was going on? What was his mind trying to communicate with this? That Tretjak was the man who was causing his nightmares?

August Maler would have figured that out without these images. Last night he had lain awake for a long time, and a long time in a hospital means an eternity. At half past five, dinner was served. And then what? Maler had the room to himself, since heart transplant patients always had a room to themselves. At one point he had fallen asleep and had dreamt of Laura Müller, the beautiful girl, and that he had sex with her. He was sleeping with the woman whose heart was beating inside him. When he woke with a jolt, he still remembered the dream. He found it so revolting that he went to the bathroom and threw up. He brushed his teeth and then looked into the mirror. Nice to know, he thought, whose heart I now have inside me. Thank you very much, Mr Tretjak.

Maler did not tell the professor about the delusional images or about his last dream either. He asked to be given something to help him sleep, 'but I don't want to dream.' The nurses refused to give him a sleeping pill, saying 'you are taking so many drugs already.'

The professor, however, said: 'OK, I'll have them give you something. Take two of these pills and an earthquake in your room will not wake you.'

'That sounds great,' Maler said. And because he wanted the professor to stay a little, he asked which patients he was planning to perform transplants on next. He always asked that question, it was almost a ritual now. Maler asked about the work of the professor, and then the professor asked about the work of the inspector.

'A little girl, seriously ill, a new heart is her only chance. Three years old,' the professor said. There was a problem, though: there were practically no hearts for three-year-olds. 'We have to go by an alternative route.'

'An alternative route?', Maler asked.

'We have to make a bigger heart smaller. I will scrape off enough so it fits.'

Maler shuddered: 'My God, the poor child.'

'No, no, don't worry, it will work. I'm sure of that.'

And then the professor returned the question: 'And what are you working on at the moment? You were talking about a serial killer the other day…'

'Maybe you read about it in the papers. The guy who scooped out his victims' eyes. That's the kind of thing I have to deal with.'

'I hardly read the papers,' the professor said, 'and definitely not that kind of story.'

Maler briefly sketched the facts of the case. Several murders, no apparent connection. In the centre a dubious businessman, whose business it was to fix people's lives.

'He is from Munich. His name is Gabriel Tretjak. Do you know him?'

'No, never heard of him.'

'Well, in any case,' Maler continued, 'it finally emerged that the murderer was Tretjak's father. A family tragedy, a Shakespearean drama. The murderer killed himself and explained it all in a letter.'

'Congratulations,' the professor said, 'then the case is closed, isn't it? Then it's not really true what you just said, that you have to catch a serial killer.'

'Yes, the case appears to be solved.' Maler hesitated. 'But something is still bothering me about it.'

'But it shouldn't. I like my job, because it deals with clear questions: does the heart function healthily, or doesn't it? Yes or no? Everything in between, I can't stand. This should be your rule as well. One goes crazy if one lets go of clear questions. Believe me.'

The professor looked at his wristwatch, a simple Swatch, and said good-bye. 'I'll come back tomorrow.'

August Maler remained in his hospital room. He thought: why did I tell the professor that I have some doubts about whether the case is really solved? The investigations were complete and the case had been closed, by Maler himself as a matter of fact. Signed and sealed. He had never been somebody who considered it part of his job to ponder too long. So why this now? The clear questions the professor had been speaking about were: is Paul Tretjak the murderer? Yes or no? The evidence gave a clear answer. Was the case solved or not? Yes or no?

It took a while for Maler to sit up in bed. And to say in a loud, inappropriately loud, voice: 'No. No, I don't believe it is.'

There was a knock on the door. Dinner was served on a tray, two rolls, two pieces of sausage, two slices of cheese, butter. And tea, herbal tea. He decided to wait a bit before he ate dinner.

Maler remembered his meeting with Paul Tretjak. Lago Maggiore, wonderful sunshine, a café directly on the lakefront. At first a seemingly nice man, who told him about the drama with his son and presented himself as somebody who wanted to make amends, to repair the relationship. Paul Tretjak explained to Maler why he thought his son Gabriel was well-suited to the task of getting Charlotte Poland's son on the right path. 'Inspector', the older Tretjak had said, 'my son would understand this Lars, and he is brutal enough to tell him what really needs to be done now.'

Maler had driven to Italy, a journey of four and a half hours, to find out what had happened ten years ago, why Paul Tretjak had asked that this question be passed on to his son Gabriel Tretjak by Charlotte Poland. He should have noticed the change immediately, because when he asked Paul Tretjak that question, there was suddenly nothing left of the softness and friendliness he had earlier sensed in the father. Paul Tretjak began talking about his other son, Gabriel's half-brother, who was a few years older. Luca was his name, said Tretjak, his mother had been Italian and had passed away long before. And ten years ago, on 11 May, the two brothers had got together. As far as Tretjak Senior knew, the meeting had taken place in the Blauen Mondschein in Bolzano, the hotel he had run once upon a time.

'That's what happened ten years ago, Inspector,' Paul Tretjak said.

'And?' Maler asked. 'And then?'

'I don't know,' Tretjak said. 'Gabriel denies that this meeting ever took place. He says that he hasn't seen Luca for over 30 years.'

'And what does Luca say?'

'Nothing at all, Inspector. Luca disappeared that day. Nobody has seen him since.'

'Did you call the police?'

'They looked into it, but then stopped. People disappear. It isn't against the law, they said. Inspector, I am convinced my son is dead.'

'May I ask what Luca wanted from Gabriel? Do you know?'

'It had to do with me,' Paul Tretjak said, 'he wanted to mediate. He wanted to bring the family back together.'

'I understand less and less, Mr Tretjak,' Maler said. 'You suspect your son of having killed your other son. But on the other hand, you want Gabriel to save your friend's son. How does that fit together?'

The old Tretjak didn't really have a sensible answer to that question. But just before Maler's departure for Munich, he had made another cryptic remark. If Maler wanted to clear up the issue about his other son, he would have to go to South Tyrol. To Jenesien, a small mountain village above Bolzano. 'Ask for the man who lives with the eagles. That is an interesting lead for you, Inspector,' Tretjak had said. Maler just let him stand there and, annoyed by it all, had started driving back to Munich.

Lying in his hospital room, he bit into his sausage roll. Maybe it was logical after all: a mad old man, who commits mad murders – out of revenge on his son? He briefly investigated the matter of Gabriel Tretjak's half-brother. But without any results – or rather, with the following result: Luca Tretjak? There was no person by that name. There was no information, nothing, nowhere. Maler finished the sausage roll and allowed himself to think for one moment: a man commits a murder and then expunges the identity of his victim. If there is no body, there is no murder. A perfect murder. Committed by the Fixer. At least the theory would appeal to Gabriel Tretjak, Maler thought.

He didn't touch the tea. He knew it tasted ghastly. It was a little before six o'clock. Maler decided to grant himself a coffee in the sad cafeteria of the clinic.

# 3

At one minute past six o'clock, Fiona Neustadt closed the door of the room on the cancer ward. 'Drink a schnapps, toasting me as usual,' he had said on parting. 'I can't join you, I can't manage it anymore.'

She hadn't expected that, although she of course knew how ill he was. He had continuously talked about this being the last time. And about what he still wanted to tell her. What advice he still had for the coming weeks. What she should definitely pay attention to. And he had become a bit sentimental. He was proud of her, he had said, he had always believed in her, in contrast to many other people, and today he knew that he had been right to place his trust in her. 'Bye-bye, my girl.'

Fiona Neustadt walked along the long grey corridor of the cancer ward and started to observe herself objectively. As if she was accompanied by cameras. How did she appear, walking along like this? A pretty, young woman, for sure, that's what she was, but could one notice the emotion, the sense of shock at the realisation that she had just said good-bye to a person who meant so much to her? More than that, the person who was most important in her life? He had always seen her the way she really was, he had always appreciated the special core of her. He had known how valuable she was, what she was capable of.

She wished that people would notice this very special mourning she was in, that her pain would show on her face. She was waiting at the lift. She had this gift, of being able to look at herself with extreme detachment, to take a position outside herself and to thereby keep her distance. That's how she never lost control, how she kept an overview. That was maybe her biggest strength, she thought, when the lift arrived. She pressed the button for the ground floor. She still wanted to go to the cafeteria. To drink a schnapps as a toast to him, as she had promised. She always kept her promises.

Her ability to look at herself from the outside went even further, Fiona Neustadt thought, when she got out of the big metallic lift and walked along the long grey corridor in the direction of the cafeteria. Using this method she could split herself incessantly; she was never only one person, and was therefore always stronger than other people. Controlled schizophrenia, she thought, and had to smile.

For example, this morning: for the first time in a long time, she had woken up alone in her flat. And she didn't just get up. She had watched herself doing it. As somebody who loved and desired her. Not Gabriel, or any specific man. Just man as a prototype. She had felt her own looks on her skin, in the bathroom, under the shower as well. She had felt strong by way of this detached self-projection.

Fiona Neustadt stood at the self-service counter of the cafeteria and bought a small bottle of brandy. She took a big water glass and poured in the brandy. Right now she also felt strong. What kind of woman does this so matter of factly, drinking brandy in the hospital's cafeteria? She wanted to sit in a corner, and found a place at the window overlooking the big parking lot. The sun was still shining. What a contrast to the room on the cancer ward.

'Ms Neustadt?'

She looked up and saw a man in a blue bathrobe, pyjamas and trainers standing in front of her. She needed a moment to recognise him.

'Inspector! Well hello, what are you doing here?'

'I'm here as a patient for a few days. Nothing serious. Only a few tests. And you? What are you doing here?'

'I've been here to see my Dad. Unfortunately it is serious, very serious. To put it bluntly: my father is dying.'

'Oh, I'm sorry to hear that.'

'Please sit down,' she said.

Maler sat down and both were quiet for a moment. Not an easy occasion for pleasant small talk. A young woman wrapped in the pain of mourning, and an inspector wrapped in a blue bathrobe. Maler's first question didn't lighten the mood.

'Tell me,' Maler asked, 'I don't want to be nosy, but how does an attractive young woman become a tax inspector?'

'What kind of a question is that?'

'I'm really interested,' said Maler.

'Why did you become a cop?' asked Fiona Neustadt.

'OK, I understand. Stupid question. Then I'll ask something else: How is Mr Tretjak?'

'He has to live with the fact that his father is a serial killer. But otherwise he is fine, I think.'

'It's nice that you two are a couple now,' was the inspector's last attempt.

Fiona Neustadt took a large gulp of the brandy. She then got up and extended her hand towards him. 'Inspector, I've got to go. Good-bye.'

She did not see how August Maler returned to his room, to the pills the professor had had send there. But when she had left the hospital, outside in the parking lot in the sun, she asked herself whether she had made a mistake.

# 4

The tablets the professor had given him had worked. In fact, they had worked so well that Inspector Maler needed some time to realise who was standing in front of his bed when he woke the next morning. It was after eight, and his breakfast had been waiting for him on his night stand for two hours. He had not even been conscious of it being brought in.

Rainer Gritz stood at his bedside, his young companion, whom he had come to trust. Everything was happening in slow motion with Maler, but slowly his body functions were picking up speed. Gritz's words were also reaching his brain painfully slowly. A new case, a new murder. A bank employee was lying in his flat, poisoned. Some very strange poison, something exotic, Maler understood.

'But Boss,' said Gritz, 'that's not all.'

And what he said next made Maler wake up rather quickly. There was a connection to the previous series of murders? Charlotte Poland?

'You know, the writer with the disturbed son, the friend of the old Tretjak. She was also at the funeral, I saw her there.'

Charlotte Poland, Gritz explained, had met the murdered bank employee, officially on totally normal bank business. But his colleague had declared that the banker had been totally beside himself after the appointment.

'I have viewed the tapes of the bank's CCTV camera,' said Gritz. 'You could see him nervously pacing up and down the corridor after she had left. The guy was finished. And you know when this meeting took place? Two hours before the dinner with Gabriel Tretjak in the Osteria at which we arrested him.'

'Have you reached Charlotte Poland already?'

'Yes. She says it was a completely ordinary conversation. She had sought advice about what to do with her money. She didn't remember any details.'

When Rainer Gritz left the hospital room, he added: 'Boss, I don't like the look on your face.'

Maler, in the meantime, had sat up in his bed. He thought, well he is right, this Gritz, I don't like the look on my face either. And then suddenly the inspector had another thought. My God. Maler heaved himself out of bed, went over to the wardrobe, and got his mobile out of his jacket. He pushed a few buttons and then dialled the number of the forensic pathologist.

# 5

Charlotte Poland typed the last sentences of her latest novel into the computer. She was sitting at the small desk of her hotel room in the Tucher Park Hilton in Munich. She had ordered a big pot of tea, Darjeeling, the Risheehat variety. Not one of the common Darjeelings, a pretty expensive one, which the hotel procured especially for her at Dallmayr, Munich's famous delicatessen. 'Of course we'll get you that tea, we'd be delighted,' the receptionist had said. The aroma of Risheehat was part of writing for her, as well as the minor stomach ache which reliably occurred after consuming the fourth cup. She waited for the pain, she liked it.

She took another sip from the white porcelain cup and then wrote the very last sentence: *In the end, it had been easy. In the end, it was always easy.*

Charlotte Poland was pleased with the idea of how her publisher and lover would react when he read the new book. Of course, she had told him that he had to expect a completely different book this time, a radical, a courageous one. Yes, yes, he had replied, as you wish, he was looking forward to it. 'Think of your readers, though,' he had said. 'They want to read a Poland again, nothing else. There is enough of everything else around, but there is only one Poland.' The old charmer.

*In the end, it had been easy. In the end, it was always easy.* The last sentence of a novel about a brutal female killer. In a way, she thought, the book was not that much different from her earlier books. It also dealt with the magician's trick of hidden depths, the secret compartment beneath the false bottom of a box, in the life of her protagonist. A woman who notices that nothing is as it seems, who understands that everything around her is lies, fraud and hypocrisy. The only difference in the new novel was the series of logical steps her heroine chose to take as a consequence of that realisation. In the past, her novels had been a declaration of love for hypocrisy: whoever recognises hypocrisy lives wonderfully happily with it ever after. Now that was all turned around. This time her heroine shouted against hypocrisy, this time she destroyed the lie, and the destruction was literal. A woman was seeking the truth, and ran amok. Her motive: fury at the world. Her solution: violent revenge upon the world.

Charlotte Poland opened the email account on her computer and sent the manuscript to her publisher. The computer registered the time sent as 7.34am. It was 354 pages long, while her other works had all been about 200 pages longer. The truth, she thought, was briefer after all.

She dialled the number for room service on the hotel telephone and ordered a glass of champagne. A little early, she thought, but a small celebration was in order. Service in the Hilton was good, and the glass of champagne was delivered exactly six and a half minutes later. She gave the waiter a ten-euro tip, and when he had left, she posed in front of the mirror and grinned: cheers, Mrs Poland, to the murderess!

With the story of the murderess, she had wanted to answer one question in particular: how much guilt can one person stand? How many illegal acts can a conscience tolerate? Conscience – what a word, Poland thought. If you killed a nasty person, wasn't that a much more moral act than watching him perpetrate his nastiness? It was good that she had done a lot of research for her book, she thought. It was good that she knew what she was writing about.

'My conscience can stand a lot,' Charlotte Poland said aloud in the direction of her mirror image. 'My conscience will have to put up with a lot in the future.'

She finished the champagne. And for a moment she thought of Mr Borbely, the pudgy bank employee. Was anybody sad that this smarmy creature was no longer alive? Well, she thought, he was bound to have had a mother at least. A mother who was suffering now. She checked herself as if to take her temperature. She listened to a voice inside herself – and was content. The end of Mr Borbely didn't bother her, not a bit. It didn't even marginally touch her conscience. It bounced off, without leaving any measurable reaction.

Charlotte Poland had checked into the Hilton for six months. For the time being. How things were going to pan out, she didn't know. She had a very definite sensation that she didn't have a future. The hotel seemed the appropriate place for such a sensation. The first three weeks had passed now, and living here was pleasantly easy. The Hilton was in the middle of the English Garden, Munich's vast park, and was the ideal place for her to live for various reasons. One could go for a walk whenever one wanted. Early in the morning, in the middle of the night, whenever one couldn't sleep. She now could distinguish exactly between the various shades of grey and black one encountered in the park, at two o'clock in the middle of the night or four; the grey of the morning just before six o'clock versus the one at half past seven.

The hotel had to be in Munich, the city where her son lived. But she wanted to be as far away as possible from the borough of Haar in the east of Munich. She drove there every second day, and she needed the distance, the half an hour it took her by car, to gather her strength.

She had known the Tucher Park Hilton for a long time. A few times she had met her publisher there for sex in the afternoon. Even then she had liked the seclusion, the green, the illusion of a country estate. The publisher had asked her out for a date a few times recently, 'to take your mind off things'. But Charlotte Poland kept putting him off until another time, and at one point he had intelligently stopped asking. Maybe the flame of passion was not burning as bright anymore, but maybe, she thought, there was another reason as well: maybe another feeling had taken hold of her, an all-consuming one. It was a feeling which it had taken her many sentences and pages in her new novel to describe, because the one or two words which existed for it didn't seem appropriate. Rage or fury – these words described only a momentary state, something violent, that came on quickly, and then equally quickly dissipated.

She always went in the morning. She drove through the city and breathed a sigh of relief at every traffic light which turned red because it extended the journey time.

The borough of Haar. There were many cities with quarters which were identified by one single concept or institution. With Haar, it was the district hospital. Signs pointing in its direction started appearing long before one got close to it. It was not a normal hospital, it was a hospital for the mentally ill. One could also say it was a city of the insane. A wall surrounded the compound, which consisted of various old buildings of elaborate architecture. The enclosed area had been filled in more densely over time with more modern buildings.

Charlotte Poland always parked outside the compound walls, although she could have driven her car into the grounds. She walked the rest of the way. It was a beautiful route, past big trees. She had to go to House No. 10, from the outside a particularly beautiful old building. Here as well, one could enjoy the illusion of being on a country estate. It housed the particularly tough cases, the pathological ones, human beings which a judge had decided should be locked up for a long time for what they had done, because they constituted a danger to the community.

For the past three weeks, she had come here every other day. Normally she didn't see the other patients in House No. 10, since during visiting hours in the morning they were all in their rooms. Only once she had gone to the kitchen to ask for some cutlery and a plate. A big, pale man had stood there, making himself a cup of coffee. He was very friendly, handed her the plastic cutlery and the plate and asked who she was visiting. This was the start of a conversation, and at one point the man had said that it had been hard at the beginning to accept the patients in here, to accept that they were human beings too, just a bit different, a bit more honest. Honest, that's what he had said. Charlotte Poland had not asked him why he was here. Later on, she had made enquiries with the nurse.

'He likes dead corpses,' the nurse had said. She did not really understand, Charlotte Poland had said. 'Well,' the nurse explained, 'he dug up corpses in the graveyard and took them home with him. And sometimes that was too exhausting, so he got himself dead bodies in other ways. Do you understand now?' And then she had added: 'He once told me why he likes doing that. He wants to get under their skin. Yes, that's how he put it.'

A few days later, she had seen the man walking in the park with an elderly woman. She had waited until the woman came out of House No. 10 alone. She had asked her when she had first noticed something odd about her son. The woman said, quite early on, her son had taken dead animals to bed with him, mice, and then a dead cat. Back then, she had thought and hoped that this would pass one day.

Lars was in Room No. 10. House No. 10, Room No. 10, the symmetry made it easy to remember. A double room, but he was alone, since the doctors had said that it was out of the question that he could share the room with anyone. And they had told her that they could not allow her to go into the room with her son alone. Or at least they would insist on a straitjacket if she did. Her son was dangerous. Her son could attack her.

'My son won't hurt me, I know that,' Charlotte Poland had said.

'You might not be able to judge that correctly,' had been the doctors' response.

'And if he harms me, that's my business. I take complete responsibility, I'll sign anything.'

'No, we in House No. 10 are responsible. You, at least as far as the law is concerned, have nothing more to do with your son,' the doctor had said.

Lars was usually lying on the bed, or sometimes he was sitting on a chair, somehow bent over. Blond and slim, the straitjacket made him look even thinner than he was already.

'Hello, Mama. How nice that you have come. I am glad.' Those were his words, every time.

'Hello, Lars. I am glad too,' she said. And then most of the time she asked: 'How are you?'

'Fine, Mama, not bad actually.'

During her first visits, Lars had asked his mother to talk about the future, about her plans, about trips, about food, about dreams. Lars had loved that ever since he had been a little boy. 'Mama, tell me...'

Charlotte Poland had liked it too, even here in Room No. 10. For a moment she could escape it all that way. But then the doctors had found out about these conversations. And had forbidden them emphatically: 'Mrs Poland, for your son every concept of the future is absolute poison. Every time he experiences that it is like a new hit of a drug, which pulls him further into his illness. Normally imagination is something good, but with Lars it isn't. Your son, Mrs Poland, has lost any connection to reality. We all have to try to lead him back into reality.'

'What else should I talk about with my son?'

'Ask him what he is thinking about right now. Ask him what is on his mind right now.'

Since then, it had always been quiet in Room No. 10 when Charlotte Poland was visiting her son.

'Tell me about our plans, Mama.'

'No, Lars. The doctors say that's not good for you. Why don't you tell me what you are thinking about now, how you are feeling.'

'I don't know,' Lars said.

And then they were silent, both of them.

On the morning that she had finished her novel, the senior consultant, the head of House No. 10, asked Charlotte Poland to come to her office. It was located in the house opposite, the administrative building, which did not have a number. She hated these conversations, and the fading effect of the champagne didn't make things any better. When she got into her car and drove back in the direction of the city, she still had the voice of the senior consultant in her ears. 'Mrs Poland, the deterioration in your son's condition is dramatic. There has been a development, a sort of feedback of various negative factors, which we so far haven't been able to stop. On the one hand, there is the psychiatric diagnosis, his inability to be aware of his own identity. In addition there was excessive drug abuse, which has led to his brain being damaged, which has furthered the symptoms of the dissolution of his sense of self.'

'And what am I supposed to do with this information?' Charlotte Poland had asked.

'You should prepare yourself for the fact that your son will never in his life leave the psychiatric ward. We thought you should know that.'

In the car, Charlotte Poland searched for a radio channel which played only music. She couldn't tolerate any more voices or talking. She found something classical. She sensed her rage. About her husband, her soon-to-be ex-husband, who had asked after Lars maybe three times since they had separated, a maximum of three times. Rage about the doctors, who had never helped one bit, but who never gave the impression that they felt they had failed in any way.

Rage about Paul Tretjak. She had really believed this

man, that he wanted to do good. A dreamer, a sensitive visionary. When they met by chance at the Lago Maggiore, she had thought that a man with his kind of history could turn around her son's life. She now realised what kind of man she had been dealing with. A human being who was rotten to the core, who was obsessed with his own self-pity. How could she have been so wrong about this man?

And the other Tretjak? The son Gabriel, who had been called a monster by his own father? The pretty boy, who considered himself to be a latter-day James Bond? Who supposedly could fix anything, if he only wanted to. Fixer! What a name for a man who had no idea about the abyss in his own family history.

Charlotte Poland parked the car in the hotel lot. By now it was midday. The air was muggy; there would be a thunderstorm soon for sure. That would be good. She went to the front desk and got her room key. Her favourite receptionist, Helmut Gruber, was on duty. Gruber handed her the key and said: 'Mr Tretjak was here. He left the message that he was going to be in the English Garden. The man said you knew where.'

'Thank you, Helmut,' Charlotte Poland said. 'Yes, I know where.'

# 6

Late on Monday morning, Gabriel Tretjak went to a branch of his bank and arranged a transfer of funds. How much is the life of a human being worth? he asked himself. And immediately tried to forget the question. 50,000 euros. Transferred to Carolina Lanner. Maybe she would find the transfer of money insulting. Especially coming from him. But in Tretjak's experience, on the whole, money calmed nerves, whatever life threw at you, especially a lot of money. He was sure she was going to keep the money. Tomorrow he was going to send her a text message, but not before tomorrow, when the money would have reached her account. He had already drafted the message: *Nothing can bring back your beloved mother. But she would surely be happy if this money supported your café a little. Gabriel Tretjak.*

He left the bank on Sendlinger Street and sensed in himself some little bit of vitality. He had finally done something again. He had transferred some money, had had a few letters typed into a bank computer, at least that was something. In the morning he had called the estate agent, yes, he was going to take the flat, immediately. Only one big room, with a doorman downstairs in the building, not far from the Isar River, only a short distance from the zoo. He had made a decision, placed a telephone call, at least that was something.

Tretjak had not returned to his flat at the St-Anna-Platz after the murder of Rosa Lanner. Even the thought of turning the keys in the lock induced physical pain. He had known immediately that this location didn't exist anymore for him. Because of her murder there, only the past could now exist in those rooms. And the past was not a category in his life. There could be no other choice but to get rid of the flat as quickly as possible.

When the police let him go after a night in the cells, he had stayed in the Hotel Vier Jahreszeiten, one of the best addresses in town. Then he had changed his hotel every two days, partly because that had structured the days, checking out, checking in, so that at least he was doing something. He felt best when he was with Fiona, when he stayed with her overnight. When he woke up in the middle of the night and felt her beside him. When the fear came and he heard her breathe. He felt calmer when Fiona was there.

In fact, it helped him if anybody was there. Tretjak sat in crowded restaurants and tried to start a conversation with the punters there. He got into a taxi and told the driver to show him Munich, that he was a tourist with only a little time to spare, just passing through. Those trips could last a couple of hours. Tretjak asked lots of questions, questions about Munich, the answers to which he already knew. Whoever is still talking is not dead, that's what he had once read in some poem.

Gabriel Tretjak could no longer stand to be alone. And this had to happen to him, the very one who had considered himself the master of being alone, who had always thought that being by yourself was the only true elixir of life. Tretjak knew what was behind his not being able to be alone anymore: he couldn't stand himself any longer. But he didn't know anything more than that. A centrifugal force had taken hold of him. He felt like he was going to disintegrate into his component parts if he sat still or stood there, concentrating only on himself. Only movement protected him, movement just for its own sake, without concept, without plan. Or when Fiona casually kissed him.

In other words, exactly those things which had never helped him in the past helped him now. His life had been turned upside down and he had no logical explanation for why this had come to pass. And he had no idea how his life was supposed to continue. It drove him crazy that he had no answers to the question: what was happening to him here?

Tretjak had stopped taking Tavor two days ago. In the end, he had been popping pills like cough drops. But he had hardly noticed any relief anymore. The very last time he had taken it, he had even thought that the stuff was causing a completely new kind of fear in him.

It is said that such crises are the hours of true friends, those you can call in the middle of the night and say: I need you. I need your help. Can you come over? The problem was that Gabriel Tretjak's friends were of a different nature. They knew other sorts of telephone calls from Tretjak: you have to immediately do this and that for me. Don't ask why, just do it. And it worked the other way around as well. They contacted Tretjak saying: can you do me a favour? They knew they could depend on one another. They were friends, but they had their own unique code. A code which should not be violated.

But still Tretjak had done just that, in his way. He had sent an email to Stefan Treysa over the weekend: *I'm not feeling well. I would like to ask you for advice. I have a proposal: you are a therapist, aren't you? Or you were a therapist once upon a time. I would like to make an appointment with you, as a patient. Just one hour. I fear I won't make it any other way.*

Only a few minutes later Treysa answered: *Of course. Monday at 12.30, at my office on Buttermelcher Street?*

Tretjak looked at his watch, he still had an hour. He walked down Sendlinger Street, turned left in the direction of Mueller Street, straight and then right onto Hans-Sachs Street. He came to the Hierlmaier Antiquarian Bookshop. He entered the shop, and the ring of the door's bell summoned a very large man from the back of the shop, whose belly was so big that his blue work apron hardly closed around it.

'*Servus*, Mr Tretjak,' Max Hierlmaier said, using the traditionally more intimate Bavarian version of 'Hello'.

'*Servus*, Mr Hierlmaier. I have a job for you. A flat in Munich. Everything that is in the study has to be transported into another flat. Everything else in the flat should be cleared out, sold or otherwise disposed of.'

Max Hierlmaier knew about this kind of removal. He

had organised them a dozen times at Tretjak's behest. Little to take along, lots to throw away, that was the rule. Tretjak had once explained it to him: 'People don't want to carry too much ballast into their new life.'

Hierlmaier asked for the name of the flat's owner. 'It's in my name. It's about me this time. It is a private move, you might say.'

'I see,' Hierlmaier said, 'I'll take care of it personally, if that's the case. I'm interested to find out what your home looks like. I believe that you can read a lot about people when you see their flats.'

'You won't find a lot to read in my home, I'm afraid.'

'Mr Tretjak, I tell you: nothing is a lot as well.'

Tretjak finally told him that he shouldn't be surprised to still find traces that the police had been in the flat. The police had combed the flat for evidence for days, and then cleaned it afterwards.

'OK,' Hierlmaier said, 'not a problem.'

Tretjak left the shop and, walking in the direction of Buttermelcher Street, thought of the only enquiry he had responded to in the past few weeks. Apart from that one, he had completely gone to ground. No matter what method people had used to try to contact him, the sender had received the same reply: Gabriel Tretjak was not reachable for the foreseeable future, he would neither read nor listen to any enquiry. On that point Rainer Gritz had been mistaken, there were by no means fewer enquiries than before. But he had sent a response to one person. She had recounted her life in just a few lines: she was an affluent lady, without any family, and had been the mistress of a very famous Munich celebrity, a fact which nobody had been allowed to know. Now the man had died. And with him had gone her life, her past. She wanted to change this retrospectively, wanted as many people to find out about the truth as possible, about the fact that she had existed and that she still did. She wanted her life back, at least to be able to talk about it and remember it. *That's all I want to achieve,* the woman had written, *really. I cannot organise this myself. Can you?*

Surprising himself, Tretjak had answered: *Yes, I can. But I have to ask you to be patient. I still need a little time.*

He got the response he had expected: *I have waited such a long time. A few more months won't make a difference.*

He found the idea intriguing: it was not like the other cases, when he had had to correct the past, this time he had to prepare a grand entrance for the past. It was mad that he had even sent the email. Did he ever want to work again? Would he be able to? Wasn't it completely clear that it was over? That the Fixer couldn't fix anything anymore? Too much had happened, there was not one single stone left in place from his old life, he thought. On the other hand: could he ever really stop doing what he was doing? He had to think of Dimitri Steiner and his death. With people like us, Tretjak thought, in the end there is always a reckoning. Those kinds of thoughts drove him crazy, and yet he couldn't stop them.

Tretjak had reached Buttermelcher Street. Still seven

minutes to go until half past. He was standing in front of a shop selling leather garments: the window display was mainly made up of chains and collars with spikes on them, and in between stood naked male display dummies brandishing whips. For a split second he changed the subject of his thoughts: he knew a few homosexuals, and all of them were polite and sensitive human beings. How did that go together with the whips? Was he missing something?

It was one of those autumn days which can make Munich sparkle like no other city. That set off his next chain of thoughts: would he miss Munich if he left? How would it be if he went away and then returned to the city, would he feel like he was in an old movie which had continued to run without him? Tretjak liked Fiona's plans to go away together, for example to Brazil, a good place to live, or to Moscow, good for business. He liked her enthusiasm, her strength, which had started to pull him along.

Stefan Treysa had made coffee, and on the table a plate of buttered pretzels was waiting. As usual, Treysa was alone in the office, except of course for the parrot, who was quickly making himself heard with loud cries of 'woof'. They were sitting on two office chairs opposite each other, with the small table bearing the pretzels between them. Tretjak thought that his friend looked even smaller, even thinner than usual.

Treysa started with a short introduction on the role of a therapist. In principle, it was impossible to be the therapist of a person one knew very well, a family member or a friend. A therapist always had to be able to keep his distance, to take an outside view, to be able to interfere effectively. A therapist should never be part of the system, which he was supposed to judge. Treysa smiled: 'All right, let's attempt the impossible,' he said. 'We have 45 minutes. I would suggest that the next session be tomorrow. We can discuss how to proceed then.'

Tretjak nodded.

'I'm asking you what I always ask at the beginning: why are you here?'

'Because I feel bad. Really bad. I can't sleep. I'm afraid. I'm not taking the tablets anymore. Maybe you'll say that is good news, but it's not. I know that it sounds idiotic, but with the tablets I still somehow had the feeling of being in control. But then I felt as if exactly this attempt to stay in control was making things even worse. I feel completely helpless, I think for the first time in my life.'

'I don't believe that. I think you only blocked help-lessness from your life. And now it's back.'

Tretjak was silent.

'Gabriel, I'm going to summarise what has happened in the past months. There were several murders, grue-some murders. Acquaintances, close acquaintances of yours were killed. And your cleaning lady. A poor, elderly lady. And who did all this? Your father. Let me repeat this: your father committed these murders, your father with whom you have always had a disturbed relationship.'

'I know what has happened. You don't have to tell me the story again.'

'Yes, I do have to. Because I'm telling you for a very specific reason. How can a man who has experienced such horror not be in a crisis? How can a man who has lived through all that not think that the ground beneath his feet is trembling? Let me put it simply: there has never been a man who has had more reason to be in a crisis than you.' Treysa took a gulp of his coffee and said: 'Could it be that you should acknowledge this fact, before we talk about everything else?'

'No', Tretjak said.

'What, no?'

'You know me, Stefan. I have a philosophy of life, to which everything else is subordinated. I live by that philosophy. You can call it a crutch, I don't care. An important pillar of that philosophy is that I cut off everything behind me. What is past is past. Doesn't make a difference anymore. Nothing that happened a long time ago, nothing that happened a few years ago, not even what went on the day before yesterday. That is my principle.'

'Yes, I know,' Treysa said. 'And there were moments when you had me almost convinced. A life without a past? That's a real challenge for a psychologist.'

'But right now it doesn't seem to work,' said Tretjak, 'just when it is supposed to. Because every indication is that all the evil lies in the past. The murders, my father, everything. You know that I've been trained in the techniques of expunging the past. I've tried everything, but nothing has worked. Everything is bubbling up, so that I've got the feeling that I consist only of the past. I'm dreaming you can't imagine what kind of dreams.'

'Tell me one dream.'

'One comes back every night. I'm a little boy, about ten years old, and I'm walking across a meadow, holding an older man's hand, towards a clearing in a forest. Then the man says to me, "do you see the bird there, the big bird?" And I'm actually seeing a big bird hop into the meadow, a crow, black, as big as a human being. I want to run towards it. "No", says the man, "I don't mean the little bird, I mean the big bird, the really big bird. Look carefully!" And then I see it. There is no clearing in front of us, but everything in front of us is just one giant bird, an eagle as big as a hundred trees. I feel that I am gasping with excitement. And then I wake up and I'm drenched in sweat.'

'Interesting dream,' Treysa said.

Tretjak took one of the pretzels and said: 'What is this all about? What, may I ask, is the message?'

'Of the cuff I would say that the little boy, the little Gabriel, was not allowed to be a child. He sees only the small bird, not the big one. One thing is clear: your childhood is coming to the fore with this dream.' Treysa also reached for a pretzel. 'Do you remember poor Professor Kerkhoff and his thesis about the Factory of the Soul?'

'Yes,' Tretjak replied, 'I remember well. I've got to thinking about it quite often lately.' Images appeared in Tretjak's mind's eye, brief clips. The arrogant face of

Harry Kerkhoff. The strange message about the race-horse in the hotel restaurant in Sri Lanka. Then the news of Kerkhoff's murder. That's how everything started, the whole nightmare. 'Yes,' he repeated, 'I often think of Harry.'

Treysa once more summarised Kerkhoff's thesis. 'Kerkhoff was a biochemist and brain specialist, not a friend of psychology. "If one absolutely has to work with this strange term, the 'soul'," he had always pontificated, "then one has to imagine the soul to be something like a factory." And he had thought of a factory with huge machines, which perform various functions. The machines produce, repress, plan, and when the human being feels fine these machines work perfectly and in harmony. In that case, nobody would think about stopping the machines or questioning them. Kerkhoff was convinced that it was best to just leave everything the way it was. If that human being, however, wasn't feeling so good, then it was time to go into the engine room and check out what was defective.'

Tretjak was able to almost automatically complete Kerkhoff's theory: if everything is functioning well, you still need to oil and fuel the machines. 'He always told me, OK, you block out the past, but you therefore have to provide your soul with sufficient other stuff. You, for example, have to become a megalomaniac...'

'That was Kerkhoff's idiosyncratic method...' said Treysa, and had to laugh.

'Yes, megalomania was his thing, wasn't it? And in a

way, it's mine as well. Kerkhoff told me that you have to
be successful, very successful, you have to be diligent,
you have to create your own world of experience. You
cannot allow your soul even the briefest moment to turn
around and look back.' Tretjak paused. 'Now it obviously has turned around.'

Stefan Treysa stood up. And then he sat down again.
'Yes, well, no wonder with all that has happened. The
factory has been damaged from the outside. And we
now have to get into the engine room and start up the
machines again.' It was totally silent in the room, and
nothing could be heard outside either, not even the
parrot. 'Tell me about your Fiona. What kind of story
is that? I've seen you two a couple of times and you look
good together.'

'She thought she had caught a cool guy. And what has
she got now? A ruin.'

'Some women like that. Have you got plans?'

'Fiona always makes plans. Start anew somewhere
else, go away. The two of us.'

'And you?'

Tretjak thought about it. He thought for a long time,
too long in fact to say just something casual. 'I mistrust
her. I feel mistrustful. I ask myself why she is saying what
she says, doing what she does. I ask myself whether there
is an ulterior motive. This is what I think. I can't help it.'

'Is there a reason for this?'

'I don't know. I don't mistrust only her. I don't trust
anybody. Even you. I can imagine that when I leave here,

you'll call somebody to tell him how to get me. Because you are a part of a big conspiracy. I'm constantly imagining these kinds of things.'

'I'm not surprised. With your kind of job, I would think the same way. Particularly considering what happened to you.'

'Stefan, you asked me about Fiona. I think this woman is terrific. At times I even think I love her. But how is that going to work with a guy like me who is so overly suspicious? I'm damaged, really damaged. A guy like that should keep his hands off nice women.'

'Hmm,' Stefan Treysa said, 'maybe that's right.'

'There is something else,' Tretjak said, 'I've given you my father's letter to read, his farewell letter. What do you think?'

'I've never read something so terrible. I use the word very rarely, it doesn't really belong to my vocabulary, but that letter is really evil. I can't think of another word for it.'

'Yes, I agree,' Tretjak said, 'but there is something wrong with that letter. Why did my father commit suicide at that very moment? He kills my cleaning lady and then himself. Why? Why doesn't he continue? Why doesn't he totally let loose it and do God knows what? I don't understand. And there is one point in that letter which is particularly strange. I don't know whether you remember. He writes…'

'Be quiet,' Treysa said, 'I don't want to hear any more about it. This letter is a hypnotic work. Your father wrote it with only one intention: it is supposed to take over your mind again and again, to create obsessive negative thoughts in you. He would be content if he could see you now. His plan is about to work. If it was ever sensible to expunge something from memory, then it is this letter. Expunge it, Gabriel. Expunge it forever.'

'But this is not just about me,' Tretjak said, 'this is about a case, which has to be solved. And maybe I can do that.'

'I want to tell you something else now: you know the term "comfort zone", don't you?'

'No,' Tretjak said, 'I don't know that term.'

'Nothing defines a human being more than his comfort zone. That is, how he has grown accustomed to think, how he has grown accustomed to live. And with you I would add: how he has grown accustomed to solve a problem or not. A human being arranges his comfort zone and fights tooth and nail against any attempt to force him to leave it. He finds reasons, logical reasons, all sorts of reasons, which prevent him from moving into another zone.'

'I'm not inventing anything.'

'Yes, you are,' Treysa said. 'You are falling back into your old routine: I want to solve a case and I'm applying my rules to do that. But this time it's not your case. There is no more case. Your father is the culprit, end of story. And you shouldn't get entangled in your father's spider web, but instead you have to take care of yourself. You have to get out of your tried and tested comfort zone. This is now all about Gabriel Tretjak, about your soul. You can't waste any time, none at all. You know yourself how serious the situation is.'

'What do you mean, serious?'

'You know that best of all. In addition, you are addicted to a certain medication, and it's not going to be that easy to come off it.' Treysa looked at his watch. 'The hour is over. We'll meet again tomorrow. And then we'll enter the engine room.'

They said good-bye at the office door, and Tretjak had already walked down a few steps when he turned around one more time. Treysa nodded at him. Saying good-bye and then turning around one more time – he hadn't done that for a long time, Tretjak thought.

Treysa and he had first met a few years ago on a long train journey, on the Orient Express from Vienna to Istanbul. Tretjak had given the trip to a girlfriend as a birthday present, a terrific journey, with a sleeping carriage, total luxury. The neighbouring compartment was occupied by Mr and Mrs Treysa. They saw one another at breakfast and then again at dinner. They talked, and they liked each other. It had been a fun week as a foursome. When they said good-bye in Istanbul, they exchanged numbers but they didn't see each other again. But a few months later, Tretjak attended a reception at the Munich House of Literature, feeling a bit tense as he was about to organise the uncomfortable meeting of three people who were very important for a case he was working on at the time. And suddenly Stefan Treysa was standing in front of him, the small, slim man. Tretjak could really not handle him at that moment and overlooked him as arrogantly as he could – and he could be very arrogant. Treysa immediately understood, grinned, and walked on. Tretjak had liked that grin. He called Treysa the very next day. In a way, their friendship had started with a lie.

Gabriel Tretjak walked down Buttermelcher Street in the direction of the Viktualienmarkt. He turned on his mobile. There was a message from Lichtinger. It read: *I've been thinking a lot. I'm sure you have challenged a completely different power. Gabriel, this is about a bigger dimension. You have to think in a different way, totally different. I believe I can help you.*

# 7

When she had got up that morning, the forensic pathologist had briefly considered trying the new restaurant around the corner that day. Filled veal breast, one of her many favourite dishes. It wouldn't be very good for her diet, but she had read somewhere that if one had to sin, then it would be better at lunch time, definitely not in the evening. The anticipated filled veal breast put her in a good mood that morning, which was promising to be a quiet day. But then Maler called.

She asked herself whether these inspectors knew what consequences their calls had. In this case, she had to ruin two of her colleagues' plans to have a quiet weekend, as she needed them for a new post-mortem and the subsequent lab examinations. She had to tell a third colleague to be on stand-by in case he was also needed. She called the office of the public prosecutor and asked permission to exhume three bodies. She called three different cemeteries and told them to instruct their workers to dig up the bodies. She had to do all that herself because her secretary had stayed at home with gastric flu and because everything was quicker when one did it oneself anyway.

Maler had actually asked only one question: whether she, the forensic scientist, could exclude the possibility that the three previous victims, the two professors and the cleaning lady, had been poisoned, just like the newly dead man, the bank employee. No, she couldn't, she had answered quite quickly. She had wondered herself why none of the victims' bodies had displayed any defensive wounds, and had finally come to the conclusion that the extremely professional positioning of the stabs to the livers had led to shock, which had paralysed everything. Had she overlooked something? No, she didn't really blame herself. This is what her profession was like: once one discovered one cause of death, why look for another one? A deadly stab to the liver – who would think that poison also could play a role? What sense was there in that? But Maler was right, she couldn't rule it out. So to work, she thought.

The forensic pathologist liked August Maler. He was one of these men, who became ever rarer these days, where you could see that he argued a point with himself long before he bothered others with it. That gave him a quiet, serene aura. The pathologist liked to work with the inspector, and also with his assistant, who was another quiet one. There were so many hectic types in the police force, and they all became more hectic with time, with a hectic job, in hectic times. Awful.

During their telephone conversation, she had also given Maler the final report from the post-mortem on the bank employee. The man had been killed with a care-fully-placed injection of pure heroin, mixed with snake poison. And this time there were signs of a struggle: the bank employee had clearly fought back, and had then been tied up. The man had had to watch, the pathologist said, how the deadly injection was administered. This murder had been a demonstration.

# PART 3

# AT THE LAKE

# 1

*We were alone only one single time. We played ball. In the meadow with the birch tree. But you don't remember. You have forgotten. It was a big yellow plastic ball with red stars on it. Never again. My father suddenly had to leave. Never again did I have you all to myself. But on that day, I did.*

She stood behind a projection on a wall, about a hundred metres above the little harbour of Maccagno, and observed the ferry port. Maccagno was not a big town, but had a surprising number of churches. One of them was built on a rock, directly along and above the lakeshore, like a castle. The main street no longer led up around it, but through a tunnel in the rock. One could climb up on a paved path and look down from a sort of terrace in front of the church. A relatively old wall surrounded the terrace.

She saw the ferry cut a straight line through the leaden grey water. The old Alpino. And she saw how Tretjak walked along the wooden planks of the landing dock and stopped next to the railing. He had his hands deep inside his coat pockets. From above, where she stood, she could also see the small Piazza Roma with its palm trees, the few parking places, the pretty bar and the hotel Torre Imperial. It had turned cool in the past few days. That could sometimes happen rather rapidly. The town was preparing for hibernation. The square was empty, and the bar, as well as the hotel, were already illuminated.

She had stood in the living room, she remembered it precisely, in the middle of the living room, and she had seen him sit on the terrace, seen him read the newspaper. She had stood like that for a while, quiet as a mouse, in that ridiculous blue-checkered little dress, much too childish for her age – after all, she was eleven, almost eleven, and her heart had beaten so strongly it could be seen through the material. But then she had gathered all her courage. She remembered the look of her feet in the sandals on the stone slabs, how they made one step after another. Don't stumble, not now... And then she had positioned herself in front of him, and had almost run out of air because of her beating heart. 'Shall we play ball for a while?'

*You smelt so good. And you put the newspaper aside and looked at me, and you smiled and said my name. And then you said: 'All right. We shall.' And then we played, in the meadow with the birch tree, throwing the ball to each other. And the sun was directly behind you; sometimes I couldn't really see you. And I thought, this will never stop, it will never be over. And somehow the little girl was right, wasn't she? Why haven't you recognised me? The sun, back then, was behind you, not me. You could see me. Why haven't you recognised me?*

She saw how the ferry landed. A man with a bicycle disembarked, a small boy with him. And a woman got off. There we go, she thought, and pulled herself subconsciously closer to the shelter of the wall. She observed how the woman approached Tretjak, put down her bag, and exchanged a few words with him. Then he took the bag, and both walked side by side along the promenade towards the Piazza Roma. They appear to be two totally normal people, she thought up there on her post. Man picks up woman from ferry and takes her to hotel. Nobody would suspect anything else. Not even now, when they checked into the hotel, she thought and smiled. The fact that, on this night, all the rooms had been booked ahead of time and paid for, the fact that all of them were empty except the one that they were being shown to right now – who would have noticed or cared?

*Every time you were at our home, I stayed close to you. As close as possible, that is. One evening you men sat in the living room, you, my father and two other guys who I didn't know. I was next door in the little television room, you probably didn't even know that it existed. The door was closed and I could hear only the voices. I could hardly understand anything, but that didn't matter. You didn't say much, but I waited for your voice only. The television was on very low, I had stopped watching it altogether, and I lay on the sofa and waited for your voice. Sometimes it was only one word, between the other voices and the clinking of glasses. The smoke of the cigars and cigarettes seeped through the gap under the door, and between my legs I had a pillow, a big blue one. I only wore a tee-shirt and my knickers, and it got warmer and warmer there, and I heard your voice and rubbed myself against the pillow. And I kept on rubbing against the pillow, and then it started, and I almost couldn't breathe, and it was incredibly beautiful. That's something you can be proud of, my first orgasm. Some women never have one their whole lives.*

Now a corpulent man with an absurd red pointed hat came towards the two figures on the promenade, a kind of German camping tourist, she thought. Left over from the season. The man asked Tretjak something, obviously the way to somewhere, as Tretjak made some signs with his hand before walking on. Charlotte Poland stayed by his side during the brief interruption. This was the right moment to send the prepared text message. Of course, she couldn't hear from up here near the church exactly how the message arrived on Charlotte Poland's phone. But one could almost imagine the beep. At least she saw how the novelist reacted, as she took the mobile from her coat and looked at the display. What an exciting thought: both people down there believed that it was they who determined what happened and what would happen.

*You don't doubt that, do you, Gabriel, not for a second, do you? You are afraid, I know it, but you think you know what you are afraid of. And you think you know what you have to do.*

She looked on as the two crossed the main street which separated the lake from the harbour and the promenade from the town itself. As they crossed the Piazza Roma and disappeared into the entrance of the Hotel Torre Imperial. The glass door with the three gold stars on it still swung back and forth for a little while.

# 2

She had thought of so many possible eventualities. That much, the investigation was to prove later on. She had, for example, succeeded in reprogramming the telephone exchange of the Munich Inland Revenue Branch I so that every call to Fiona Neustadt would automatically be redirected to her mobile phone. She therefore always knew who wanted to speak to Fiona Neustadt and could listen in. She had pretended to be an employee of the telephone company, from the maintenance department. Obviously she had spent a quiet half hour in a room full of monitors and telecommunication devices. The most complicated part had been to redirect all calls from police headquarters which were intended to reach Fiona Neustadt. Redirection meant that none of these calls reached Ms Neustadt. All calls, including those from the mobile phones of the Homicide Squad, went directly to her. Only once had there been a knock on the door. A nice secretary had asked whether she would like a cup of coffee. Even that secretary was interviewed later.

She had thought of so many possible eventualities. What she hadn't considered, however, was one of Rainer Gritz's particular characteristics, which was widely known and ridiculed by his colleagues in the Homicide Squad. He hated making telephone calls, tried to avoid them whenever possible. He sent emails, and much preferred going somewhere to have a look himself, to gain many impressions at the same time, as he put it. 'On the telephone I'm only 20 percent,' he had once told Maler.

Rainer Gritz lived in a district of Munich called Schwanthaler Höhe, alone in a two-room apartment. Two weeks out of the year he cursed the area, when only a few streets away the Oktoberfest rollicked about down on the Theresienwiese. Otherwise he liked living there very much. Not far from his flat ran Landsberger Street, where Munich's Inland Revenue Division I was located. For some time Gritz had had a mind to look up Fiona Neustadt personally, but it had never worked out timewise so far. Gritz was always the first into the office of the Homicide Squad each morning. When he passed the Inland Revenue building just before seven, it was still completely dark, and when he drove back at some point in the evening, it was dark again. But one morning it worked. It was just before half past eight when he parked in front of the Inland Revenue building. The evening before, they had celebrated the birthday of a colleague from the Vice Squad in a small pub. It had been quite late when he got home.

Rainer Gritz had that certain special feeling quite often, and although he hadn't been with the Homicide Squad for a long time yet, his colleagues already took this special feeling seriously, as it had often proven to be extremely useful. Gritz himself would not have spoken of a feeling, more of a course of events which hadn't been completed. In this case, he wanted to check two contrasting images, which in his mind didn't quite fit together – on the one hand, the woman who, almost theatrically clad in a chic black dress, walked up the hill at the Lago Maggiore beside Gabriel Tretjak to attend the funeral of a murderer. And on the other hand there was the tax inspector with heaps of files in front of her. Gritz wanted to have a look at the conventional side of this contrast. He wanted to see the complete picture of Fiona Neustadt. As the official reason for his visit, he would ask whether he could take a look at the final report on Tretjak's tax inspection.

I'll just walk into the Inland Revenue, Gritz thought. There was indeed no doorman, no central information desk, no receptionist, nothing. Only a large black directory board, on which the names of the officials were listed in white letters. *Neustadt, Room 237, Building II, Tax Affairs.* Gritz took the stairs to the second floor and turned right, into Building II. The linoleum flooring was grey and a bit sticky. The windowless hallway had a white swinging door at the end with matt milky glass. In the passageway to the next hallway he met a woman with a flower pot in her hand. If he had to describe the character of government offices like this one, Gritz thought, he would try with this scene: in places like these, women always walked the hallways holding flower pots in their hands.

Room 237. A white door, with a black sign with two

names on it: Neustadt, Pfister. Gritz knocked, briefly waited for an answer, and when he heard nothing, carefully opened the door. A double desk stood in the middle of the room. On the left side sat a bald man with a beard, and on the right sat a woman, maybe 50 years of age, wearing a blouse with a flower pattern, slightly corpulent.

'I beg your pardon, I'm looking for Ms Neustadt,' Gritz said.

'Yes,' the woman answered, looking up from her files.

'Fiona Neustadt?' said Gritz.

'Yessss!' said the woman, and this time she not only sounded indifferent, but also slightly irritated.

'There has to be a misunderstanding, I'm looking for another Ms Neustadt,' Gritz said and tried to lend a little more authority to his voice.

'I am Fiona Neustadt. And I work here. Could you please tell me what this is all about?'

The rest of the conversation can be summarised as follows: the woman at the desk became friendlier when she heard that Gritz was from the police; a sort of colleague, she felt. She became a little nervous, however, when she started to comprehend that there was another woman who called herself a tax inspector and, what is more, who called herself Fiona Neustadt. And the woman became slightly hysterical, and asked her persistently silent bearded colleague for a glass of water, when she realised that the other Ms Neustadt might be involved in a series of murders.

'Do you have any idea,' Gritz asked, 'why somebody has assumed your identity? Do you deal with special tax cases?'

'I have no idea,' she said, 'I deal with bog standard cases. Nothing dramatic. When it becomes dramatic, we hand over the cases to the appropriate people in the Commission for the Investigation of Suspected Tax Evasion.'

'Ms Neustadt,' Gritz said, then corrected himself, 'the fake Ms Neustadt was dealing with the tax affairs of Gabriel Tretjak. At least that's what she claimed she was doing. Could you have a look at whether you have an open file dealing with that tax investigation?'

'Yes, of course.'

Gritz had already sat down on the visitor's chair in front of her desk.

'Gabriel Tretjak, St-Anna-Platz. No, there is no current tax investigation dealing with him. Nothing. He has never been suspicious. From a tax point of view, the man is completely clean.'

When Gritz left the Inland Revenue building, he couldn't wait to make the telephone call. He dialled Maler's number, which was saved under *Boss* in his speed-dial.

'Yes, what's up?' Maler answered.

Gritz ignored Maler's somewhat subdued voice and immediately launched into it: 'There is something new, Boss. This Fiona Neustadt is not a tax official. She has to be somebody completely different.'

'Come again?' Maler asked.

Gritz told him about his visit to the Inland Revenue, about the real Ms Neustadt, and about the fact that there had never been a tax inspection of Tretjak's affairs. He ended his report with the question: 'What do we do now, Boss?'

# 3

*Do you know how many times I asked after you? Suddenly you didn't come to us anymore and they all pretended you didn't exist. Nobody talked about you anymore, at least not in my presence. I was only briefly told that you had gone abroad. Once, through an open door, I heard a man, a Russian, who spoke with an accent, ask my father: 'Could it be that Gabriel has deceived us all?' I couldn't hear my father's answer because he closed the door.*

She walked down the path which led from the church to the Piazza Roma and consisted partly of steps. The church clock tolled twice; it was half past six. A metallic thunderclap announced the evening train from Luino to Locarno. The tracks ran, like the road, along the lake shore, and here in town just above the Piazza between the church and the steep mountain slope which rose above the lake. She stopped in the square, for a moment hesitating, and then finally sat down on a bench underneath a palm tree diagonally across from the entrance of the hotel. The train had now reached the height of the square and made a lot of noise. It must have been the third time that she checked in the pockets of her anorak to see whether she had everything that she would need in the coming minutes. She thought of her father and had to smile. In the end, he had been the winner, even back then. And it would turn out the same way for her. She was the best, she knew that. Again she had to smile. She had that in black and white. It was official.

*You brought fear to my family. I had never seen my father so afraid. Do you know that I had a scarf of yours? You had forgotten it and I snatched it. Cashmere, with your smell on it. Believe me, I sniffed every molecule of your scent out of it until only a distant echo remained, and I so loved the material and hated it so. Each night I fell asleep with it, not for just for a few days, but for a few weeks. For years, do you understand? Love can build bridges, so the saying goes. Bullshit. Although... it is building one right now, isn't it? You do love, as you say. You do believe me, don't you? I have delivered the murderess to you. The evidence. That's why you have asked her to come here. What are you doing with her right now? Do people change their smell during their life time? I often asked myself that question, when we met. I didn't find your smell again. But then in your bathroom at the St-Anna-Platz, there it suddenly was again, it hung in your towels, in your wardrobes, in your bathrobe – and I almost fainted.*

She looked over at the hotel. Except for the entrance hall and the empty restaurant only one room was illuminated, at the very top, on the fourth floor, at the corner of the building. The curtains had been drawn. Obviously the two inhabitants were not interested in the view of the lake, which shimmered, pale in the fading light. It took her a while to realise that the noise which lay in the evening air and mixed with the engine noises of the passing cars was her mobile phone. This number had not yet existed for very long, very few people had it, and she was not accustomed to the ringtone yet. She rummaged around for the phone, looked at the lit-up display and frowned. The hospital in Munich? Now? Why?

'Hello?' she said.

# 4

The nurse had taken his temperature this morning. At seven, it had been 38.5 degrees Celsius, a fever, and by nine it had risen again to 39.0. Maler knew what a fever meant: the body had assembled its defences – if he were still a healthy normal man that would be no reason for alarm, just a sign that his immune system was fighting bacteria or an infection. But in the case of transplant patients, fever was feared, as it was always possible that his body's defences had identified the foreign organ as the enemy.

The nurse had just noted down 39.0 degrees and shot him a worried glance when Gritz called with his news. Shortly after that, the ward doctor had shown up in his room and told him that, unfortunately, the blood tests had shown that the rejection level had increased. 2a. Still no reason to panic, but they would have to do some more tests, and this evening they were going to transfer him into an isolation ward where, with less risk of an infection, they could close down his immune system for a while. The doctor also said that he had informed the professor, who would probably visit him later on in the isolation ward.

August Maler was afraid. He didn't want to be isolated, didn't want the whole thing to start again, the nightmares, the passage. And he was afraid, because he clung to his life, to his wife, to his family and even to his job. How far would the fever rise? He felt his heart beat, which was not a good feeling as his heart was beating irregularly; it stumbled. Please, body, he thought, leave my heart alone.

But he knew he should not surrender to fear. Maler still had to do something and he had to find the right moment for it, between the tests and the transfer to the isolation ward.

It was already evening when the right moment finally arrived. Maler felt exhausted and weak, and in the meantime the fever had risen to almost 40 degrees. He didn't have a lot of time, a few minutes max, before the male nurse was supposed to arrive to take him to the other ward. Maler put on his bathrobe and raced out of his room down the hall towards the lift. He was lucky that no nurse saw him. He went up two floors and then turned left towards oncology, the cancer ward. Maler knocked on the door of the nurses' room. A Sister Judith opened and looked at him inquisitively: 'Yes?'

Maler had thought up a story which he now recounted: he had played chess in the cafeteria with a patient who had terminal cancer, who had come to the clinic to die. And now he wanted to enquire after him, but he had forgotten his name. A nice man, not very old yet, maybe 60 or so. Maler was lucky with Sister Judith, who was known to be quite talkative. She said she had four patients on the ward at the moment who were dying, two women, two men. But the men were much too ill to play chess, and had been that ill for a long time. Mr Leucht and Mr Braun, no, no, neither could be the man he was looking for.

'Has one of them got a daughter, who comes to visit him regularly?' Maler asked.

'No, Mr Leucht is always visited by his son. And Mr Braun has no visitors. But hang on, you are right, there was a patient, also terminally ill, who might have been able to play chess. He used walk about the ward, and he had a daughter who came to visit him a few times. But he is no longer here, he was moved to a hospice in Solln yesterday. Shall I give you the address?'

Maler nodded.

'Well,' Sister Judith said, 'the patient was called Martin Krabbe, and the telephone number of the hospice is…'

Krabbe, Martin Krabbe. Maler didn't listen to the nurse any longer. This was the man that Dimitri Steiner had said he should talk with. The man who had been spoken of with a mixture of fear and respect by Steiner. And that had meant something with a guy like Steiner. Gritz had tried to interview Krabbe, but he had already been too ill, the police had been told. Should he have just acted? Maler knew that all this was not good for his heart, but he heard himself ask: 'That's him, Sister, the one I'm looking for. Do you have a number for the daughter, so I can call her directly?'

'Yes, we always have the telephone numbers of the

relatives.' She leafed through the card index and wrote the mobile phone number on a note pad. 'Nora Krabbe is her name.'

It was a professional reflex which made Maler ask whether he could just briefly use the telephone here on the table. He dialled the mobile number.

It rang a few times before she answered.

'Hello?'

He immediately recognised her voice. 'Good evening,' he said, 'this is Inspector Maler from the hospital. Good evening, Ms Neustadt, or no, Ms Krabbe, which is the correct name? And what is your correct job title?'

It clicked and the line went dead. Maler redialled, but it was dead again. She had turned off the mobile. August Maler said good-bye to the stunned Sister Judith and went back to his own ward. In the lift he noticed that he felt faint, just for a moment. He had to call Gritz immediately. When he arrived at his room, there were already two doctors and two nurses waiting in front of the door.

August Maler wanted to say something, apologise somehow, but he couldn't anymore. He heard the excited words of the medics, then it went black in front of his eyes.

# 5

Charlotte Poland felt her knees knock while she was standing at the reception desk of the Hotel Torre Imperial. She tried not to show it. She didn't hear what the receptionist was talking about, the most beautiful corner room, view of the lake and so on. The air around her felt like cotton or wool. Everything was somehow muffled. Her left hand was still in her coat pocket and clutched the telephone on which she had received the message a few minutes ago. It felt hot. She saw Gabriel Tretjak walking towards the lift, but she didn't have the strength to follow him. But when he turned around, looked at her with his black eyes and said 'Come', she also didn't have the strength not to follow him.

The human brain hates nothing more than sheer happenstance or coincidence, an event which is unpredicted and unpredictable. That is why the human brain always looks for hidden rules, laws and messages. The unpredictable is dangerous. If the event continues to occur, the brain immediately sets the priorities and concentrates totally on the processing of the event. It may be, for example, some awful sight or bad news. Researchers call it a new stimulus, a new experience which forces the brain to react in an unusual way: it cuts itself off completely from any new information until the new stimulus is processed. Doctors know that patients who find out that they have been diagnosed with cancer cannot absorb anything else after that, and later cannot remember what was talked about.

Charlotte Poland could not have said what colour the walls of the hotel room were, what material the floor was covered with, how many pictures hung on the walls, whether there was a mirror in the lift. Presumably she couldn't have even answered the question at that moment of why she was here. Tretjak's call, saying that he wanted to meet her, that he had a new plan which concerned her son, all that was far, far away. Also the time last summer, when he had finally found Lars and repeatedly offered to help, as if he had sensed a certain commonality with him, even a closeness – everything was expunged. Her brain was concerned only with processing the text message, and forbade any distraction.

While Tretjak, in his black cashmere coat, unlocked the door to Room 405, turned on the light, walked to the window and drew the curtains, and still in his coat sat down on one of the two armchairs, unfolded a piece of paper and started to ask her questions, Charlotte Poland's brain repeated the text message. Again and again.

*Under no circumstances should you meet Gabriel. I've found out something dreadful. Paul Tretjak was innocent. Your life is in danger. Don't believe one word Gabriel tells you.*

And Charlotte Poland's brain also repeated again

and again the name of the person who had signed the message: *Fiona Neustadt.*

The furniture of Room 405 consisted of a big bed, a wardrobe and a small corner seating arrangement with two armchairs. The bed was covered with a dark green throw. The wardrobe was made from dark wood, as was the floor. The armchairs were dark green as well, the colour of the walls was ochre, the curtains white. Above the bed hung a framed black and white photograph. It showed the small harbour of Maccagno, as it had been a long time ago, maybe a hundred years. Slowly, all of this crept into Charlotte Poland's perception. She saw that the piece of paper Tretjak had unfolded was some kind of parchment with colourful decorations in the margins, and that coats of arms could be made out. And she also heard what Gabriel Tretjak was saying.

A new stimulus also sets off a second effect in the human brain: once the shocking event has been digested, the blockage is lifted. Then the reverse happens: the brain has a particularly acute perception of everything that is happening.

'I'm going to bring the story to an end now,' Gabriel Tretjak said. 'And your silence won't help you. I will find out the truth. Everything, even whether you had an affair with my father.'

Charlotte Poland looked at him. She felt a sensation rise inside her, which she initially couldn't identify. But then it became clear to her: it was the urge to laugh. Was that his question? Was that what was bothering him?

She looked him in the eyes and the urge to laugh was
gone. No, she wanted to say. There was nothing going
on with your father. But in that moment she understood
that that his eyes were not fixed on her, but on a point
directly behind her.

# 6

The forensic pathologist hadn't been able to reach Inspector Maler, and had already left two messages on his voicemail: 'Please call me back, Inspector, I've got news for you.' Strange, she thought, that he doesn't get in touch. Normally it didn't take him more than 20 minutes.

Then she sent an email to Rainer Gritz. She remembered that he had once told her, don't call me, send me an email, that's much faster. Firstly, she wrote that the results of the new post-mortem of the three exhumed bodies were ready. In brief: there were no signs of poison in any of the bodies, and the knife wounds to the liver and the heart remained the causes of death. From her point of view, there was no connection between the first three murders and the violent death of the bank employee.

Then she wrote: *Secondly: I have noticed something curious. No idea whether it means anything. I've checked the DNA samples of Paul Tretjak one more time, which he left behind after his suicide – and compared them to the traces of DNA previously found on the first three bodies. It is without any doubt Paul Tretjak's DNA on those three bodies, as we had said before, but there is something else. In all three cases, something is added to the DNA, a sort of massage oil, or an essence of it.* She pondered for a brief moment whether to include a concluding sentence, whether anybody would wonder how she knew that, and then she wrote: *It is the kind of oil that is frequently used during sex.*

# 7

*I am the best. Even the police have to learn this now. This Inspector Maler can come in his bathrobe if he wishes. You didn't recognise me, Gabriel. What do you think: would everything have been different, if you had looked at your tax inspector and had simply said my name, like you did back then on the terrace?* Nora, yes, let's play ball. *Dimitri also didn't recognise me, the pig. He didn't have much time, that much I have to admit. Old men are so vain, can't face the fact that they are no longer in charge. Why else did he tell the inspector about my father? To be important one more time, to be a part of it one more time. It was not good for you, Dimitri. My father had also thrown money in his direction so he would suffocate the investigations, which would have led the Russians to us. Father was so desperate, he was so afraid of the Russians, once I even saw him cry. What would they have done to him if they had found out that you cheated them all, that you collected the money for nothing? Brazil. Are you still thinking, Gabriel? You don't need to anymore. Your money is already on its way there, I arranged it all today. But it's travelling in my name. Nora. Do you remember?*

She heard his voice through the door. He talked about the piece of paper she had given him, which she told him she had seen in Charlotte Poland's handbag during the funeral and had later stolen during dinner in the restaurant. He probably didn't know how valuable the sheet that he held in his hand was. But all that was of little consequence now. Downstairs in the Piazza a car honked. She herself stood completely still, directly behind the door. Between her nose and the metallic numbers 405 were only ten centimetres. She sensed her heartbeat slip downwards to her wrists. Stay calm, she thought, totally calm. Assume an outside perspective. Who is standing here? A woman, who knows what needs to be done. Who knows how to do it. A woman, who is not to be dissuaded. Name: Fiona Neustadt. A woman, who, after all this, won't exist anymore. Who has nothing to lose. She was rummaging around in her pockets. Knife. Stiletto needle. Telephone. Pistol.

*Why doesn't the writer slut answer? Why is she not to be heard? Did you sleep with her? Oh no, you love me, you say. Father had his affairs with women better organised. They were brought to him. Discreetly by taxi, in the middle of the night. Sometimes two at a time. They always went next door, to the medical suite. I got it quite quickly, when I was still small. In the dark I ran over there and listened at the door… Like now. Life, a chain of repetitions. Apropos repetition: I gave you a hint, you and the police. It took a lot of effort to procure the Udine papers. All originals, no fakes. For you, Gabriel, nothing was too expensive or difficult. You should have looked up the illuminated manuscript of the city of Udine. Betrayal is the theme. But you didn't understand anything. As always. You didn't understand me.*

She took the gun from her pocket and released the safety catch. She placed her left hand on the door handle, concentrated and pushed it down in a very slow but even movement, millimetre by millimetre. In case it was locked she had brought along the second key. But it wasn't locked. Gently she pushed open the door. Gabriel Tretjak's voice became clear and pronounced.

'... did you have an affair with my father?'

Charlotte Poland sat with her back towards her. Gabriel looked towards the door. When he saw her, she pointed the gun at him.

'Hello, Gabriel,' she said. 'No, she didn't have an affair with your father. *I* fucked your dad. He was good, the old guy. Didn't need a sky full of stars to get it up.'

# 8

Maresciallo Mario Facchetti was not lucky in love. His appearance was not the problem: he was of average height, average weight, his red hair was cut short as was proper for a *carabiniere*. His eyes were a strikingly radiant blue. What he was lacking was a certain light touch, charm, an ability to flirt. Mario Facchetti always appeared serious, and when there were women around, he appeared even more serious. Then he had the feeling that he was tensing up inside. He didn't know what to say; he remained silent and thought about what he should say, and then he had even less of an idea what to say. For somebody like him, therefore, this Wednesday night had a special significance.

A money courier of the Banco Populare, which was located directly opposite the police station in Luino, had had her eye on *Il Maresciallo* for quite some time. In fact, so obviously had she had her eye on him that his colleagues had already teased him about it. Much too often, she parked her bullet-proof little Fiat in one of the places normally reserved for police cars outside the building. She parked and then came inside for a chat. Stella was her name, and she looked slightly Arab with her thick black hair. She had a beautifully-shaped mouth and, yes, Mario Facchetti had to admit, a pretty behind.

At one point Facchetti had gathered up all his courage and had asked her out to dinner. She had agreed immediately, and tonight was the big night. Facchetti had booked a table in the Ristorante Camino for eight o'clock. They wanted to meet early at half past seven to have a drink at the comfortable bar. It was the best restaurant in Luino, and actually far too expensive for Facchetti. But what the heck, he was *Il Maresciallo*, after all. In his profession he had had better luck than he had in romance. He was one of the four group leaders of the Luino police and he was only 29 years old.

It was a quarter to seven and he was sitting at his desk wondering whether he should keep his dark blue uniform on for dinner or not. He had been told several times that the uniform suited him very well, that it looked impressive. And Stella had got to know him in uniform. He would give the impression of being a very busy man, who had just come from doing his duty – that couldn't be wrong. On the other hand, it wasn't really relaxed or cool, was it? Maybe it would be more attractive to just show up in jeans and a freshly-ironed white shirt, suggesting: look, I can be totally different.

Facchetti's office was on the ground floor of a venerable building with an eagle on the gable. He looked across to the square where the lights were already illuminated. If he leaned forward a bit, he could even see the lake. It was almost completely dark outside, and his desk lamp shone down onto two reports from colleagues, which he could either read now or put off with no problem.

Tomorrow morning would be early enough. The theft of a bicycle and the burglary of a holiday home.

He looked at his watch for the umpteenth time. It was still a quarter to seven. He could have left, there were enough of his colleagues in the duty room. But Mario Facchetti was a diligent policeman. His duty ended at seven, and that was it.

The call that would fundamentally change *Il Maresciallo's* plans for the evening arrived at six minutes to seven. Mario Facchetti was the last link in a short chain of urgent calls: Munich-Milano, Milano-Varese, Varese-Luino. Facchetti listened for about three minutes, took notes, asked a few questions, again took notes – and finally called all the available men to his office. Shortly afterwards three blue Alfa Romeos set off, in the direction of Maccagno, specifically to the Hotel Torre Imperial.

In the history of physics, a certain experiment had driven the leading scientists all over the world crazy because nobody could find an explanation for the result. No matter how many times the experiment was repeated, the result always stayed the same. They shot a particle – an electron – at a lead plate with two slits located very close together to determine which slit it would fly through. For this purpose, a camera had been attached to the back of the plate. What disturbed the scientists was the result the camera was showing: the electron had flown through both slits simultaneously. But an electron cannot split itself! Only quantum physics had provided the explanation: the electron, according to the quantum physicists, is not a particle at all but a relativity wave. Which means that each particle always takes every possible path simultaneously – not just two paths as in the experiment, but an infinite number.

Since both *Il Maresciallo* Mario Facchetti and the money courier Stella Scipio were composed of electrons, one could say that their love story, in some possible sphere of relativity, started that evening. But it is not documented anywhere. What is, however, documented is the Newtonian rather than the quantum reality of that Wednesday evening in October: the reality of the flashing blue lights of three vehicles chasing along the road by the bank of the Lago Maggiore. The sirens had not been turned on. In the first car sat Mario Facchetti. He had received pretty clear instructions. It was only seven kilometres from Luino to Maccagno. In the tunnel before the entrance to the town, Facchetti gave the order by radio to also switch off the blue lights.

# 9

Tretjak was not afraid anymore. And he knew that that was not just the result of the two Tavor tablets he had swallowed before the ferry arrived. Had his friend Stefan Treysa ever in his life been in a similar situation? Psychologists. The hour is up. See you again next time. But no, you couldn't say that now. Tretjak was calm and not afraid. Fiona was about to chain him and Charlotte to the radiator with handcuffs. With great dexterity she did this with only one hand, while holding the gun in her other hand. Once she had pressed its barrel between his eyes at his forehead, suddenly, pretty roughly, and then had laughed briefly. Tretjak was also not afraid of the gun.

This is how it had always been in his life. When he knew exactly what was going to happen, he was not afraid. Even as a child this had been the case. And now he knew exactly what was going to happen.

Downstairs, directly in front of the entrance of the hotel, in an archway which led to the yard, a Toyota minivan was parked. It looked like a vehicle from a building site, dirty, with the faded logo of a roofing tile company on its sides. But in fact, it was packed up to the roof with explosives. When Fiona was finished here, she would go, lock the room behind her, and leave the hotel. And then detonate the bomb in the van. It would blow up the van, the hotel, and probably several other buildings as well.

Tretjak looked at Charlotte Poland. She appeared completely apathetic, as if she was paralysed. He was sorry he couldn't help her. Somehow by now he was almost fond of her. The woman with the screwed-up son. Maybe she was thinking of her son right now, right here contorted on the floor, with her hands chained behind her back. Thinking about what would happen to him if she came to any harm. But maybe she was not thinking of anything at all.

The feeling that was rising inside Tretjak was grotesque, but it was real. He suddenly felt free – although he was being tied up in that very moment. For 20 years now, he had been pursued by the smell of rotten parts of his life. And now, here at the lake, all this would come to an end.

'We are cut from the same cloth, Fiona,' Tretjak said. 'You should take me along.'

She stood up and looked at him. Her eyes were dead. Tretjak wondered whether she was on drugs.

'We two from the same cloth?' she said in a flat, toneless voice. 'You are so far removed from understanding anything. You were always so far off.'

'I know a number,' said Tretjak and added: 'BR69Q345.'

'And? What is this to me?'

'Think, Fiona,' he answered. It would not change

anything but it pleased him to throw her off course. His old game: when did who get what information?

'I wish you hell, Gabriel,' she said. And in the next moment the door shut behind her. One could hear the key turn in the lock. In the corner, behind the second green armchair, Charlotte Poland began to cry.

# 10

*In Munich, you tested a girl and said she was a genius. In Antwerp, you tested the same girl and said she was crazy. That's how far you were, so hopelessly far you all were from understanding one another, from understanding me, the truth about me. In a moment we'll ignite a few fireworks. After that the world will look a bit different, at least my world will.*

She didn't take the lift, but the stairs. Almost without making a noise, she glided down the carpet on the steps. The stairs led into the entrance hall just behind the reception desk. She paused and observed the back of the receptionist. He was the only person in the hotel with whom she had had any dealings. He was a doughy sort of guy, today wearing a blue-and-white striped shirt. She wanted to make sure, even though he had no reason to leave his post right now. With her eyes she followed the stripes of his shirt on the right side of his back from the shoulder downwards. She reached into the inside pocket of her anorak – the stiletto needle was inside its sheath, sown into the lining, with the knife beside it. It was fast, it was soundless. Then the doughy guy was lying on the floor, spread out behind the reception desk and staring up at the ceiling with a fixed, surprised look on his face.

*Unable to find my place in reality? Incapable of adjusting my own expectations to the actual circumstances? Sorry, but I can't agree with this expert report. That's what you emailed my father, Doctor Know-it-all Kufner. And you groped my ass which was also an interesting way to adjust expectations to actual circumstances. What kind of a game was that, Gabriel? Yes, maybe we are cut from the same cloth. But you have to die now.*

She went through the entrance door into the Piazza. Just to the right, in the archway, was the delivery van. In front of the bar someone was smoking. She sensed a sudden craving for a cigarette. She hadn't smoked for a long time. She toyed with the idea of asking the guy for one. But then she remembered the inspector's call. One could locate a mobile phone. She would have plenty of time to smoke a cigarette later, she thought and continued on her way. She first crossed the Piazza, then the main street, then walked along the Promenade to the ferry dock, stopped and turned around.

A quiet picture, a beautiful composition of light, shadow and the contours of the buildings. To the right and above, the discreetly-lit church, from where she had watched everything a short while ago. In front of her, the Piazza with the palm trees, the street lights, the bar, the two stone benches. To the left, the Hotel Torre Imperial. Above all of this, the roofs of the town, which hugged the steep slope of the mountain and melted into the darkness. The air was fresh and crystal clear. *BR69Q345.* She heard Gabriel Tretjak's voice in her head, as it enunciated these letters and numbers. Suddenly her brain translated the voice into written symbols. Symbols she had written herself. Symbols written today. Symbols which had been filled in on a form.

And now she knew what it was. It was the code for the transaction by which she had transferred 1.2 million euros, Tretjak's cash, to Brazil this morning. She felt herself become hot all of a sudden, and her thoughts started to race.

*Back then, during the test at the Ministry, this also happened, my thoughts were racing, there was a whirlpool in my mind. Then I looked at you, Dad, and it was over. Look, I am calm. I am totally calm. And I am the best.*

She took out her mobile phone, and punched in on the display the word *end*. She let the view of the Piazza sink in, and then she pressed the key which triggered the detonation.

# 11

Mario Facchetti had dispersed his men around the Piazza. The police vehicles had been parked out of sight on the hard shoulder inside the tunnel under the church. One of the men stood outside the bar, smoking, and had thrown a civilian coat over his uniform. Two had taken positions in the courtyard behind the hotel, one more up at the church. *Il Maresciallo* himself and another of his men stood in the open waiting room of the ferry port. Everything was dark here, because after seven in the evening no more ferries were scheduled to land in little Maccagno.

He had seen the woman leave the hotel and ordered his man to duck. He himself had stepped behind a pillar. That had to be the suspect coming towards him, finally stopping and then turning around. Facchetti stood not five metres away from her. He opened the leather holster of his service pistol. He had been told that although the woman didn't look it, she was extremely dangerous. He observed how she was pushing buttons on her phone and decided: now. He nodded towards his colleague, and together they crossed the few metres very quickly, simultaneously drawing their weapons.

In Maresciallo Facchetti's report, it would say later that Nora Krabbe, aka Fiona Neustadt, had not resisted her arrest. She had seemed confused and surprised, and had repeatedly pushed a button on her mobile phone until it had been taken away from her.

# 12

From far away, he had seen Sergeant Rainer Gritz standing outside the gate. He had to be over two metres tall. Like a small lighthouse he was standing there, with the collar of his blue raincoat turned up. Gabriel Tretjak told the taxi driver to stop near the figure standing there, it would not be necessary to drive into the clinic compound.

He had landed at 13.20 at Munich's Franz Joseph Strauß airport. Lufthansa LH 701 from Bordeaux. From the airport, one could reach the Haar district by using the motorway for almost the entire distance, and at midday there was hardly any traffic, so it had taken the taxi only about 30 minutes. It was an overcast November day, a Tuesday, wet, cold, unpleasant.

Six weeks had passed since Fiona's arrest in Maccagno. Gabriel Tretjak found that they had passed quickly. He had moved into the new apartment but it would only be a temporary move – that much he knew already. This flat was a transition – from a highly unpleasant phase of his life into a hopefully better one. He knew that he was going to move out again soon, even though Stefan Treysa often said during their sessions: 'You have to build deeper foundations in your life, not always such shallow ones. That's important.'

The trip to France had also been Treysa's idea. A

crackpot idea, as it turned out. Tretjak had told him about his memory of a holiday. It had been the only holiday that the Tretjaks had ever spent together as a family. Father, mother and two children. All in one big orange tent, directly by the sea, the Atlantic, behind a big sand dune, in the middle of the pine forest. Lit-et-Mixe, the town had been called, that was still its name. The sea was also still there, and the big waves. Even the camping ground still existed, slightly more landscaped but fundamentally the same. Of course, it was closed in November. Tretjak had taken a room in a *pension*. It had rained cats and dogs, but he had still gone to the beach a couple of times, totally alone on this mass of sand several kilometres long. But he had felt nothing. How old would he have been back then? Seven? He remembered a volleyball game the four of them had played. And a terrible thunderstorm, when lightning had hit one of the pine trees. That's about it. The call from Sergeant Gritz had come as a welcome reason to cut short his stay.

'How is your boss, by the way, Inspector Maler?' Tretjak asked, as they walked side by side across the grounds of the Haar District Hospital. Top security wing, that's where they were heading. House No. 10. Room 34/B. Nora Krabbe. Two men in white coats came towards them in hurried steps. They looked very cold.

'Not well, I'm afraid,' Gritz answered. 'The doctors still haven't been able to get the effects of a serious organ rejection under control. He is back in the ICU.' The young policeman sighed. 'I went to see him yesterday, but there was no point, he was talking complete gibberish.'

'I'm sorry to hear that,' Tretjak said.

For a short while they walked on in silence. Rainer Gritz had called Tretjak because the police were about to close the investigation. He wanted to share with him what they had found out. And maybe discuss with him a few last outstanding questions.

Nora Krabbe, Gabriel Tretjak was told, had rummaged through her father's computer. And had put in Gabriel Tretjak's name. That's how she had come across an email in which her father had asked him for advice. That had been three years ago. Tretjak remembered well. He had been surprised that Krabbe had made contact with him – after all that time and everything that had happened. His daughter was worrying him, the email said. He had written about huge psychological problems. In his answer, Tretjak had given him two names: Harry Kerkhoff and Norbert Kufner, one a brain specialist, the other a psychiatrist. And he had made appointments with both of them. He hadn't done any more than that.

'You know,' he said to Gritz, 'I couldn't even remember the daughter's name.'

'It was the complete opposite on the other side,' Gritz said. 'Our experts talked about an abnormal obsession with you.' He looked at Tretjak sideways as if expecting a commentary. But Tretjak felt no urge to comment. 'With regard to the experts,' Gritz eventually continued, 'Kerkhoff and Kufner came to the same conclusions back then as our experts today: schizophrenia, symptoms of a multiple personality disorder, a completely dislocated value system, self-harming behaviour. The reports were, of course, meant for the father. But the daughter secretly read them.'

Gritz continued to talk: he spoke of the connection between the expert reports and him, Tretjak, of an investigation and an increasingly focused idea, an obsession becoming a fixation. 'In the end she sent you an email. She had your address, of course. But she changed the name of the sender. Inland Revenue Munich I.'

'Yes, I should have questioned that,' Tretjak said. 'Despite emails, the Internet and everything else, the Inland Revenue still sends everything via snail mail.'

They had reached House No. 10. Gritz paused and opened his briefcase. 'I've brought something for you,' he said.

He took from it a file containing about 200 pieces of paper. Tretjak recognised the kind of paper – even in black and white, the decorations were visible.

'This is a copy of the notes Nora Krabbe took,' Gritz said. 'From the moment she sent you the email as your tax inspector, she kept a diary, containing all the minutiae. Granted, it is sometimes not at all easy to understand the entries. They follow their own peculiar logic, if you understand what I mean, and they are the expression of a pretty pathological emotional world. But I thought you might be interested. After all, you were...' Gritz blushed slightly and then didn't finish the sentence. He was holding the file in his hand a little uncertainly. 'Do you want to have them?'

Tretjak was thinking of Stefan Treysa. Your past is important, Gabriel. You have to take an interest in it.

'No,' he said. 'Thank you, but I'm not going to read that.' And he watched as Gritz stashed the pile in his case again.

They entered the building. Tretjak followed Gritz to the left towards the reinforced glass gate. They had to endure a series of security checks: an x-ray similar to that at the airport, a metal detector, filling in two forms, emptying pockets. Gritz continued talking while all this was happening. Tretjak knew how difficult it could be to collect information, and he got the impression that Gritz wanted to shine a bit with all he knew.

Nora Krabbe, Gritz told Tretjak, had been brought up by her father, the ear, nose and throat specialist physician Martin Krabbe. No siblings. And no mother. According to the research done by the police, Dr Krabbe had paid off the mother, a Ukrainian, immediately after Nora's birth. When she was a young girl, Nora Krabbe had been enrolled in a series of tests run by the Bavarian Ministry of Culture, which studied highly gifted children. At the end of the tests, they had determined that she had an extremely high IQ and some kind of extraordinary talent, which needed a particularly supportive educational environment. In fact, her results were the best in the whole of Bavaria. However, according to Gritz, the tests had been pretty questionable. They had never been repeated.

'That was a time when they believed they should identify and study gifted children. The thesis was that the education system destroyed such exceptional talent and should be reformed.'

'Yes,' Tretjak replied, 'the consequences can still be seen today. Every mother whose child causes problems suspects that it is gifted.'

He had to think of Lars Poland. Was this Gritz aware that here, in House No. 10, in a different part of it, but House No. 10 nonetheless, a second person also connected with the case was incarcerated?

They now stood at the beginning of a long hallway with several broad white doors on the left and the right of it. They were supposed to wait for an official.

'Is she in a state...', Tretjak was searching for the right word, '... a fit state to be interrogated?'

Rainer Gritz seemed to also have to think about how to answer: 'I would put it this way: she *was* in a fit enough state for some of the time. There were several statements which have cleared up a few things, especially about the crimes, very concrete things.'

Gritz spoke of the perfect handling of the stiletto, which she had learned from her father, and of Kerkhoff's body, which she had loaded from the boot of her car into some horse box which she had seen at a motorway service station, purely by chance and on impulse. She had liked what had been written on the outside of it: *Nu Pagadi.* Just you wait. After all, she did know a little Russian. Gritz said that Nora Krabbe had been to Tretjak's flat and murdered the cleaning lady just before going on her excursion to the Isar River. But Tretjak was interested in something different. He looked at the officer.

'What do you mean by: she *was* in a fit enough state to be interrogated?'

Gritz looked down to the floor. 'What you will see now will shock you a bit, Mr Tretjak.' He cleared his throat. 'Frau Krabbe cut out both of her eyes with a knife two weeks ago.'

Tretjak didn't feel anything. He saw the hallway, he saw the doors, he saw the security officer in a pale blue uniform approach at a leisurely pace from the other side of the hallway. 'Why did she do that?'

'We don't know. Since then she has been in an aggressive state, in which she is even withdrawing from her conversations with the psychologist. Don't be frightened, she is wearing a black eye patch and she looks different in other ways as well, because of the medication, you know.'

They had started walking, and followed the officers up to the penultimate door. The man unlocked the door and let them enter. He stayed outside and then locked the door behind them.

'Get lost, Gabriel,' Nora Krabbe said.

Tretjak looked at Gritz in surprise. He hadn't uttered a word yet. Was she really blind?

'I can smell you,' Nora said, as if she had noticed his surprise. 'Get lost,' she repeated.

Her hair had been shaved off, presumably because of

her eye injury. She appeared swollen in a way, at least ten kilos heavier. The black eye patch over both her eyes made her look helpless. Suddenly she stood up, pulled her shirt over her head, tossed it behind her and grabbed her breasts. With an intentionally distorted childish voice she said: 'Or would you like to play ball a bit?'

When they were outside again in the beautiful park, Tretjak wondered whether the dreadful events were easier to bear when they were decorated with trees and flowers. Police Detective Sergeant Rainer Gritz said he was still wondering about some other things as well, and wanted to ask Tretjak about them. For example, it was still unresolved who had killed Borbely, the bank employee. They were assuming that it was a revenge killing within the drug scene, since they had uncovered Borbely's links to drug dealers. Tretjak was thinking of Charlotte Poland. Of the scene when she had been so desperate, so near collapse, that she had told him everything, including about this Borbely guy. And had finally asked him: 'Can you help me?'

They had to stop to let a little vehicle pass which swept the paths. Tretjak sensed that Gritz was looking at him quizzically. In the past, he sometimes unintentionally had a traitorous smirk around his mouth, but a few years ago he had consulted an expert on mimicry about how to get rid of it. Thank goodness for that, he thought now.

'One thing interests me, Mr Tretjak,' said Gritz. 'You

knew *before* the fateful events in Maccagno that your girlfriend was behind the murders. How did you find that out?'

In the pocket of his cashmere coat Tretjak felt the little bottle with his rescue drops. A homeopathic remedy, which Treysa swore by. Tretjak had promised to give the stuff a chance, at least for its placebo effect. But he didn't want to let on in front of Gritz, and left the bottle in his pocket.

'The letter my father had supposedly written contained a mistake,' he said. 'An important mistake.'

He explained to Gritz how his father had always described their last meeting to everybody: he, Gabriel, had walked away without turning around.

Gritz nodded: 'That's what is said in the letter, as if it was an accusation.'

'But that's not the way it happened,' Tretjak said. 'He was the one who was standing in the doorway. I was the one who said: "Or is there still some way in which we could change our story?" And he walked away without turning around. He would never have described this scene wrongly to me, even if he blamed me when he told this story to others.'

Gritz stopped and looked at him: 'But from that you knew only that your father was not the murderer. But you didn't know yet that it was Ms Neustadt, I mean Ms Krabbe.'

Tretjak smiled up to the two-metre man. 'You figured it out as well, Mr Gritz. Leave me with the comfort that I can be faster and better than the police in certain respects, at least.'

When they were outside the big gate again, Tretjak waved over a taxi from the stand on the other side of the street. He recognised the same driver from before, who in the meantime had obviously advanced to the first position in the waiting queue. The man was wearing a turban.

Tretjak opened the back door of the car and shook Sergeant Gritz's hand to say good-bye.

'Tell me,' Tretjak asked, 'what were the strange injuries on her body? She was covered with cuts.'

'Her *mistakes*. She has said that she is drawing up an account of all the mistakes she made,' Gritz answered. 'Every mistake is recorded with one cut.' She had done all that in one day, he explained. With a fork. She hadn't been given knives. Now she wasn't given even forks anymore. And she had always been talking about her biggest mistake, Gritz added. 'Something about a red pointed hat.' He looked at Tretjak enquiringly. 'Does that mean anything to you?'

Tretjak shook his head. 'I've no idea what that means.' He got into the taxi and closed the door. Luigi deserved to be left alone.

# 13

The guy with the red pointed hat, who had briefly caught Nora Krabbe's eye at the ferry dock below, was fundamentally a genial, easy-going man. Luigi was his first name, and that's what everybody in town called him. A tourist he was not. He was the landlord of the inn down at the water's edge, with the large windows through which one could see the Lago Maggiore as a glistening sea during the daytime and as a black nothing at night. It was not an exciting restaurant, but the ravioli was good and so was the wine, especially the Valpolicella. Luigi was convinced that he served the best Valpolicella in the whole lake region. Clear, pure taste, with no blend.

The nice Luigi, whom everybody knew and liked, was, however, only one side of this man. For many years, Luigi had been on the payroll of the Italian secret police. He was a simple informer, but he worked on cases in a grey, morally questionable zone. What exactly he did, probably only he knew. It seemed also to be clear that he had other employers, people who rejected law and order out of principle. In his view, these roles didn't contradict each other, quite the contrary, and Luigi had always fared well with that business philosophy: all is well as long as everyone profits from my work. If they don't profit anymore, then I've got a problem.

He had met Gabriel Tretjak a few years ago. They had had dealings with each other only for a few days, but those days had been intense. There had been a moment back then when Luigi had been afraid, a feeling which only very rarely took hold of him. Tretjak had helped him, and you don't forget that, especially not if you are a man like Luigi. He hadn't hesitated for one second when Tretjak had called last September and asked him for a favour.

Gabriel Tretjak had asked whether he could check around in Maccagno and the surrounding towns. Was there anything out of the ordinary happening, did there seem to be something special in the offing? That was all.

Luigi had understood early in his life that you could talk to a hundred people and not find out anything if they were the wrong ones. And you could talk to three and comprehend everything if they were the right people. This time it had been four people in the end with whom he had spoken. After that, he had been certain that there was indeed something special coming in those autumn days.

There was something big and something small, which Luigi believed might interest Tretjak. The something small was: somebody had booked all the rooms in the Hotel Torre Imperial. And paid in advance. Supposedly because of a class reunion. But nobody knew anything about a party. The something big was: somebody had bought a considerable amount of explosives. In that case, the research had been particularly simple: the man from whom the woman had ordered the explosives was an old school friend of Luigi. They knew each other from the most varied stages of life.

When Luigi had informed Tretjak, he had asked whether there was anything else he could organise for him. He should make sure that the explosive was delivered but would not explode. 'Sure thing,' Luigi had said, 'will do.'

It was now late afternoon on the Lago Maggiore. Luigi liked November. The inn was still empty, and it would be more than an hour before the first guests arrived. Not many in this season. Luigi sat alone in the empty restaurant, and the few noises he could hear came only from the kitchen. He opened a bottle of wine, just for himself, his most expensive wine, an Amarone, the big brother of the Valpolicella. He poured himself a glass of the wine and swished it around the sides of the glass, once, twice, again and again. An explosive which was not going to explode. Luigi liked that kind of a job. That kind of thing could happen more often as far as he was concerned. He thought back to the moment when he had given Tretjak the agreed sign at the ferry port to say that everything had been arranged. Then he took a sip of the wonderful Amarone and thought how pleasant life was.

# Epilogue

*In the end there was always something left over, one final piece of the puzzle. That had been Rainer Gritz's experience in his policeman's life so far: there was always something that still had to be resolved at the end.*

*This time, the last piece of the puzzle lay in South Tyrol, in a village above Bolzano, a long way up, enclosed by mountains. It was 21 December. There was no snow in Munich. The air had been soft and clear when Gritz got going at seven o'clock that morning. His GPS told him he would reach Bolzano at 11.12am.*

*August Maler had told him about the man who lived with the eagles. Tretjak Senior had provided that lead. The man with the eagles could clear up the mystery of what had happened between Tretjak's two sons back then, ten years ago. Why the one son had disappeared and the other wouldn't comment on it.*

*Rainer Gritz had liked puzzles as a child. To put together the full picture bit by bit, that was what thrilled him. He had never told anybody in the police about this childhood passion, not even Maler. It seemed a bit too banal. As a child to play with puzzles, as a grown-up to hunt criminals.*

*But now, alone in the car, he was allowed to think how the puzzle-principle suited him. To complete something, to tick the box. In this case, it was particularly important to him. Never before had he had to deal with such depravities. Nora Krabbe's diary: one could not imagine anything more horrible. A thoroughly evil young woman who had perpetrated thoroughly evil deeds. And when she could not do evil to the outside world anymore she began to direct the evil against herself. But it wasn't so much the cruelty which Rainer Gritz found hard to take, which didn't let him sleep and tied him to the table in his little kitchen for hours, drinking one peppermint tea after another. It was not the brutality, which sometimes almost drove him mad. It was the sense of uncertainty in this case, which he had never been able to shake: what was reality, what was imagination? What could you believe and what should you believe? This double game of facts and suggestion – in the world of Gabriel Tretjak, all this could co-exist side by side, in fact such a fog was in a way the foundation of his business. In the world of the Detective Sergeant of the Homicide Squad, everything was reduced to the simple question: what was true and what wasn't. Whenever in the course of this investigation one had thought:* that's how it must have happened! *something had changed. Whenever one had thought that one understood this Gabriel Tretjak, something happened which altered everything. The man remained a mysterious, curious figure to him and he would not put anything past him.*

*There was, for example, the matter of the blood at the farmyard, Tretjak's refuge, where he looked up into the stars. Gritz had the whole farm searched, for all kinds of clues. They found traces of blood in several places, not even dry yet.*

*Gritz had been sure that this lead would solve the case. One day later the result of the forensic investigation was: rabbit blood, from a freshly slaughtered animal. What had that been all about? What was the meaning of that crap?*

*Or this story with the brothers: Gritz suspected that the meeting of the two brothers ten years ago had actually never taken place. Maybe the mad Nora Krabbe had only persuaded the old Tretjak that it had, to reawaken his wrath against Gabriel. On the other hand, there had been no sign of that brother since that time. Where the hell was he? What was he doing? Had he been murdered? Had he assumed another identity? What was real and what not?*

*Gritz did not tend to show great emotion, but now at the wheel of his car, pondering everything, he was shaking. Just a few more kilometres, he thought, then closure, tick that box. Finally. Please. Or did that have to remain a wish? Could a puzzle ever be completed if the rules of the game were constantly redrawn?*

*It was 11.07am when he reached Bolzano. Five minutes quicker than the GPS had calculated, he thought. It had started to snow. His police-issued BMW had winter tyres and he had also brought along the snow chains. The road which led up to the village was marked on the map only as a thin line, but his GPS said he should use it. When he drove up the road, he thought: the GPS doesn't know how wide a BMW can be.*

*The road up to the village of Jenesien ran through a forest, was very steep and very narrow, and became even steeper and narrower the further he climbed it. It felt like being stuck in a drainpipe. And it was snowing more and more heavily. He turned the wipers up to the highest setting. He didn't listen to music anymore. Three kilometres to go, the navigation system pronounced. The wheels were starting to slip, but the car was still pulling itself upwards. Gritz had called his colleague in South Tyrol to ask whether he knew anything about this eagle-man. The colleague said that he would need to make some enquiries, and had called back the next day. Yes, such a man existed in Jenesien. Had to be a strange kind of a guy. He lived in a remodelled citadel, a little outside the village, on the edge of a forest. He wasn't there for months on end, but at the moment, so the information said that his colleague had received, the guy was in residence. There had been some trouble in the past, because he had gathered some youths around him who were attracted to him. He was rumoured to be a Satanist or something like that, so the colleague said. But that had not turned out to be the case. The community had met with him, and since then there had been no problems between them.*

*Gritz had reached the village. It was snowing very hard. It was a small village, and despite the weather, Gritz could see the silhouettes of an idyllic setting all around him. Ponies in the meadows, to the left goats and sheep. Forests, the shadow of the mountains. A few pretty farmhouses. What a beautiful village, he thought. Maybe one day he should spend his summer holidays here.*

*Gritz asked a farmer's wife who was herding two cows in front of her how to get to the citadel. He had to leave the car behind and walk the last part of the way. After a few hundred metres, he was sinking into the snow which came up above the edge of his shoes. His feet were wet and freezing when he reached the citadel and the man who was loading logs onto a wheelbarrow in its yard. When Gritz came closer and recognised him, he knew that he wasn't going to able to complete the puzzle.*

*'Good day,' Gritz said when he was almost standing in front of him.*

*The man had not seen him yet and turned around.*

*'Good day,' said Joseph Lichtinger.*

*When Gritz left the yard of the citadel, he had to free his car from a thick blanket of snow. It had continued to snow, while they had sat together, the strange priest and the long, thin inspector. What could one believe, what should one believe? As he drove off, it started to get dark. Gritz turned on the lights. No, there had been no closure. Nothing was clear. Except one thing: it wasn't eagles who had chosen the citadel as their kind of flight hub. They were falcons. But they were so gigantic that one could bloody easily mistake them for eagles. In Celtic mythology, Gritz knew, falcons were messengers between this world and the next. And he knew another thing now, glancing at his navigation system:* traffic jam on the Brenner Pass – no alternative route possible.

## THE END